UNAUTHORIZED VERSIONS

by the same editor

The Faber Book of
English History in Verse

I have no gun
but I can spit
(*Eyre Methuen*)

London Lines
(*Methuen*)

UNAUTHORIZED VERSIONS
Poems and their Parodies
Edited by KENNETH BAKER

faber and faber
LONDON · BOSTON

First published in 1990
by Faber and Faber Limited
3 Queen Square London WC1N 3AU

Photoset by Wilmaset Birkenhead Wirral
Printed in Great Britain by Clays Ltd, St Ives plc

A CIP record for this book is available from the British Library.

ISBN 0–571–14122–6

CONTENTS

INTRODUCTION: THE PURPOSE OF PARODY

The purpose of parody is pleasure. The parodies in this book should make you laugh or smile. The writers certainly had that intention and I think they succeed.

Dr Johnson defined parody as 'a kind of writing, in which the words of an author or his thoughts are taken, and by a slight change adapted to some new purpose' and the verb 'to parody' has come to mean 'to ridicule through imitation'. In order to appreciate the art of parody, we have to start with some knowledge of the words of the original writer, for without them the point will be lost or blunted. That is why, in this anthology, I have included the original poem on the left-hand page and the parody alongside it on the right. For much of the pleasure of reading a parody is to see how clever the writer has been in adapting or altering the original. Moreover, some of the poems that have been parodied may not, alas, be as familiar to readers as they once were. A helping hand is needed.

I have decided to include only parodies of poems and passages of dramatic verse. There have been some splendid prose parodies – the best, in my view, being those by Max Beerbohm in *A Christmas Garland*. They are so good that I have sometimes thought it would be amusing to ask exam students at universities to comment on them, without revealing that they were parodies, and to see how many twigged. Successful prose parodies, however, tend to be long, and the use of excerpts cannot do them justice where the effect is sustained over more than a few pages. Poetic parodies are generally shorter and their impact can be appreciated more readily and quickly. They have to achieve their sharpness and force within a much smaller span. They are altogether more accessible.

You will find in this book a number of different types of parody, each with a different aim. Some of the pieces that I have included are not parodies in the strict Johnsonian sense but are more akin to pastiche or burlesque. We are in an area of fine distinctions here, for in most dictionaries a subsidiary meaning of 'pastiche' or 'burlesque' is 'parody'. A clear example of burlesque is Tom Lehrer's version of Gilbert's song, the 'modern major-general', where Lehrer applies to Sullivan's well-known tune a bravura display of versification, accommodating all the elements in the Periodic Table. But this is an extreme case and the dividing lines are not always so easily drawn.

I have, none the less, identified five main types of parody in all. The first includes parodies that openly attack the original writer by alluding to one of his or her most famous or characteristic poems. The Victorian poet J. K. Stephen took the great sonnet by Wordsworth which begins,

> Two Voices are there; one is of the sea,
> One of the mountains; each a mighty Voice,

in order to describe the two facets of Wordsworth's poetic personality – the sublime and the ridiculous. And one of the Voices was, in Stephen's opinion, *very* ridiculous, being that of

> an old half-witted sheep
> Which bleats articulate monotony,
> And indicates that two and one are three,
> That grass is green, lakes damp, and mountains steep . . .

Another example of this type of parody, from the present century, is J. B. Morton's poetic attack on the mawkishness of A. A. Milne:

> Hush, hush,
> Nobody cares!
> Christopher Robin
> Has
> Fallen
> Down-
> Stairs.

And Chesterton uses Byron's characteristic manner to satirize the rumbustious Byronic lifestyle, ending it with a couplet about the dandy who

> sinks above his bills with bubbling groan,
> 'Absconded; gone abroad; address unknown.'

The second category takes a well-known text like Hamlet's soliloquy beginning 'To be, or not to be' and sticks as closely to it as possible, often using the same words at the beginnings of lines and even, if rhyme is involved, the same rhyming words. I found an example in a book of Victorian wit and humour, where Hamlet's soliloquy is adapted to express the anxiety and hesitancy felt before visiting a dentist. This sort of clever literary exercise was much favoured by minor Victorian poets and imitators. There is no attempt to ridicule; it's merely an amusing device in its own right.

In the third group, the target is the literary style of the poet, though the parodist may not necessarily have any particular poem in mind. One of the finest of these is William Empson's 'Just a Smack at Auden', which neatly captures the spirit of Auden's work at a certain time:

> Waiting for the end, boys, waiting for the end.
> What is there to be or do?
> What's become of me or you?
> Are we kind or are we true?
> Sitting two and two, boys, waiting for the end.

Another outstanding example is 'Chard Whitlow', the parody of T. S. Eliot by Henry Reed, who was himself a fine poet and wrote one of the most celebrated poems of the Second World War, 'Naming of Parts'. His parody is an ingenious collage of allusions to many different passages from Eliot's work and Eliot himself is reported to have admired it. I have also included Dylan Thomas's and John Davenport's parody of Stephen Spender, which evokes

Spender's characteristic themes and manner without sticking closely to any single poem. Similarly, Wendy Cope's parodies of Ted Hughes and Craig Raine are not related line for line to any particular piece, but they capture the flavour of the originals, I think, almost perfectly. I find little rancour in parodies of this sort; much more, admiration for the original. They convey what might even be described as a sense of literary fellowship. As Owen Seaman once wrote, 'only a man's friend, in the sense of one who is closely in touch with his work, has the right to parody him.'

The fourth category is where the parodist sets out to reverse completely the meaning of a vulnerable piece of verse. A good example is Shirley Brooks's treatment of Burns's 'For A' That and A' That', in which Burns extols the dignity and nobility of the poor. Brooks sticks very closely to Burns's words in order to sing the virtues of the rich. Here the parodist delights in sending up the solemnity or pious sentiments of the original. The Monty Python team did just that in their version of the hymn 'All things bright and beautiful', included here.

The fifth category is now the most common. In this case, the parodist takes a famous original and uses it as a model to comment upon some topical event, political figure or social development. Thus we have Roger Woddis borrowing the form of Christopher Logue's 'I Shall Vote Labour' in order to satirize the former Alliance parties in a piece called 'I Shall Vote Centre'. Or there is Sagittarius reworking Poe's 'The Raven' in her attack on Mussolini; or Paul Griffin adapting Belloc's 'Tarantella' for the sake of a comment on the hazards of modern Spanish holidays; or Simon Rae invoking one of Cat Stevens's lyrics to criticize Stevens's own attitude to Salman Rushdie and *The Satanic Verses*. Most parodies of this kind, however, are liable to date, and only a few stand the test of time when the subject they address has lingered in the collective memory.

Some of the items I have chosen for this book have

become so well known in their own right that they are often remembered and quoted without its being realized that they are parodies. Lewis Carroll wrote many that have achieved this status, 'The Lobster Quadrille', 'Father William' and 'The Song of the Mock Turtle' all being parodies of rather solemn pieces popular in his day but now largely forgotten. The middle and end of the nineteenth century was an especially fruitful time for the writing of parodies, and some of the finest and wittiest were composed by gifted minor poets such as J. K. Stephen, A. C. Hilton, Shirley Brooks, C. S. Calverley and Owen Seaman. Sadly, a number of these died young.

This has happily not been the case where our most accomplished recent parodists are concerned. Under the pseudonym Sagittarius, Olga Katzin Miller wrote weekly parodies for the *New Statesman* during the 1930s, 1940s and 1950s. She lived to a great age and I was lucky enough to meet her two or three times before she died. I recall her saying once that she would be very happy if she could be remembered for a line as haunting as Browning's 'What of soul was left, I wonder, when the kissing had to stop?' from 'A Toccata of Galuppi's'. She earns her place, at any rate, in any good anthology of parodies.

She was followed, as house parodist, by Roger Woddis, who has been wonderfully inventive for years. I first read his work when Richard Crossman was Editor of the *New Statesman*. I once said to Crossman that I didn't believe there was such a person as Roger Woddis, that there must be a team. He assured me that Woddis did exist and I have since been able to confirm this, having met the man himself. He continues to produce a huge number of fine parodies for the *New Statesman*, *Punch* and the *Radio Times*. He does this with great humour and spirit, and also with some humility. He wrote to me: 'After a lifetime of this curious trade, I'm still not sure what rings a bell.'

There are other excellent contemporary parodists,

notably Wendy Cope, Gavin Ewart and Simon Rae, who now writes regularly for the *Weekend Guardian*. The urge to parody is also given a frequent outlet in the competition pages of the *New Statesman* and the *Spectator*. I have included here a number of poems that have appeared in those columns over the last forty years. An identifiable group of gifted competitors exists. The pivot of this group is E. O. Parrott, who not only enters the competitions but often sets them as well. He is a brave spirit who has marvellously managed to overcome the affliction of near-blindness. I am grateful to him for putting me in touch with some of his colleagues: Martin Fagg, Stanley J. Sharpless, Paul Griffin, Mary Holtby, Noël Petty and Bill Greenwell. They are well represented in this collection.

I have enjoyed compiling this anthology, not least because I have had to spend time tracking down many of the original poems. Interestingly, the most frequently parodied poets seem to be Wordsworth, Tennyson, Browning, Kipling, Chesterton and Betjeman, and I have had to exclude innumerable parodies of their work. Poets of a more advanced style, on the other hand, have rather daunted the parodists, perhaps because their characteristic verse patterns are less readily recognizable, or because they have not written so many memorable lines. I might add that it wasn't easy to find decent parodies of Donne, Herbert, Marvell, Blake, Byron or Hopkins.

In case anyone should doubt its value, let me end by quoting one of the great poets of the twentieth century in support of the art of parody. In his essay 'The Poet and the City', W. H. Auden invokes his 'daydream College for Bards', in which a significant part of the set-up and curriculum would be as follows: 'The college library would contain no books of literary criticism, and the only critical exercise required of students would be the writing of parodies.'

Kenneth Baker, 1990

UNAUTHORIZED VERSIONS

MRS C. F. ALEXANDER (1818–95)

'All things bright and beautiful'

All things bright and beautiful,
   All creatures great and small,
All things wise and wonderful,
   The Lord God made them all.

Each little flower that opens,
   Each little bird that sings,
He made their glowing colours,
   He made their tiny wings.

The rich man in his castle,
   The poor man at his gate,
God made them, high or lowly,
   And order'd their estate.

The purple headed mountain,
   The river running by,
The sunset and the morning,
   That brightens up the sky.

    *

He gave us eyes to see them,
   And lips that we might tell
How great is God Almighty,
   Who has made all things well.

All Things Dull and Ugly

All things dull and ugly
All creatures short and squat
All things rude and nasty
The Lord God made the lot.

Each little snake that poisons
Each little wasp that stings
He made their brutish venom
He made their horrid wings.

All things sick and cancerous
All evil great and small
All things foul and dangerous
The Lord God made them all.

Each nasty little hornet
Each beastly little squid
Who made the spikey urchin,
Who made the sharks? He did.

All things scabbed and ulcerous
All pox both great and small
Putrid, foul and gangrenous,
The Lord God made them all.
Amen.

MONTY PYTHON

ANONYMOUS

Sumer is icumen in

   Sing! cuccu, nu. Sing! cuccu.
   Sing! cuccu. Sing! cuccu, nu.

Sumer is icumen in –
Lhude sing! cuccu.
Groweth sed and bloweth med
And springth the wude nu –
Sing! cuccu.

Awe bleteth after lomb,
Lhouth after calve cu,
Bulluc sterteth, bucke verteth,
Murie sing! cuccu.
Cuccu, cuccu,
Well singes thu, cuccu –
Ne swik thu naver nu!

'What are little boys made of?'

What are little boys made of?
What are little boys made of?
   Frogs and snails,
   And puppy-dogs' tails,
That's what little boys are made of.

What are little girls made of?
What are little girls made of?
   Sugar and spice
   And all that's nice,
That's what little girls are made of.

Ancient Music

Winter is icummen in,
Lhude sing Goddamm,
Raineth drop and staineth slop,
And how the wind doth ramm!
        Sing: Goddamm.
Skiddeth bus and sloppeth us,
An ague hath my ham.
Freezeth river, turneth liver,
        Damn you, sing: Goddamm.
Goddamm, Goddamm, 'tis why I am, Goddamm.
        So 'gainst the winter's balm.
Sing goddamm, damm, sing Goddamm,
Sing goddamm, sing goddamm, DAMM.

                EZRA POUND

Nursery Rhyme

What are the suburbs made of?
Fridges and freezers and eyebrow tweezers –
that's what the suburbs are made of!

What are the fine houses made of?
Clusters and clarets and 24-carats –
that's what fine houses are made of!

What are the tenements made of?
Dry rot and dampness, congestion and crampness –
that's what the tenements are made of!

                GAVIN EWART

'Who killed Cock Robin?'

Who killed Cock Robin?
I, said the Sparrow,
With my bow and arrow,
I killed Cock Robin.

Who saw him die?
I, said the Fly,
With my little eye,
I saw him die.

Who caught his blood?
I, said the Fish,
With my little dish
I caught his blood.

Who'll make the shroud?
I, said the Beetle,
With my thread and needle
I'll make the shroud.

Who'll dig his grave?
I, said the Owl,
With my pick and shovel,
I'll dig his grave.

Who'll be the parson?
I, said the Rook,
With my little book,
I'll be the parson.

Who'll be the clerk?
I, said the Lark,
If it's not in the dark,
I'll be the clerk.

John Keats

Who kill'd John Keats?
  'I,' says the Quarterly,
So savage and Tartarly;
  ''Twas one of my feats.'

Who shot the arrow?
  'The poet-priest Milman
(So ready to kill man),
  Or Southey, or Barrow.'

GEORGE GORDON, LORD BYRON

Keats published his first poem in 1816 and just five years later he
died of consumption. After the publication of *Endymion* in 1818,
he was viciously attacked in *Blackwood's Magazine*, where
reference to his medical training was dragged in: 'It is a better and
wiser thing to be a starved apothecary than a starved poet; so back
to the shop, Mr John, back to "plasters, pills and ointment boxes".
But for heaven's sake, young Sangrado, be a little more sparing of
extenuatives and soporifics in your practice than you have been in
your poetry.'

  John Wilson Croker also attacked Keats, in the *Quarterly
Review*, as did Henry Hart Milman, who in 1821 became the
Professor of Poetry at Oxford. And who has heard of Milman
now? Hazlitt was also attacked and responded with a libel writ,
but Keats was not so robust. In this indignant obituary Byron
helped to create the myth that Keats had been hounded to his
death by the critics. Not so, I think. Keats was himself quite clear
about his own significance, once remarking, 'I think I shall be
among the English poets after my death.'

Who'll carry the link?
I, said the Linnet,
I'll fetch it in a minute,
I'll carry the link.

Who'll be chief mourner?
I, said the Dove,
I'll mourn for my love,
I'll be chief mourner.

Who'll carry the coffin?
I, said the Kite,
If it's not through the night,
I'll carry the coffin.

Who'll bear the pall?
We, said the Wren,
Both the cock and the hen,
We'll bear the pall.

Who'll sing a psalm?
I, said the Thrush,
As she sat on a bush,
I'll sing a psalm.

Who'll toll the bell?
I, said the Bull,
Because I can pull,
I'll toll the bell.

All the birds of the air
Fell a-sighing and a-sobbing,
When they heard the bell toll
For poor Cock Robin.

This was first published in 1744 and some have claimed that it refers to the intrigues which led to the fall of Sir Robert Walpole. Others point to a traditional song going back to the thirteenth century.

The New Knighthood

Who gives him the Bath?
'I,' said the wet,
Rank Jungle-sweat,
'I'll give him the Bath!'

Who lays on the sword?
'I,' said the Sun,
'Before he has done,
'I'll lay on the sword.'

Who fastens his belt?
'I,' said Short-Rations,
'I know all the fashions
'Of tightening a belt!'

Who gives him his spur?
'I,' said his Chief,
Exacting and brief,
'I'll give him the spur.'

Who'll shake his hand?
'I,' said the Fever,
'And I'm no deceiver,
'I'll shake his hand.'

Who brings him the wine?
'I,' said Quinine,
'It's a habit of mine.
'I'll come with his wine.'

Who'll choose him for Knight?
'I,' said his Mother,
'Before any other,
'My very own Knight.'

And after this fashion, adventure to seek,
Was Sir Galahad made – as it might be last week!

RUDYARD KIPLING

God Rest You Merry

God rest you merry, Gentlemen,
   Let nothing you dismay,
For Jesus Christ our Saviour
   Was born upon this day,
To save us all from Satan's power
   When we were gone astray:

   O tidings of comfort and joy.

In Bethlehem in Jewry
   This blessèd babe was born,
And laid within a manger,
   Upon this blessèd morn;
The which his mother Mary
   Nothing did take in scorn:

   O tidings of comfort and joy.

    *

But when to Bethlehem they came,
   Whereat this infant lay,
They found him in a manger,
   Where oxen feed on hay;
His mother Mary kneeling,
   Unto the Lord did pray:

   O tidings of comfort and joy.

Now to the Lord sing praises,
   All you within this place,
And with true love and brotherhood
   Each other now embrace;
This holy tide of Christmas
   All others doth deface:

   O tidings of comfort and joy.

A Christmas Carol

The Chief Constable has issued a statement declaring that carol
singing in the streets by children is illegal, and morally and
physically injurious. He appeals to the public to discourage the
practice. – *Daily Paper*

God rest you merry gentlemen,
Let nothing you dismay;
The Herald Angels cannot sing,
The cops arrest them on the wing,
And warn them of the docketing
Of anything they say.

God rest you merry gentlemen,
May nothing you dismay:
On your reposeful cities lie
Deep silence, broken only by
The motor horn's melodious cry,
The hooter's happy bray.

So, when the song of children ceased
And Herod was obeyed,
In his high hall Corinthian
With purple and with peacock fan,
Rested that merry gentleman;
And nothing him dismayed.

G. K. CHESTERTON

from The Cutty Wren

O where are you going, says Milder to Malder,
O, I cannot tell, says Festel to Fose,
We're going to the woods, says John the Red Nose,
We're going to the woods, says John the Red Nose.

O, what will you do there, says Milder to Malder,
O, I cannot tell, says Festel to Fose,
We'll shoot the Cutty Wren, says John the Red Nose,
We'll shoot the Cutty Wren, says John the Red Nose.

O, how will you shoot her, says Milder to Malder,
O, I cannot tell, says Festel to Fose,
With arrows and bows, says John the Red Nose,
With arrows and bows, says John the Red Nose.

O, that will not do, says Milder to Malder,
O, what will do then, says Festel to Fose,
Big guns and cannons, says John the Red Nose,
Big guns and cannons, says John the Red Nose . . .

' "O *where are you going?" said reader to rider*'

'O where are you going?' said reader to rider,
'That valley is fatal when furnaces burn,
Yonder's the midden whose odours will madden,
That gap is the grave where the tall return.'

'O do you imagine,' said fearer to farer,
'That dusk will delay on your path to the pass,
Your diligent looking discover the lacking
Your footsteps feel from granite to grass?'

'O what was that bird,' said horror to hearer,
'Did you see that shape in the twisted trees?
Behind you swiftly the figure comes softly,
The spot on your skin is a shocking disease.'

'Out of this house' — said rider to reader,
'Yours never will' — said farer to fearer,
'They're looking for you' — said hearer to horror,
As he left them there, as he left them there.

W. H. AUDEN

Here Auden parodies the alliteration and rhythm of an old
English folk song, to his own characteristic poetic ends.

'O to scuttle from the battle'

O to scuttle from the battle and to settle on an atoll far
  from brutal mortal neath a wattle portal!
To keep little mottled cattle and to whittle down one's
  chattels and not hurtle after brittle yellow metal!
To listen, non-committal, to the anecdotal local tittle-
  tattle on a settle round the kettle,
Never startled by a rattle more than betel-nuts a-prattle
  or the myrtle-petals' subtle throttled chortle!
But I'll bet that what'll happen if you footle round an
  atoll is you'll get in rotten fettle living totally on turtle,
  nettles, cuttle-fish or beetles, victuals fatal to the natal
  élan-vital,
And hit the bottle.
I guess I'd settle
For somewhere ethical and practical like Bootle.

This celebrated tongue-twister first appeared in *Punch* and I have
heard its authorship attributed to one Justin Richardson. In 1987,
Spectator readers were invited to compose up-to-date versions.

'I could have been Lord Dacre'

I could have been Lord Dacre or a balalaika-maker,
A docker or a vicar or a pickled-pepper-picker,
A shorter Peter Walker or a meeker Kenneth Baker
Or a lucre-laden Laker or an even slicker Whicker . . .
I could have been a hookah-smoker hunkering in Mecca,
A liquor-wrecked old busker or a biker or a trucker,
A darker Charlie Parker or a sleeker Chubby Checker,
A stoker or a broker or a gee-gee-backing sucker . . .
I could have been a soccer striker hooked on beta-
    blockers,
A double-decker-wrecker or a knicker-dropping hooker,
A knocker-back of hock or one of oakier Riojas . . .
But I'm only Jeffrey Archer and I'll *never* win the Booker!

PETER NORMAN

W. H. AUDEN (1907–73)

from Miss Gee

Let me tell you a little story
    About Miss Edith Gee;
She lived in Clevedon Terrace
    At Number 83.

She'd a slight squint in her left eye,
    Her lips they were thin and small,
She had narrow sloping shoulders
    And she had no bust at all.

     *

She bicycled down to the doctor,
    And rang the surgery bell;
'O, doctor, I've a pain inside me,
    And I don't feel very well.'

Doctor Thomas looked her over,
    And then he looked some more;
Walked over to his wash-basin,
    Said: 'Why didn't you come before?'

Doctor Thomas sat over his dinner,
    Though his wife was waiting to ring;
Rolling his bread into pellets,
    Said: 'Cancer's a funny thing . . .'

     *

They took Miss Gee to the hospital,
    She lay there a total wreck,
Lay in the ward for women
    With the bedclothes right up to her neck.

A Moral Tale

'No one ever has the authority to destroy unborn life.' – *The Pope*

Let me tell you a little story
   About Miss Edith Gee;
She lacked the kind of figure
   That decorates page 3.

She had narrow sloping shoulders
   And she had no bust at all,
But one evening on the common
   In fear she gave her all.

She did not love the stranger,
   She had to yield to force,
And more than her eyes were swollen
   As nature took its course.

She went to Doctor Brady,
   He rubbed his shaven chin;
'To do the thing you ask me
   Would be a mortal sin.'

And since he thought it sinful
   To end an unborn life,
She ended in a back street
   Beneath a rusty knife.

And now in Hell she suffers
   For all Eternity;
There never was a lady
   As wicked as Miss Gee.

ROGER WODDIS

They laid her on the table,
    The students began to laugh;
And Mr Rose the surgeon
    He cut Miss Gee in half.

Mr Rose he turned to his students,
    Said: 'Gentlemen, if you please,
We seldom see a sarcoma
    As far advanced as this.'

They took her off the table,
    They wheeled away Miss Gee
Down to another department
    Where they study Anatomy.

They hung her from the ceiling,
    Yes, they hung up Miss Gee;
And a couple of Oxford Groupers
    Carefully dissected her knee.

from The Dog Beneath the Skin

NINEVEH GIRLS [*sing*].
    We are girls of different ages,
    All sorts of girls at all sorts of stages, we've
        Come to delight you,
        Come to excite you,
        Come to present our revue!
    Fair girls, dear girls,
    Dark girls, stark girls,
    Glad girls, bad girls,
    Poor girls, we've-met-before-girls, we
        All would welcome you.

Roger Woddis wrote this in 1979, at the time of Pope John Paul
II's triumphal and much-publicized tour of Ireland and the United
States, when His Holiness took the opportunity to reaffirm the
Roman Catholic Church's opposition to birth-control and
abortion.

Just a Smack at Auden

Waiting for the end, boys, waiting for the end.
What is there to be or do?
What's become of me or you?
Are we kind or are we true?
Sitting two and two, boys, waiting for the end.

Shall I build a tower, boys, knowing it will rend
Crack upon the hour, boys, waiting for the end?
Shall I pluck a flower, boys, shall I save or spend?
All turns sour, boys, waiting for the end.

Desires, ambitions, anxieties fill us,
We come from brick rectories and sham-Tudor villas,
    It's our profession
    To cure your depression
    And banish those melancholy blues.
Old girls, bold girls,
Shy girls, fly girls,
Kiss-girls, sis-girls,
Lean girls, do-you-get-what-I-mean-girls, you
    Only have to choose.

We lift our legs for your masculine inspection,
You can admire us without our correction, we
    Do this nightly,
    We hope we're not unsightly
    Or all our labours are vain!
Neat girls, sweet girls,
Gym girls, slim girls,
Meek girls, technique girls,
Pat girls, come-up-to-my-flat-girls, we
    Hope to see you again!

There is no one poem that will quite match Empson's famous
'Smack', but this chorus from the play Auden wrote in
collaboration with Christopher Isherwood shows at least
something of the slangy idiom and cabaret jauntiness that Empson
picked up. Auden later wrote a generous tribute to Empson, which
begins:

    As *quid pro quo* for your enchanting verses,
    when approached by Sheffield, at first I wondered
    if I could manage *Just a Smack at Empson*,
        but nothing occurred.

Shall I send a wire, boys? Where is there to send?
All are under fire, boys, waiting for the end.
Shall I turn a sire, boys? Shall I choose a friend?
The fat is in the pyre, boys, waiting for the end.

Shall I make it clear, boys, for all to apprehend,
Those that will not hear, boys, waiting for the end,
Knowing it is near, boys, trying to pretend,
Sitting in cold fear, boys, waiting for the end?

Shall we send a cable, boys, accurately penned,
Knowing we are able, boys, waiting for the end,
Via the Tower of Babel, boys? Christ will not ascend.
He's hiding in his stable, boys, waiting for the end.

Shall we blow a bubble, boys, glittering to distend,
Hiding from our trouble, boys, waiting for the end?
When you build on rubble, boys, Nature will append
Double and re-double, boys, waiting for the end.

Shall we make a tale, boys, that things are sure to mend,
Playing bluff and hale, boys, waiting for the end?
It will be born stale, boys, stinking to offend,
Dying ere it fail, boys, waiting for the end.

Shall we go all wild, boys, waste and make them lend,
Playing at the child, boys, waiting for the end?
It has all been filed, boys, history has a trend,
Each of us enisled, boys, waiting for the end.

What was said by Marx, boys, what did he perpend?
No good being sparks, boys, waiting for the end.
Treason of the clerks, boys, curtains that descend,
Lights becoming darks, boys, waiting for the end.

Waiting for the end, boys, waiting for the end.
Not a chance of blend, boys, things have got to tend.
Think of those who vend, boys, think of how we wend,
Waiting for the end, boys, waiting for the end.

                                        WILLIAM EMPSON

ALFRED AUSTIN (1835–1913)

from Jameson's Ride

Wrong! Is it wrong? Well, may be:
   But I'm going, boys, all the same.
Do they think me a Burgher's baby,
   To be scared by a scolding name?
They may argue, and prate, and order;
   Go, tell them to save their breath:
Then, over the Transvaal border,
   And gallop for life or death!

Let lawyers and statesmen addle
   Their pates over points of law;
If sound be our sword, and saddle,
   And gun-gear, who cares one straw?
When men of our own blood pray us
   To ride to their kinsfolk's aid,
Not Heaven itself shall stay us
   From the rescue they call a raid.

     *

So we forded and galloped forward,
   As hard as our beasts could pelt,
First eastward, then trending northward,
   Right over the rolling veldt;
Till we came on the Burghers lying
   In a hollow with hills behind,
And their bullets came hissing, flying,
   Like hail on an Arctic wind!

Right sweet is the marksman's rattle,
   And sweeter the cannon's roar,
But 'tis bitterly bad to battle,

England's Alfred Abroad

[M. Alfred Austin, poète-lauréat d'Angleterre, vient d'arriver à
Nice, où il a devancé la Reine. Il était, hier, dans les jardins de
Monte-Carlo. Sera-ce sous notre ciel qu'il écrira son premier
poème? – *Menton-Mondain.*]

Wrong? are they wrong? Of course they are,
    I venture to reply;
For I bore 'my first' (and, I hope, my worst)
    A month or so gone by;
And I can't repeat it under this
    Or any other sky.

What! has the public never heard
    In these benighted climes
That nascent note of my Laureate throat,
    That fluty fitte of rhymes
Which occupied about a half
    A column of the *Times?*

They little know what they have lost,
    Nor what a carnal beano
They might have spent in the thick of Lent
    If only Daniel Leno
Had sung them *Jameson's Ride* and knocked
    The Monaco Casino.

                *

Nay! this is life! to take a turn
    On Fortune's captious crust;
To pluck the day in a human way
    Like men of common dust;

Beleaguered, and one to four.
I can tell you it wasn't a trifle
    To swarm over Krugersdorp glen,
As they plied us with round and rifle,
    And ploughed us, again – and again.

*

I suppose we were wrong, were madmen,
    Still I think at the Judgment Day,
When God sifts the good from the bad men,
    There'll be something more to say.
We were wrong, but we aren't half sorry,
    And, as one of the baffled band,
I would rather have had that foray,
    Than the crushings of all the Rand.

After Tennyson's death in 1892, the post of Poet Laureate was left vacant for three years, largely because the leading poet of the day, Swinburne, was *persona non grata* to the Establishment. Then, surprisingly, Alfred Austin was appointed, and with reckless haste he sent this poem to *The Times*, praising Jameson's foolhardy ride into the Transvaal – an escapade which the Government itself had immediately repudiated. Jameson eventually got fifteen months in gaol. Austin never really recovered from the avalanche of criticism with which his poem was greeted, for even Queen Victoria complained about it to the Prince Minister. Mark Twain, visiting London, described it as 'a Poet Laureate explosion of coloured fireworks which filled the world's sky with giddy splendours'.

But O! if England's only bard
  Should absolutely bust!

A laureate never borrows on
  His coming quarter's pay;
And I mean to stop or ever I pop
  My crown of peerless bay;
So I'll take the next *rapide* to Nice,
  And the 'bus to Cimiez.

OWEN SEAMAN

Sir Owen Seaman was the son of a florist in Sloane Street, and the
modest income from that business saw him to Cambridge and a
career of intermittent schoolteaching. He was a donnish bachelor
who liked cricket and sailing, but he also developed a talent for
light verse. This led to his becoming the Editor of *Punch* from
1906 to 1932, when that weekly magazine and its main political
cartoon carried real influence. His first book of parodies, *The
Battle of the Bays* of 1895, parodied all contenders for the Poet
Laureateship. Seaman was a skilful parodist, though too often his
targets were minor poets celebrated in their day, but now not read
or even remembered.

HILAIRE BELLOC (1870–1953)

Noël

On a winter's night long time ago
  (*The bells ring loud and the bells ring low*),
When high howled wind, and down fell snow
  (Carillon, Carilla).
Saint Joseph he and Nostre Dame,
Riding on an ass, full weary came
From Nazareth into Bethlehem.
  And the small child Jesus smile on you.

And Bethlehem inn they stood before
  (*The bells ring less and the bells ring more*),
The landlord bade them begone from his door
  (Carillon, Carilla).
'Poor folk' (says he), 'must lie where they may,
For the Duke of Jewry comes this way,
With all his train on a Christmas Day.'
  And the small child Jesus smile on you.

Tarantella

Do you remember an Inn,
Miranda?
Do you remember an Inn?
And the tedding and the spreading
Of the straw for a bedding,
And the fleas that tease in the High Pyrenees,
And the wine that tasted of the tar?
And the cheers and the jeers of the young muleteers
(Under the vine of the dark verandah)?
Do you remember an Inn, Miranda,

After Hilaire Belloc

One Christmas Night in Pontgibaud
   (*Pom-pom, rub-a-dub-dub*)
A man with a drum went to and fro
   (*Two merry eyes, two cheeks chub*)
Nor not a citril within, without,
But heard the racket and heard the rout
And marvelled what it was all about
   (*And who shall shrive Beelzebub?*)

He whacked so hard the drum was split
   (*Pom-pom, rub-a-dub-dum*)
Out lept Saint Gabriel from it
   (*Praeclarissimus Omnium*)
Who spread his wings and up he went
Nor ever paused in his ascent
Till he had reached the firmament
   (*Benedicamus Dominum*).

MAX BEERBOHM

New Tarantella

Do you remember an Inn,
Matilda?
Do you remember an Inn?
And the clangs and the bangs
Of the gangs from the builder?
Do you remember an Inn,
Matilda?
Do you remember an Inn?
And the porter mixing mortar
With a bucketful of water,

Do you remember an Inn?
And the cheers and the jeers of the young muleteers
Who hadn't got a penny,
And who weren't paying any,
And the hammer at the doors and the Din?
And the Hip! Hop! Hap!
Of the clap
Of the hands to the twirl and the swirl
Of the girl gone chancing,
Glancing,
Dancing,
Backing and advancing,
Snapping of a clapper to the spin
Out and in —
And the Ting, Tong, Tang of the Guitar!
Do you remember an Inn,
Miranda?
Do you remember an Inn?

    Never more;
    Miranda,
    Never more.
    Only the high peaks hoar:
    And Aragon a torrent at the door.
    No sound
    In the walls of the Halls where falls
    The tread
    Of the feet of the dead to the ground
    No sound:
    But the boom
    Of the far Waterfall like Doom.

Fatigue

I'm tired of Love: I'm still more tired of Rhyme.
But Money gives me pleasure all the time.

And the floorless, doorless room?
And the stamp, stamp, stamp
Of the tramp in the damp
Of the workmen marching,
Putting up the arching,
Knocking off the copper from the roof;
And the woof! and the grrr!
And the stir
Of the long-tailed cur
Snapping at the chappies in the gloom?

    Nevermore,
    Matilda,
    Nevermore;
    No Inn without a window or a door;
    Only a neat,
    Complete Hotel,
    Not a cell with a smell
    On the Costa del Sol,
    Not a hol
    Like Hell.

PAUL GRIFFIN

Variation on Belloc's 'Fatigue'

I hardly ever tire of love or rhyme —
That's why I'm poor and have a rotten time.

WENDY COPE

JOHN BETJEMAN (1906–84)

How to Get On in Society

Phone for the fish knives Norman,
  As cook is a little unnerved;
Your kiddies have crumpled the serviettes
  And I must have things daintily served.

Are the requisites all in the toilet?
  The frills round the cutlets can wait
Till the girl has replenished the cruets
  And switched on the logs in the grate.

It's ever so close in the lounge dear,
  But the vestibule's comfy for tea,
And Howard is out riding on horseback
  So do come and take some with me.

Now here is a fork for your pastries
  And do use the couch for your feet;
I know what I wanted to ask you –
  Is trifle sufficient for sweet?

Milk and then just as it comes dear?
  I'm afraid the preserve's full of stones.
Beg pardon, I'm soiling the doileys
  With afternoon tea-cake and scones.

'Would you care for a smoke or a sherry?'

Would you care for a smoke or a sherry?
  The cocktail cabinet's there.
No, the savoury spread and the vitamin bread's
  In the cubby hole under the stair.

Has Uncle gone out on his cycle?
  He left making terrible sounds,
Saying 'Just what the medico ordered'.
  I'm afraid he'll get lost in the grounds.

We've several new gnomes in the rockery
  And his eyesight's not dreadfully strong.
Bring the flash from my handbag. Good gracious,
  He's had a mishap! Hark, the gong.

Just leave your bootees in the hallway
  Till the cloakroom is free, there's a pet.
My friend left his mac in the dining recess
  And ruined our condiment set!

Yes, this costume was made for my Auntie.
  She said I must have a new gown.
I wear any old bags in the country,
  But one has to be soignée in town.

MOPEV

Betjeman's famous poem on social solecisms appeared in *Time and Tide* in 1951, and he himself invited readers to compose further verses in the same metre and on the same theme. He judged this pseudonymous effort 'better than my own'.

On Seeing an Old Poet in the Café Royal

I saw him in the Café Royal,
  Very old and very grand.
Modernistic shone the lamplight
  There in London's fairyland.
'Devilled chicken. Devilled whitebait.
  Devil if I understand.

'Where is Oscar? Where is Bosie?
  Have I seen that man before?
And the old one in the corner,
  Is it really Wratislaw?'
Scent of Tutti-Frutti-Sen-Sen
  And cheroots upon the floor.

Betjeman, 1984

I saw him in the Airstrip Gardens
    (Fahrenheit at 451)
Feeding automative orchids
    With a little plastic bun,
While above his brickwork cranium
    Burned the trapped and troubled sun.

'Where is Piper? Where is Pontefract?
    (Devil take my boiling pate!)
Where is Pam? and where's Myfanwy?
    Don't remind me of the date!
Can it be that I am *really*
    Knocking on for 78?

'In my splendid State Apartment
    Underneath a secret lock
Finger now forbidden treasures
    (Pray for me St Enodoc!):
TV plate and concrete lamp-post
    And a single nylon sock.

'Take your ease, pale-haired admirer,
    As I, half the century saner,
Pour a vintage Mazawattee
    Through the Marks and Spencer strainer
In a *genuine* British Railways
    (Luton made) cardboard container.

'Though they say my verse-compulsion
    Lacks an interstellar drive,
Reading Beverley and Daphne
    Keeps *my* sense of words alive.
Lord, but *how* much beauty was there
    Back in 1955!'

                              CHARLES CAUSLEY

Business Girls

From the geyser ventilators
  Autumn winds are blowing down
On a thousand business women
  Having baths in Camden Town.

Waste pipes chuckle into runnels,
  Steam's escaping here and there,
Morning trains through Camden cutting
  Shake the Crescent and the Square.

Early nip of changeful autumn,
  Dahlias glimpsed through garden doors,
At the back precarious bathrooms
  Jutting out from upper floors,

And behind their frail partitions
  Business women lie and soak,
Seeing through the draughty skylight
  Flying clouds and railway smoke.

Rest you there, poor unbelov'd ones,
  Lap your loneliness in heat.
All too soon the tiny breakfast,
  Trolley-bus and windy street!

Place Names of China

Bolding Vedas! Shanks New Nisa!
Trusty Lichfield swirls it down
To filter beds on Ruislip Marshes
From my loo in Kentish Town.

The Burlington! The Rochester!
Oh those names of childhood loos –
Nursie knocking at the door
'Have you done your Number Twos?'

Lady typist – office party –
Golly! All that gassy beer!
Tripping home down Hendon Parkway
To her Improved Windermere.

Chelsea buns and Lounge Bar pasties
All swilled down with Benskin's Pale,
Purified and cleansed by charcoal,
Fill the taps in Colindale.

Here I sit, alone and sixty,
Bald, and fat, and full of sin,
Cold the seat and loud the cistern,
As I read the Harpic tin.

ALAN BENNETT

WILLIAM BLAKE (1757–1827)

Jerusalem

And did those feet in ancient time
Walk upon England's mountains green?
And was the holy Lamb of God
On England's pleasant pastures seen?

And did the Countenance Divine
Shine forth upon our clouded hills?
And was Jerusalem builded here
Among these dark Satanic Mills?

Bring me my Bow of burning gold!
Bring me my Arrows of desire!
Bring me my Spear! O clouds, unfold!
Bring me my Chariot of fire!

I will not cease from Mental Fight,
Nor shall my Sword sleep in my hand,
Till we have built Jerusalem
In England's green and pleasant land.

from Auguries of Innocence

The bat that flits at close of eve
Has left the brain that won't believe.

The New Jerusalem

And did these feet, in pre-war days,
  Walk along England's lighted streets?
And were shop-windows all ablaze,
  And coppers silent on their beats?
And did that Corporation bus
  Shine forth in splendour from afar?
And was it mere child's play for us
  To dodge the swiftly-moving car?

Bring me my torch of waning power!
  Bring me my phosphor button bright!
Bring me my stick – O, dreadful hour!
  That brings the darkness of the night!
I will not cease from pavement taps,
  Nor shall my stick sleep in my hand
Till I have tested all the gaps
  In England's blind and shuttered land!

ALLAN M. LAING

Allan M. Laing was a Liverpool Scot who started to enter literary
competitions in the 1930s and continued until well after the
Second World War. He won so many that an anthology of his
work alone was published in 1941. His 'New Jerusalem' describes
the wartime black-out, when windows were sealed so that no chink
of light could give help to the German bombers.

'The bat that blocks at close of play'

The bat that blocks at close of play
Stays to hit another day.

JOYCE JOHNSON

RUPERT BROOKE (1887–1915)

The Soldier

If I should die, think only this of me:
    That there's some corner of a foreign field
That is for ever England. There shall be
    In that rich earth a richer dust concealed;
A dust whom England bore, shaped, made aware,
    Gave, once, her flowers to love, her ways to roam,
A body of England's, breathing English air,
    Washed by the rivers, blest by suns of home.

And think, this heart, all evil shed away,
    A pulse in the eternal mind, no less
        Gives somewhere back the thoughts by England
            given;
Her sights and sounds; dreams happy as her day;
    And laughter, learnt of friends; and gentleness,
        In hearts at peace, under an English heaven.

The Doctor

The result of the SDP's ballot on merger with the Liberals follows
three days after the centenary of the birth of Rupert Brooke

If I should lose, think only this of me:
   That there's some lesion, when the wound has healed,
That is for ever bleeding. There shall be
   In years to come a larger lust revealed;
A lust to lead that overrides despair,
   Though it makes Roy and Bill and Shirley foam
And even drives boy David to declare
   That Number Ten is not my natural home.

To think that I will simply sail away,
   If all those merger maniacs say 'Yes',
     Is to believe there is no God in heaven.
Whatever friends and foes alike may say,
   Unmindful of the ego I possess,
     I'm damned if I'll just be our man in Devon.

ROGER WODDIS

After the General Election of 1987, David Steel set out to break
what had been the temporary 'Alliance Party' and to force a
merger between his Liberal Party and the Social Democratic Party
led by David Owen. Dr Owen realized that his smaller party would
be overwhelmed by the Liberals and that he would have to accept
their non-nuclear defence policy. Although the other members of
the 'gang of four' who had founded the SDP – Roy Jenkins, Shirley
Williams and Bill Rodgers – favoured a merger, Owen, together
with two other MPs, decided to hold out against it. Within nine
months of the election, the Alliance had foundered on the pique of
David Steel and the pride of David Owen.

T. E. BROWN (1830–97)

My Garden

A garden is a lovesome thing, God wot!
Rose plot,
Fringed pool,
Ferned grot –
The veriest school
Of peace; and yet the fool
Contends that God is not –
Not God! in gardens! when the eve is cool?
Nay, but I have a sign;
'Tis very sure God walks in mine.

This is the most famous poem by the Manx poet who, while
teaching at Oxford and Bristol, wrote many verses in Manx
dialect, though not in the Manx language. They are vigorous and
show a great disdain for what Brown called 'cockney balderdash'.

My Garden

A garden is a loathsome thing, God wot!
Black spot,
  Fat slug,
Dank grot.
  Who'd be a mug
  Trudging with spade and trug?
Not this poor clot!
  I'll soon be shot
  Of worm and snail and bug.
For now I've got
A sign: *To Let, new-dug,*
One Garden Plot.

                    P. R. HINES

ELIZABETH BARRETT BROWNING (1806–61)

'How do I love thee?'

How do I love thee? Let me count the ways.
I love thee to the depth and breadth and height
My soul can reach, when feeling out of sight
For the ends of Being and ideal Grace.
I love thee to the level of every day's
Most quiet need, by sun and candle-light.
I love thee freely, as men strive for right;
I love thee purely, as they turn from praise.
I love thee with the passion put to use
In my old griefs, and with my childhood's faith.
I love thee with a love I seemed to lose
With my lost saints – I love thee with the breath,
Smiles, tears, of all my life! – and, if God choose,
I shall but love thee better after death.

Sonnet

How do I hate you? Let me count the ways:
I hate your greying hair, now almost white,
Your blotchy skin, a most repellent sight,
The eyes that stare back in a sort of daze,
The turned-up nose, the hollow that betrays
The missing dentures, taken out at night,
Receding chin, whose contour isn't quite
Masked by the scraggy beard – in a phrase,
I hate the sight of you, as every morn,
We meet each other in our favourite place,
And casually, as to the manner born,
You make your all too customary grimace,
Something between disgust, boredom and scorn;
God, how I loathe you, shaving-mirror face.

                              STANLEY J. SHARPLESS

ROBERT BROWNING (1812–89)

Home-Thoughts, from Abroad

Oh, to be in England
Now that April's there,
And whoever wakes in England
Sees, some morning, unaware,
That the lowest boughs and the brushwood sheaf
Round the elm-tree bole are in tiny leaf,
While the chaffinch sings on the orchard bough
In England – now!

And after April, when May follows,
And the whitethroat builds, and all the swallows!
Hark, where my blossomed pear-tree in the hedge
Leans to the field and scatters on the clover
Blossoms and dewdrops – at the bent spray's edge –
That's the wise thrush; he sings each song twice over,
Lest you should think he never could recapture
The first fine careless rapture!
And though the fields look rough with hoary dew,
All will be gay when noontide wakes anew
The buttercups, the little children's dower
– Far brighter than this gaudy melon-flower!

Home Truths from Abroad

Oh, to be in England
Now that April's there,
And whoever wakes in England
Sees some morning, in despair,
There's a horrible fog i' the heart o' the town,
And the greasy pavement is damp and brown;
While the rain-drop falls from the laden bough,
In England – now!

And after April when May follows,
How foolish seem the returning swallows.
Hark! how the east wind sweeps along the street,
And how we give one universal sneeze!
The hapless lambs at thought of mint-sauce bleat,
And ducks are conscious of the coming peas.

Lest you should think the Spring is really present,
A biting frost will come to make things pleasant,
And though the reckless flowers begin to blow,
They'd better far have nestled down below;
And English spring sets men and women frowning,
Despite the rhapsodies of Robert Browning.

ANONYMOUS

from Soliloquy of the Spanish Cloister

Gr-r-r – there go, my heart's abhorrence!
   Water your damned flower-pots, do!
If hate killed men, Brother Lawrence,
   God's blood, would not mine kill you!
What? your myrtle-bush wants trimming?
   Oh, that rose has prior claims –
Needs its leaden vase filled brimming?
   Hell dry you up with its flames!

At the meal we sit together:
   Salve tibi! I must hear
Wise talk of the kind of weather,
   Sort of season, time of year:
Not a plenteous cork-crop: scarcely
   Dare we hope oak-galls, I doubt:
What's the Latin name for 'parsley'?
   What's the Greek name for Swine's Snout?

    *

There's a great text in Galatians,
   Once you trip on it, entails
Twenty-nine distinct damnations,
   One sure, if another fails:
If I trip him just a-dying,
   Sure of heaven as sure can be,
Spin him round and send him flying
   Off to hell, a Manichee?

    *

Or, there's Satan! – one might venture
   Pledge one's soul to him, yet leave

From a Spanish Cloister

Grrr – what's that? A dog? A poet?
  Uttering his damnations thus –
If hate killed things, Brother Browning,
  God's Word, would not hate kill us?

If we ever meet together,
  Salve tibi! I might hear
How you know poor monks are really
  So much worse than they appear.

There's a great text in Corinthians
  Hinting that our faith entails
Something else, that never faileth,
  Yet in you, perhaps, it fails.

But if *plena gratia* chokes you,
  You at least can teach us how
To converse in wordless noises,
  Hy, zi; hullo! – Grrr – Bow-wow!

G. K. CHESTERTON

Browning was lionized by society and ladies craved a lock of his hair. Other writers took a cooler view of him, and Hopkins made the comment that 'he had all the gifts but the one needful – the pearls without the string.' They were, however, pearls of the very best quality, and have been much imitated and parodied.

Perhaps the text from Galatians which Browning had in mind for this jealous and hateful monk was from chapter V, verses 14 and 15:

Such a flaw in the indenture
    As he'd miss till, past retrieve,
Blasted lay that rose-acacia
    We're so proud of! *Hy, Zy, Hine* . . .
'St, there's Vespers! *Plena gratiâ*
    Ave, Virgo! Gr-r-r – you swine!

A Toccata of Galuppi's

Oh, Galuppi, Baldassaro, this is very sad to find!
I can hardly misconceive you; it would prove me deaf
    and blind;
But although I give you credit, 'tis with such a heavy
    mind!

Here you come with your old music, and here's all the
    good it brings.
What, they lived once thus at Venice, where the
    merchants were the kings,
Where St Mark's is, where the Doges used to wed the sea
    with rings?

Ay, because the sea's the street there; and 'tis arched by
    . . . what you call
. . . Shylock's bridge with houses on it, where they kept
    the carnival!
I was never out of England – it's as if I saw it all!

Did young people take their pleasure when the sea was
    warm in May?
Balls and masks begun at midnight, burning ever to mid-
    day,
When they made up fresh adventures for the morrow, do
    you say?

For all the law is fulfilled in one word, even in this; Thou shalt
    love thy neighbour as thyself.
But if ye bite and devour one another, take heed that ye be not
    consumed one of another.

Chesterton in this spirited parody refers to the famous passage
from Corinthians which places charity as the pre-eminent virtue:
'And now abideth faith, hope, charity, these three; but the greatest
of these is charity.'

A Nocturne at Danieli's

Caro mio, Pulcinello, kindly hear my wail of woe
Lifted from a noble structure – late Palazzo Dandolo.

This is Venice, you will gather, which is full of precious
    'stones',
Tintorettos, picture-postcards, and remains of doges'
    bones.

Not of these am I complaining; they are mostly seen by
    day,
And they only try your patience in an inoffensive way.

But at night, when over Lido rises Dian (that's the moon),
And the vicious *vaporetti* cease to vex the still lagoon;

When the final *trovatore*, singing something old and
    cheap,
Hurls his *tremolo crescendo* full against my beauty sleep;

When I hear the Riva's loungers in debate beneath my
    bower
Summing up (about 1.30) certain questions of the hour;

Then across my nervous system falls the shrill mosquito's
    boom,
And it's 'O, to be in England', where the may is on the
    bloom.

Was a lady such a lady, cheeks so round and lips so
  red, –
On her neck the small face buoyant, like a bell-flower on
  its bed,
O'er the breast's superb abundance where a man might
  base his head?

Well (and it was graceful of them) they'd break talk off
  and afford
– She, to bite her mask's black velvet, he to finger on his
  sword,
While you sat and played Toccatas, stately at the
  clavichord?

What? Those lesser thirds so plaintive, sixths diminished,
  sigh on sigh,
Told them something? Those suspensions, those solutions
  – 'Must we die?'
Those commiserating sevenths – 'Life might last! we can
  but try!'

'Were you happy?' – 'Yes.' – 'And are you still as
  happy?' – 'Yes – And you?'
– 'Then more kisses' – 'Did *I* stop them, when a million
  seemed so few?'
Hark – the dominant's persistence, till it must be
  answered to!

So an octave struck the answer. Oh, they praised you, I
  dare say!
'Brave Galuppi! that was music! good alike at grave and
  gay!
I can always leave off talking, when I hear a master play.'

Then they left you for their pleasure: till in due time, one
  by one,
Some with lives that came to nothing, some with deeds as
  well undone,

I admit the power of Music to inflate the savage breast –
There are songs devoid of language which are quite
    among the best –

But the present orchestration, with its poignant oboe part,
Is, in my obscure opinion, barely fit to rank as Art.

Will it solace me to-morrow, being bit in either eye,
To be told that this is nothing to the season in July?

Shall I go for help to Ruskin? Would it ease my pimply
    brow
If I found the doges suffered much as I am suffering now?

If identical probosces pinked the lovers who were bored
By the sentimental tinkling of Galuppi's clavichord?

That's from Browning (Robert Browning) – I have left his
    works at home,
And the poem I allude to isn't in the Tauchnitz tome;

But, if memory serves me rightly, he was very much
    concerned
At the thought that in the sequel Venice reaped what
    Venice earned.

Was he thinking of mosquitoes? Did he mean *their*
    poisoned crop?
Was it through ammonia tincture that 'the kissing had to
    stop'?

As for later loves – for Venice never quite mislaid her
    spell –
Madame Sand and dear De Musset occupied my own
    hotel!

On the very floor below me, I have heard the patron say,
They were put in No. 13 (No. 36, to-day).

But they parted – '*elle et lui*' did – and it now occurs to
    me

Death came tacitly and took them where they never see
the sun.

But when I sit down to reason, — think to take my stand
nor swerve
Till I triumph o'er a secret wrung from nature's close
reserve,
In you come with your cold music, till I creep thro' every
nerve.

Yes, you, like a ghostly cricket, creaking where a house
was burned —
'Dust and ashes, dead and done with, Venice spent what
Venice earned!
The soul, doubtless, is immortal — where a soul can be
discerned.

'Yours for instance, you know physics, something of
geology,
Mathematics are your pastime; souls shall rise in their
degree;
Butterflies may dread extinction, — you'll not die, it
cannot be!

'As for Venice and its people, merely born to bloom and
drop,
Here on earth they bore their fruitage, mirth and folly
were the crop.
What of soul was left, I wonder, when the kissing had to
stop?

'Dust and ashes!' So you creak it, and I want the heart to
scold.
Dear dead women, with such hair, too — what's become
of all the gold
Used to hang and brush their bosoms? I feel chilly and
grown old.

That mosquitoes came between them in this 'kingdom by
   the sea'.

Poor dead lovers, and such brains, too! What am I that I
   should swear
When the creatures munch my forehead, taking more than
   I can spare?

Should I live to meet the morning, should the climate
   readjust
Any reparable fragments left upon my outer crust,

Why, at least I still am extant, and a dog that sees the sun
Has the pull of Danieli's den of 'lions', dead and done.

Courage! I will keep my vigil on the balcony till day
Like a knight in full pyjamas who would rather run away.

Courage! let me ope the casement, let the shutters be
   withdrawn;
Let sirocco, breathing on me, check a tendency to yawn;
There's the sea! and – *Ecco l'alba!* Ha! (in other words)
   the Dawn!

OWEN SEAMAN

from How They Brought the Good News
from Ghent to Aix

I sprang to the stirrup, and Joris, and he;
I galloped, Dirck galloped, we galloped all three;
'Good speed!' cried the watch, as the gate-bolts undrew;
'Speed!' echoed the wall to us galloping through;
Behind shut the postern, the lights sank to rest,
And into the midnight we galloped abreast.

Not a word to each other; we kept the great pace
Neck by neck, stride by stride, never changing our place;
I turned in my saddle and made its girths tight,
Then shortened each stirrup, and set the pique right,
Rebuckled the cheek-strap, chained slacker the bit,
Nor galloped less steadily Roland a whit.

                *

So, we were left galloping, Joris and I,
Past Looz and past Tongres, no cloud in the sky;
The broad sun above laughed a pitiless laugh,
'Neath our feet broke the brittle bright stubble like chaff;
Till over by Dalhem a dome-spire sprang white,
And 'Gallop,' gasped Joris, 'for Aix is in sight!'

'How they'll greet us!' – and all in a moment his roan
Rolled neck and croup over, lay dead as a stone;
And there was my Roland to bear the whole weight
Of the news which alone could save Aix from her fate,
With his nostrils like pits full of blood to the brim,
And with circles of red for his eye-sockets' rim.

Then I cast loose my buffcoat, each holster let fall,
Shook off both my jack-boots, let go belt and all,
Stood up in the stirrup, leaned, patted his ear,
Called my Roland his pet-name, my horse without peer;
Clapped my hands, laughed and sang, any noise, bad or
     good,
Till at length into Aix Roland galloped and stood . . .

How I Brought the Good News from
Aix to Ghent, or Vice Versa

I sprang to the rollocks and Jorrocks and me,
And I galloped, you galloped, we galloped all three.
Not a word to each other: we kept changing place,
Neck to neck, back to front, ear to ear, face to face:
And we yelled once or twice, when we heard a clock chime,
'Would you kindly oblige us, *is that the right time?*'
As I galloped, you galloped, he galloped, we galloped, ye
    galloped, they two shall have galloped: *let us trot.*

I unsaddled the saddle, unbuckled the bit,
Unshackled the bridle (the thing didn't fit)
And ungalloped, ungalloped, ungalloped, ungalloped a bit.
Then I cast off my buff coat, let my bowler hat fall,
Took off both my boots and my trousers and all –
Drank off my stirrup-cup, felt a bit tight,
And unbridled the saddle: it still wasn't right.

Then all I remember is, things reeling round,
As I sat with my head 'twixt my ears on the ground –
For imagine my shame when they asked what I meant
And I had to confess that I'd been, gone and went
And *forgotten* the news I was bringing to Ghent,
Though I'd galloped and galloped and galloped and
    galloped and galloped
And galloped and galloped and galloped. (Had I not
    would have been galloped?)

ENVOI
So I sprang to a taxi and shouted 'To Aix!'
And he blew on his horn and he threw off his brakes,
And all the way back till my money was spent
We rattled and rattled and rattled and rattled and rattled
And rattled and rattled –
And eventually sent a telegram.

                                W. C. SELLAR *and* R. J. YEATMAN

J. W. BURGON (1813–88)

from Petra

Match me such marvel save in Eastern clime,
A rose-red city – 'half as old as time'!

This must be the most quoted couplet from any of the poems to
have won the Newdigate Prize for poetry at Oxford University.
Burgon wrote it in 1845, before becoming a clergyman and
disappearing into obscurity. None the less, this is a fine piece of
verse to be remembered by.

'Match me such marvel'

Match me such marvel save in college port,
The rose-red liquor, half as old as Short.

WILLIAM BASIL TICKELL JONES

William Short was an Oxford don and 'character'. He had taught
at Rugby around 1800, had become a tutor at Oxford around
1820, and still lectured at Trinity College in the 1860s. He had a
cutting turn of phrase and once told an undergraduate who had
got a local girl pregnant, 'If you marry her you are a fool; if you
don't marry her you are a blackguard; in either case you will cease
to be a member of this college.' Tickell Jones later became Bishop
of St Davids.

from *The Playboy of the Demi-World*

Aloft in Heavenly Mansions, Doubleyou One –
Just Mayfair flats, but certainly sublime –
You'll find the abode of D'Arcy Honeybunn,
A rose-red sissy half as old as time.

Peace cannot age him, and no war could kill
The genial tenant of those cosy rooms,
He's lived there always and he lives there still,
Perennial pansy, hardiest of blooms.

WILLIAM PLOMER

ROBERT BURNS (1759–96)

For A' That and A' That

Is there, for honest poverty
   That hangs his head, and a' that;
The coward-slave, we pass him by,
   We dare be poor for a' that!
For a' that, and a' that,
   Our toils obscure, and a' that,
The rank is but the guinea's stamp,
   The man's the gowd for a' that.

What though on hamely fare we dine,
   Wear hoddin grey, and a' that;
Gie fools their silks, and knaves their wine,
   A man's a man for a' that:
For a' that, and a' that,
   Their tinsel shew, and a' that;
The honest man, though e'er sae poor,
   Is king o' men for a' that.

Ye see yon birkie, ca'd a lord,
   Wha struts, and stares, and a' that;
Though hundreds worship at his word,
   He's but a coof for a' that:
For a' that, and a' that,
   His ribband, star, and a' that,
The man of independent mind,
   He looks and laughs at a' that.

A prince can mak a belted knight,
   A marquis, duke, and a' that;
But an honest man's aboon his might,
   Gude faith he manna fa' that!
For a' that, and a' that,

For A' That and A' That

More luck to honest poverty,
  It claims respect, and a' that;
But honest wealth's a better thing,
  We dare be rich for a' that.
    For a' that, and a' that,
      And spooney cant and a' that,
    A man may have a ten-pun note,
      And be a brick for a' that.

What though on soup and fish we dine,
  Wear evening togs and a' that,
A man may like good meat and wine,
  Nor be a knave for a' that.
    For a' that, and a' that,
      Their fustian talk and a' that,
    A gentleman, however clean,
      May have a heart for a' that.

You see yon prater called a Beales,
  Who bawls and brays and a' that,
Tho' hundreds cheer his blatant bosh,
  He's but a goose for a' that.
    For a' that, and a' that,
      His Bubblyjocks, and a' that,
    A man with twenty grains of sense,
      He looks and laughs at a' that.

A prince can make a belted knight,
  A marquis, duke, and a' that,
And if the title's earned, all right,
  Old England's fond of a' that.
    For a' that, and a' that,

Their dignities, and a' that,
The pith o' sense, and pride o' worth,
   Are higher ranks than a' that.

Then let us pray that come it may,
   As come it will for a' that,
That sense and worth, o'er a' the earth,
   May bear the gree, and a' that.
For a' that, and a' that,
   It's comin yet for a' that,
That man to man, the warld o'er,
   Shall brothers be for a' that.

A Red, Red Rose

My love is like a red, red rose
   That's newly sprung in June:
My love is like the melody
   That's sweetly played in tune.

As fair art thou, my bonnie lass,
   So deep in love am I:
And I will love thee still, my dear,
   Till a' the seas gang dry.

Beales' balderdash, and a' that,
A name that tells of service done
Is worth the wear, for a' that.

Then let us pray that come it may
And come it will for a' that,
That common sense may take the place
Of common cant and a' that.
For a' that, and a' that,
Who cackles trash and a' that,
Or be he lord, or be he low,
The man's an ass for a' that.

SHIRLEY BROOKS

Charles William Shirley Brooks (1816–74) was a humorous journalist and wit who, after brief careers as a lawyer and parliamentary reporter, in the 1850s took on the pseudonym 'Epicurus Rotundus' and helped Mark Lemon enliven *Punch*. In 1870 he became its Editor, dying a few years later, probably from drink. He was a gifted parodist, targeting Tennyson and Campbell in particular.

Dea ex Machina

My love is like Mies van der Rohe's
    'Machine for living'; she,
Divested of her underclothes,
    Suggests efficiency.

Her supple shoulders call to mind
    A set of bevelled gears;
Her lower jaw has been aligned
    To hinge behind her ears.

Her hips, sweet ball-and-socket joints,
    Are padded to perfection;

Till a' the seas gang dry, my dear,
  And the rocks melt wi' the sun:
And I will love thee still, my dear,
  While the sands o' life shall run.

And fare thee weel, my only love,
  And fare thee weel a while!
And I will come again, my love,
  Thou' it were ten thousand mile.

Comin' thro' the Rye

Gin a body meet a body,
  Comin' thro' the rye,
Gin a body greet a body
  Need a body cry?
    Ilka lassie has her laddie
      Ne'er a ane hae I;
    But a' the lads they smile on me
      When comin' thro' the rye.

Gin a body meet a body,
  Comin' frae the well,
Gin a body kiss a body
  Need a body tell?
    Ilka lassie, etc.

Gin a body meet a body,
  Comin' frae the toun,
Gin a body kiss a body
  Need a body gloom?
    Ilka lassie, etc.

Each knee, with its patella, points
   In just the right direction.

Her fingertips remind me of
   A digital computer;
She simply couldn't be, my love,
   A millimeter cuter.

JOHN UPDIKE

Mies van der Rohe the Dutch-born architect was one of the founders and exemplars of architectural Modernism.

Rigid Body Sings

Gin a body meet a body
   Flyin' through the air,
Gin a body hit a body,
   Will it fly? and where?
Ilka impact has its measure,
   Ne'er a' ane hae I,
Yet a' the lads they measure me,
   Or, at least, they try.

Gin a body meet a body
   Altogether free,
How they travel afterwards
   We do not always see.
Ilka problem has its method
   By analytics high;
For me, I ken na ane o' them,
   But what the waur am I?

JAMES CLERK MAXWELL

The author of this piece of whimsically versified scientific speculation was himself an eminent nineteenth-century physicist.

from To a Mouse, on Turning Her Up in Her Nest with the Plough

Wee, sleekit, cow'rin', tim'rous beastie,
O what a panic's in thy breastie!
Thou need na start awa sae hasty,
    Wi' bickering brattle!
I wad be laith to rin an' chase thee
    Wi' murd'ring pattle!

I'm truly sorry man's dominion
Has broken Nature's social union,
An' justifies that ill opinion
    Which makes thee startle
At me, thy poor earth-born companion,
    An' fellow-mortal!

 *

But, Mousie, thou art no thy lane,
In proving foresight may be vain:
The best laid schemes o' mice an' men
    Gang aft a-gley,
An' lea'e us nought but grief an' pain
    For promis'd joy.

To a Bull Moose

Braw, snortin', roarin', fearsome beastie
What a tumult's in thy breastie
Thou needna think that we will heed thee
    Or mark thy clatter
Thou canna make us believe we need thee
    By inane chatter.

Poor beastie, 'tis an ill opinion
To think we'd suffer thy dominion
Thy fate is sealed for next November
    After election
Then present boasts thou wilt remember
    With deep dejection.

So, Moosie, cease thy bragging vain
We canna hear thee wi'out pain
The best laid plans of Moose and men
    Gang aft agley
We can but hope that thine will wend
    The self-same way.

EUGENE O'NEILL

O'Neill, the famous American playwright, in his youth wrote
poems for his local newspaper, the *New London Telegraph*. Later
he dismissed these as 'smalltown jingles of my very well misspent
youth'. Some were love poems, which are moving, and some were
parodies, which are much better than he thought. A 'Bull Moose'
was a member of the Progressive Party and a follower of Theodore
Roosevelt. This poem appeared in September 1912.

GEORGE GORDON, LORD BYRON (1788–1824)

from Childe Harold's Pilgrimage

Roll on, thou deep and dark blue ocean – roll!
Ten thousand fleets sweep over thee in vain;
Man marks the earth with ruin – his control
Stops with the shore; – upon the watery plain
The wrecks are all thy deed, nor doth remain
A shadow of man's ravage, save his own,
When, for a moment, like a drop of rain,
He sinks into thy depths with bubbling groan,
Without a grave, unknell'd, uncoffin'd, and unknown.

'When we two parted'

When we two parted
    In silence and tears,
Half broken-hearted,
    To sever for years,
Pale grew thy cheek and cold,
    Colder thy kiss;
Truly that hour foretold
    Sorrow to this!

The dew of the morning
    Sunk chill on my brow;
It felt like the warning
    Of what I feel now.
Thy vows are all broken,
    And light is thy fame:
I hear thy name spoken
    And share in its shame.

The Sea Replies to Byron

Stroll on, thou dark not deep 'blue' dandy, stroll,
  Ten thousand duns call after thee in vain.
Thy tailor's marked with ruin; his control
  Stops with my shore; beyond he doth retain
No shadow of a chance of what's his own,
But sinks above his bills with bubbling groan,
'Absconded; gone abroad; address unknown.'

G. K. CHESTERTON

'When we two parted'

When we two parted
In silence and tears,
Half broken-hearted
We ordered two beers.
Pale was thy drink and mild;
Bitter my cup.
Truly the hour foretold
Time to sup up.

The brew of the morning
Hung chill on my breath.
It felt like the warning
Of half way to death.
My teeth are all broken,
Dislocated my nose.
I hear thy name spoken
And stare at my toes.

They name thee before me,
    A knell to mine ear;
A shudder comes o'er me –
    Why wert thou so dear?
They know not I knew thee
    Who knew thee too well:
Long, long shall I rue thee
    Too deeply to tell.

In secret we met:
    In silence I grieve
That thy heart could forget,
    Thy spirit deceive.
If I should meet thee
    After long years,
How should I greet thee? –
    With silence and tears.

They blame me before thee
For spilling the beer.
I couldn't afford thee.
Why wert thou so dear?
They knew not I knew thee
Who knew thee too much.
Long, long shall I rue thee
That kick in the crutch.

In secret we met.
In silence I grieve,
For my trousers are wet –
They're only loose weave.
If I should meet thee,
Heaven forfend,
How should I greet thee?
With hemlock my friend.

JOHN C. DESMOND

LEWIS CARROLL (1832–98)

Jabberwocky

'Twas brillig, and the slithy toves
    Did gyre and gimble in the wabe:
All mimsy were the borogoves,
        And the mome raths outgrabe.

'Beware the Jabberwock, my son!
    The jaws that bite, the claws that catch!
Beware the Jubjub bird, and shun
        The frumious Bandersnatch!'

He took his vorpal sword in hand:
    Long time the manxome foe he sought –
So rested he by the Tumtum tree,
        And stood awhile in thought.

And, as in uffish thought he stood,
    The Jabberwock, with eyes of flame,
Came whiffling through the tulgey wood,
        And burbled as it came!

One, two! One, two! And through and through
    The vorpal blade went snicker-snack!
He left it dead, and with its head
        He went galumphing back.

'And hast thou slain the Jabberwock?
    Come to my arms, my beamish boy!
O frabjous day! Callooh! Callay!'
        He chortled in his joy.

'Twas brillig, and the slithy toves
    Did gyre and gimble in the wabe:
All mimsy were the borogoves,
        And the mome raths outgrabe.

"Twas rollog, and the minim potes'

'Twas rollog, and the minim potes
Did mime and mimble in the cafe;
All footly were the Philerotes,
And Daycadongs outstrafe.

Beware the Yallerbock, my son!
The aims that rile, the art that racks,
Beware the Aub-Aub Bird, and shun
The stumious Beerbomax.

He took Excalibur in hand:
Long time the canxome foe he sought —
So rested he by the Jonbul tree,
And stood awhile in thought.

Then, as veep Vigo's marge he trod,
The Yallerbock, with tongue of blue,
Came piffling through the Headley Bod,
And flippered as it flew.

ANONYMOUS

The *Yellow Book*, 1894 to 1897, was the major vehicle for the decadent writers who followed in the wake of Oscar Wilde. The Bodley Head published many of their works. *Punch* commented: 'Uncleanliness is next to Bodliness.'

Max Beerbohm, in his essay, 'A Defence of Cosmetics', used the language of the ardent campaigner to claim that the era of rouge was at hand, that the mask was more important than the face. Beerbohm was really sending up the cult of Aestheticism. Wilde treated him with respect, but could not resist asking a friend, 'When you are alone with Max, does he take off his face and reveal his mask?'

GEOFFREY CHAUCER (c. 1343–1400)

from The Prologue to the Canterbury Tales

A knight ther was, and that a worthy man,
That fro the tyme that he first bigan
To ryden out, he loved chivalrye,
Trouthe and honour, fredom and curteisye.
Ful worthy was he in his lordes werre,
And therto hadde he riden (no man ferre)
As wel in Crisendom as hethenesse,
And ever honoured for his worthinesse.
   At Alisaundre he was, when it was wonne;
Ful ofte tyme he hadde the bord bigonne
Aboven alle naciouns in Pruce.
In Lettow hadde he reysed and in Ruce . . .
This ilke worthy knight had been also
Somtyme with the lord of Palatye,
Ageyn another hethen in Turkye:
And evermore he hadde a sovereyn prys.
And though that he were worthy, he was wys,
And of his port as meke as is a mayde.
He never yet no vileinye ne sayde
In al his lyf, un-to no maner wight.
He was a verray parfit gentil knight.

Chaucer: The Wogan's Tale

A Chatte-Show Host came with us, yclept Wogan,
As fam'd as any Emperour or Shogun,
Of goodly port, he smyling was, and merrie,
And known to all the companye as Terrie.
Thrice ev'ry week upon the littel screen
His jolie visage in close-uppe was seen;
From far and wide came pilgrims to his shrine,
And hard by Shepherd's Bush would wait in line.
There he, with feyned flaterye and jape,
The which kept all his faithful fannes agape,
Made conversacioun with each summon'd guest,
Contriving to turn all they said to jest,
Whereat the audience would fall about
With unconfinèd myrth, and scream and shout.
'Tis said that he was payed a wondrous fee,
The envie of all at the BBC;
Though ther were some who thought his programme
    trype,
He was a verray parfit TV type.

                    STANLEY J. SHARPLESS

G. K. CHESTERTON (1874–1936)

The Rolling English Road

Before the Roman came to Rye or out to Severn strode,
The rolling English drunkard made the rolling English road.
A reeling road, a rolling road, that rambles round the shire,
And after him the parson ran, the sexton and the squire;
A merry road, a mazy road, and such as we did tread
The night we went to Birmingham by way of Beachy Head.

I knew no harm of Bonaparte and plenty of the Squire,
And for to fight the Frenchman I did not much desire;
But I did bash their baggonets because they came arrayed
To straighten out the crooked road an English drunkard made,
Where you and I went down the lane with ale-mugs in our han
The night we went to Glastonbury by way of Goodwin Sands.

    *

My friends, we will not go again or ape an ancient rage,
Or stretch the folly of our youth to be the shame of age,
But walk with clearer eyes and ears this path that wandereth,
And see undrugged in evening light the decent inn of death;
For there is good news yet to hear and fine things to be seen,
Before we go to Paradise by way of Kensal Green.

The Rolling Chinese Wall

Before the Roman came to Rye or Caesar conquered Gaul,
The rolling Chinese drunkard made the rolling Chinese wall,
A reeling wall, a rolling wall, less straight than Brighton Pier,
For it was built by peasants who were raised on rotten beer;
A mazy wall, a crazy wall, and such as we did see,
The day we found two thousand miles was not our cup of tea.

We'd read the Thought of Chairman Mao, though he was
    round the twist,
And understood why most of them were only partly pissed;
But now it seems it's far too late to alter every bend
And straighten out the winding wall that never seems to end.
At least we had the bottle then, though never ask us how,
The day we walked to Sinkiang by way of Chu Chin Chow.

My friends, we shall not go again, by sampan, road or rail,
Or stretch our legs for umpteen *li* or sample Chinese ale,
But wait till Western expertise has added to its strength
And hardened us to hit the wall and walk along its length;
For there is good news yet to hear, though not just yet, alas,
Before we go to Paradise by courtesy of Bass.

ROGER WODDIS

This appeared in *Punch* in 1985, on the occasion when Bass, the
brewers, had won a contract to help the Chinese improve the
quality of their beer.

from The Song against Grocers

God made the wicked Grocer
For a mystery and a sign,
That men might shun the awful shops
And go to inns to dine;
Where the bacon's on the rafter
And the wine is in the wood,
And God that made good laughter
Has seen that they are good.

The evil-hearted Grocer
Would call his mother 'Ma'am',
And bow at her and bob at her,
Her aged soul to damn,
And rub his horrid hands and ask
What article was next,
Though *mortis in articulo*
Should be her proper text . . .

from When I Came Back to Fleet Street

When I came back to Fleet Street,
    Through a sunset nook at night,
And saw the old Green Dragon
    With the windows all alight,
And hailed the old Green Dragon
    And the Cock I used to know,
Where all good fellows were my friends
    A little while ago . . .

*

'God made the sex-shop keeper'

God made the sex-shop keeper
For a mystery and a sign,
That men might turn from rubber goods
And things that whirr and whine,
And go for clean and honest sex
Upon old Hampstead Heath,
With nothing but the winds above
And anoraks beneath.

He sells pink plastic ladies,
Unscrews them with a smile –
'First buy the torso, then the face,
The rest can wait a while.'
At last his videotape's run out,
He's buried 'neath plain covers
And goes before the Video King
To join his plastic lovers.

FIONA PITT-KETHLEY

A *New Statesman* competition winner.

When I Leapt over Tower Bridge

When I leapt over Tower Bridge
    There were three that watched below,
A bald man and a hairy man,
    And a man like Ikey Mo.

When I leapt over London Bridge
    They quailed to see my tears,
As terrible as a shaken sword
    And many shining spears.

Under the broad bright windows
    Of men I serve no more,
The groaning of the old great wheels
    Thickened to a throttled roar:
All buried things broke upward;
    And peered from its retreat,
Ugly and silent, like an elf,
    The secret of the street.

They did not break the padlocks,
    Or clear the wall away.
The men in debt that drank of old
    Still drink in debt to-day;
Chained to the rich by ruin,
    Cheerful in chains, as then
When old unbroken Pickwick walked
    Among the broken men.

Still he that dreams and rambles
    Through his own elfin air,
Knows that the street's a prison,
    Knows that the gates are there:
Still he that scorns or struggles
    Sees, frightful and afar,
All that they leave of rebels
    Rot high on Temple Bar.

A Cider Song

Extract from a romance which is not yet written
and probably never will be

The wine they drink in Paradise
They make in Haute Lorraine;
God brought it burning from the sod

But when I leapt over Blackfriars
    The pigeons on St Paul's
Grew ghastly white as they saw the sight
    Like an awful sun that falls;

And all along from Ludgate
    To the wonder of Charing Cross,
The devil flew through a host of hearts –
    A messenger of loss;

With a rumour of ghostly things that pass
    With a thunderous pennon of pain,
To a land where the sky is as red as the grass
    And the sun as green as the rain.

J. C. SQUIRE

from *A Downland Crisis*

The ale they drink in Giggleswick
    They brew in Biggleswade;
In Chirk and Bilbster, so they say,
    Their scores are never paid;
In Bugsworth and Fazakerley
    Their snouts are red and blue,

To be a sign and signal rod
That they that drink the blood of God
Shall never thirst again.

The wine they praise in Paradise
They make in Ponterey,
The purple wine of Paradise,
But we have better at the price;
It's wine they praise in Paradise,
It's cider that they pray.

The wine they want in Paradise
They find in Plodder's End,
The apple wine of Hereford,
Of Hafod Hill and Hereford,
Where woods went down to Hereford,
And there I had a friend.

The soft feet of the blessed go
In the soft western vales,
The road the silent saints accord,
The road from heaven to Hereford,
Where the apple wood of Hereford
Goes all the way to Wales.

But the very best tipple of all, I ween,
    Is the beer at Luton Hoo!

A man may swig at Timperley,
    And fill his paunch at Diss,
In Bootle and Balquhidder too
    A cask is not amiss.
At Cleobury Mortimer –

I've never been to Wookey,
    That lies beyond the West;
In Spofforth, or in Widnes,
    A wounded heart may rest;
But in Yealmpton, ah! in Yealmpton,
    There peace with love doth blend,
And evening comes with healing
    To Brigg and Ponder's End.

D. B. WYNDHAM LEWIS

The singer of these lines is, sadly, interrupted in the middle of the second verse, of which the rest of the words are for ever lost.

ALBERT CHEVALIER (1861–1923)

from Sich a Nice Man Too!

There's parties ad yer meets about
    Wot wins yer 'eart instanter;
They give the rest a goodish start
    And beats 'em in a canter.
There's one I know as licks 'em all,
    And that's my fellow-lodger,
He's up to ev'ry knowin' fake,
    A fair old artful dodger.

CHORUS

Sich a nice man too! Sich a very nice man,
Not a bit stuck up, no beastly affectation,
    One who somehow makes you feel
    That you really have to deal
With a gentleman by birth and education!

Chorus of a Song that Might Have Been Written by Albert Chevalier

I drops in to see young Ben
In 'is tap-room now an' then,
And I likes to see 'im gettin' on becoz
   'E's got pluck and 'e's got brains,
    And 'e takes no end o' pains,
But – 'e'll never be the man 'is Father woz.

MAX BEERBOHM

Albert Chevalier was one of the great music-hall stars and his most
popular songs were 'My Old Dutch' and 'Wot Cher! or, Knock'd
em in the The Old Kent Road'. Beerbohm, who had been a theatre
critic for twelve years, had a soft spot for the music-hall and for
some of its great performers, like Dan Leno and Chevalier. Of the
latter, he wrote: 'I had the pleasure of meeting him once, in his
later years, and was sorely tempted to offer him an idea which
might well have been conceived by himself: a song about a
publican whom the singer had known and revered, who was now
dead, whose business was carried on by his son Ben – "But 'e'll
never be the man 'is Father woz." ' Max wrote an essay, 'Music
Halls of my Youth', which he broadcast in 1942, singing this
chorus.

FRANCES CORNFORD (1886–1960)

To a Fat Lady Seen from a Train

O why do you walk through the fields in gloves,
    Missing so much and so much?
O fat white woman whom nobody loves
Why do you walk through the fields in gloves,
When the grass is soft as the breast of doves
    And shivering-sweet to the touch?
O why do you walk through the fields in gloves,
    Missing so much and so much?

The Fat White Woman Speaks

Why do you rush through the fields in trains,
Guessing so much and so much;
Why do you flash through the flowery meads,
Fat headed poet whom nobody reads;
And how do you know such a frightful lot
About people in gloves as such?

And how the devil can you be sure,
Guessing so much and so much,
How do you know but what someone who loves
Always to see me in nice white gloves
At the end of the field you are rushing by,
Is waiting for his Old Dutch?

G. K. CHESTERTON

WILLIAM JOHNSON CORY (1823–92)

Heraclitus

They told me, Heraclitus, they told me you were dead;
They brought me bitter news to hear and bitter tears to shed.
I wept as I remembered how often you and I
Had tired the sun with talking and sent him down the sky.

And now that thou art lying, my dear old Carian guest,
A handful of grey ashes, long long ago at rest,
Still are thy pleasant voices, thy nightingales, awake,
For Death, he taketh all away, but them he cannot take.

Cory's poem is in fact a translation from the Greek of Callimachus,
whose words were addressed to his fellow-poet Heraclitus of
Halicarnassus. Heraclitus's poems appear to have been known as
'nightingales' and Lemprière explains that he was 'remarkable for
the elegance of his style'. As for Cory, the only other work of his
that has survived the test of time is the 'Eton Boating Song'.

'They told me, Heraclitus'

They told me, Heraclitus, they told me you were dead.
I never knew your proper name was Heraclitus, Fred.
You made out you were working-class, you talked with
    adenoids,
And so it was a shock to learn you were a name at
    Lloyd's.

And now I'm full of doubts about the others at the squat.
Are they a load of Yuppies, or Thatcherites, or what?
Is Special Branch amongst us, camouflaged with crabs and
    fleas?
Is Kev a poncing Xenophon? Darren, Thucydides?

BRIAN FORE

'They told me, Heraclitus'

They told me, Heraclitus, they told me you were dead.
But I just wondered who you were and what on earth you
    said.

GUY HANLON

NOËL COWARD (1899–1973)

from Mrs Worthington

Regarding yours, dear Mrs Worthington,
Of Wednesday the 23rd,
Although your baby,
May be,
Keen on a stage career,
How can I make it clear,
That this is not a good idea.
For her to hope,
Dear Mrs Worthington,
Is on the face of it absurd,
Her personality
Is not in reality
Inviting enough,
Exciting enough
For this particular sphere.

Don't put your daughter on the stage, Mrs Worthington,
Don't put your daughter on the stage,
The profession is overcrowded
And the struggle's pretty tough
And admitting the fact
She's burning to act,
That isn't quite enough.
She has nice hands, to give the wretched girl her due,
But don't you think her bust is too
Developed for her age,
I repeat
Mrs Worthington,
Sweet
Mrs Worthington,
Don't put your daughter on the stage . . .

Mrs Nightingale

Regarding yours, dear Mrs Nightingale,
Of Friday, the 4th of May –
What can I candidly say –
No *wonder* you're deep in dismay!
Altho'
Dear Flo
Is clear in her tiny mind
That this gruesome grisly grind
Is her Destiny designed –
How shall we tell
The foolish gel
That a nurse is a slut, a Jezebel,
Whose lot is an utter, gutter hell
Of mangling and mopping
And sluicing and slopping
Out patients who – frankly –
Sweatily, dankly –
Only too rankly
SMELL!

Don't let your daughter be a nurse, Mrs Nightingale,
Don't let your Flossy flush the pans.
It's unbecoming her station
To moot such mutinous plans –
She'd better serve the nation
By tittling and tattling
And prettily prattling
Of nuptial bells and banns.

                    *

                                    MARTIN FAGG

Florence Nightingale rejected this advice and turned nursing into
the caring profession it is today.

WILLIAM COWPER (1731–1800)

from To Mary

The twentieth year is well-nigh past,
Since first our sky was overcast;
Ah would that this might be the last!
            My Mary!

Thy spirits have a fainter flow,
I see thee daily weaker grow –
'Twas my distress that brought thee low,
            My Mary!

Thy needles, once a shining store,
For my sake restless heretofore,
Now rust disus'd, and shine no more,
            My Mary!

For though thou gladly wouldst fulfil
The same kind office for me still,
Thy sight now seconds not thy will,
            My Mary!

Thy silver locks, once auburn bright,
Are still more lovely in my sight
Than golden beams of orient light,
            My Mary!

For could I view nor them nor thee,
What sight worth seeing could I see?
The sun would rise in vain for me,
            My Mary!

This lovely lyric was written in 1793 for Mary Unwin. She had been Cowper's landlady twenty years earlier and they had lived together after her husband's death. She helped to keep him from slipping into insanity and, when she died in 1796, he went into a sad decline.

To Mr Murray

Strahan, Tonson, Lintot of the times,
Patron and publisher of rhymes,
For thee the bard up Pindus climbs,
        My Murray.

To thee, with hope and terror dumb,
The unfledged MS authors come;
Thou printest all – and sellest some –
        My Murray.

Upon thy table's baize so green
The last new Quarterly is seen, –
But where is thy new Magazine,
        My Murray?

Along thy sprucest bookshelves shine
The works thou deemest most divine –
The 'Art of Cookery', and mine,
        My Murray.

Tours, Travels, Essays, too, I wist,
And Sermons, to thy mill bring grist;
And then thou hast the 'Navy List',
        My Murray.

And Heaven forbid I should conclude
Without 'the Board of Longitude',
Although this narrow paper would,
        My Murray.

GEORGE GORDON, LORD BYRON

Byron had a troubled relationship with his publisher, John Murray,
who occasionally censored poems by cutting lines that he thought
would offend the reading public.

e. e. cummings (1894–1962)

'o pr'

o pr
   gress verily thou art m
   mentous superc
   lossal hyperpr
   digious etc i kn
   w & if you d

   n't why g
    to yonder s
   called newsreel s
   called theatre & with your
   wn eyes beh

   ld The
        (The president The
        president of The president
        of the The)president of

        the(united The president of the
        united states The president of the united
        states of The President Of The) United States

        Of America unde negant redire quemquam supp
 sedly thr

 w
   i
    n
     g
      a
       b
        aseball

'Poets have their ear to the ground'

Poets have their ear to the ground more than most people
If only because more than most they are beating their
heads against it
Thus, Mad
          ame,
Every true artist is a p
                        i
                        o
                        neer
Eliot was streamlining in 1912
Dali's limp watches ant
                        icipated cheeseburgers
And I burr
          o
          k
          e the ground for S
                            c
                            r
                            a
                            b
                            b
                            l
                            e

                                        PETER DE VRIES

De Vries is better known as a writer of comic novels and humorous
articles, but he is adept at finding excuses to turn his hand to verse
parody. This example is from *The Tents of Wickedness*.

JOHN DAVIDSON (1857–1909)

from A Ballad of a Nun

From Eastertide to Eastertide
   For ten long years her patient knees
Engraved the stones – the fittest bride
   Of Christ in all the diocese.

She conquered every earthly lust;
   The abbess loved her more and more;
And, as a mark of perfect trust,
   Made her the keeper of the door.

          *

In winter-time when Lent drew nigh,
   And hill and plain were wrapped in snow,
She watched beneath the frosty sky
   The nearest city nightly glow.

Like peals of airy bells outworn
   Faint laughter died above her head
In gusts of broken music borne:
   'They keep the Carnival,' she said.

Her hungry heart devoured the town:
   'Heaven save me by a miracle!
Unless God sends an angel down,
   Thither I go though it were Hell.'

'Life's dearest meaning I shall probe;
   Lo! I shall taste of love at last!
Away!' She doffed her outer robe,
   And sent it sailing down the blast.

          *

A Ballad of a Bun

From Whitsuntide to Whitsuntide –
    That is to say, all through the year –
Her patient pen was occupied
    With songs and tales of pleasant cheer.

But still her talent went to waste
    Like flotsam on an open sea;
She never hit the public taste,
    Or knew the knack of Bellettrie.

Across the sounding City's fogs
    There hurtled round her weary head
The thunder of the rolling logs;
    'The Critics' Carnival!' she said.

Immortal prigs took heaven by storm,
    Prigs scattered largesses of praise;
The work of both was rather warm;
    'This is,' she said, 'the thing that pays!'

Sharp envy turned her wine to blood –
    I mean it turned her blood to wine;
And this resolve came like a flood –
    'The cake of knowledge must be mine!

'I am in Eve's predicament –
    I sha'n't be happy till I've sinned;
Away!' She lightly rose, and sent
    Her scruples sailing down the wind.

Across the sounding City's din
    She wandered, looking indiscreet,
And ultimately landed in
    The neighbourhood of Regent Street.

She reached the sounding city's gate;
  No question did the warder ask:
He passed her in: 'Welcome, wild mate!'
  He thought her some fantastic mask.

    *

Alone and watching in the street
  There stood a grave youth nobly dressed;
To him she knelt and kissed his feet;
  Her face her great desire confessed.

    *

He healed her bosom with a kiss;
  She gave him all her passion's hoard;
And sobbed and murmured ever, 'This
  Is life's great meaning, dear, my lord.

'I care not for my broken vow;
  Though God should come in thunder soon,
I am sister to the mountains now,
  And sister to the sun and moon.'

    *

At midnight from her lonely bed
  She rose, and said, 'I have had my will.'
The old ragged robe she donned, and fled
  Back to the convent on the hill.

    *

She ran across the icy plain;
  Her worn blood curdled in the blast;
Each footstep left a crimson stain;
  The white-faced moon looked on aghast.

    *

A Decadent was dribbling by;
   'Lady,' he said, 'you seem undone;
You need a panacea; try
   This sample of the Bodley bun.

'It is fulfilled of precious spice,
   Whereof I give the recipe; –
Take common dripping, stew in vice,
   And serve with vertu; taste and see!

'And lo! I brand you on the brow
   As kin to Nature's lowest germ;
You are sister to the microbe now,
   And second-cousin to the worm.'

He gave her of his golden store,
   Such hunger hovered in her look;
She took the bun, and asked for more,
   And went away and wrote a book.

To put the matter shortly, she
   Became the topic of the town;
In all the lists of Bellettrie
   Her name was regularly down.

'We recognise,' the critics wrote,
   'Maupassant's verve and Heine's wit';
Some even made a verbal note
   Of Shakespeare being out of it.

The seasons went and came again;
   At length the languid Public cried:
'It is a sorry sort of Lane
   That hardly ever turns aside.

Like tired bells chiming in their sleep,
    The wind faint peals of laughter bore;
She stopped her ears and climbed the steep,
    And thundered at the convent door.

          *

The wardress raised her tenderly;
    She touched her wet and fast-shut eyes:
'Look, sister; sister, look at me;
    Look; can you see through my disguise?'

          *

She looked and saw her own sad face,
    And trembled, wondering, 'Who art thou?'
'God sent me down to fill your place:
    I am the Virgin Mary now.'

And with the word, God's mother shone:
    The wanderer whispered, 'Mary, hail!'
The vision helped her to put on
    Bracelet and fillet, ring and veil.

'You are sister to the mountains now,
    And sister to the day and night;
Sister to God.' And on the brow
    She kissed her thrice, and left her sight . . .

John Davidson was a socialist from Scotland who wrote strange and disturbing poems that never found popularity while he was alive. He eventually committed suicide. T. S. Eliot's admiration has done something to boost his standing.

'We want a little change of air;
   On that,' they said, 'we must insist;
We cannot any longer bear
   The seedy sex-impressionist.'

Across the sounding City's din
   This rumour smote her on the ear:
'The publishers are going in
   For songs and tales of pleasant cheer!'

'Alack!' she said, 'I lost the art,
   And left my womanhood foredone,
When first I trafficked in the mart
   All for a mess of Bodley bun.

'I cannot cut my kin at will,
   Or jilt the protoplastic germ;
I am sister to the microbe still,
   And second-cousin to the worm!'

                              OWEN SEAMAN

JOHN DONNE (1572–1631)

from A Valediction: Forbidding Mourning

Our two soules therefore, which are one,
　　Though I must goe, endure not yet
A breach, but an expansion,
　　Like gold to ayery thinnesse beate.

If they be two, they are two so
　　As stiffe twin compasses are two,
Thy soule the fixt foot, makes no show
　　To move, but doth, if the'other doe.

And though it in the center sit,
　　Yet when the other far doth rome,
It leanes, and hearkens after it,
　　And growed erect, as that comes home.

On Donne's Poetry

With Donne, whose muse on dromedary trots,
Wreathe iron pokers into true-love knots;
Rhyme's sturdy cripple, fancy's maze and clue,
Wit's forge and fire-blast, meaning's press and screw.

S. T. COLERIDGE

JOHN DRINKWATER (1882–1937)

Cottage Song

Morning and night I bring
Clear water from the spring.
And through the lyric noon
I hear the larks in tune,
And when the shadows fall
There's providence for all.

My garden is alight
With currants red and white,
And my blue curtains peep
On starry courses deep,
While down her silver tides
The moon on Cotswold rides.

My path of paven grey
Is thoroughfare all day
For fellowship, till time
Bids us with candles climb
The little whitewashed stair
Above my lavender.

William Rothenstein welcomed literary friends to stay at his
cottage in Far Oakridge in the Cotswolds, and John Drinkwater
penned this poem in gratitude. Max Beerbohm also stayed there
one very cold winter during the First World War, but enjoyed it
rather less, as his parody makes clear. He dedicated it: 'For J. D.
from M. B. August 4, 1917, with 1,000,000 apologies for his
wicked echo of so lovely a poem.'

Same Cottage – but Another Song, of Another Season

Morning and night I found
White snow upon the ground,
And on the tragic well
Grey ice had cast its spell.
A dearth of wood and coal
Lay heavy on my soul.

My garden was a scene
Of weeds and nettles green,
My window-panes had holes
Through which, all night, lost souls
Peered from the desert road,
And starved cocks faintly crowed.

My path of cinders black
Had an abundant lack
Of visitors, till time
Bade us with boxes climb
The train that hurries on
To old warm Paddington.

                    MAX BEERBOHM

JOHN DRYDEN (1631–1700)

from The Hind and the Panther

A milk white *Hind*, immortal and unchang'd,
Fed on the lawns, and in the forest rang'd;
Without unspotted, innocent within,
She fear'd no danger, for she knew no sin.
Yet had she oft been chas'd with horns and hounds,
And Scythian shafts; and many winged wounds
Aim'd at Her heart; was often forc'd to fly,
And doom'd to death, though fated not to dy.
    Not so her young, for their unequal line
Was Heroe's make, half humane, half divine.
Their earthly mold obnoxious was to fate,
Th' immortal part assum'd immortal state.
Of these a slaughtered army lay in bloud,
Extended o'er the *Caledonian* wood,
Their native walk; whose vocal bloud arose,
And cry'd for pardon on their perjur'd foes;
Their fate was fruitfull, and the sanguin seed
Endu'd with souls, encreas'd the sacred breed . . .

A Fable

A dingy donkey, formal and unchanged,
Browsed in the lane and o'er the common ranged,
Proud of his ancient asinine possessions,
Free from the panniers of the grave professions,
He lived at ease; and chancing once to find
A lion's skin, the fancy took his mind
To personate the monarch of the wood;
And for a time the stratagem held good.
He moved with so majestical a pace
That bears and wolves and all the savage race
Gazed in admiring awe, ranging aloof
Not over-anxious for a clearer proof –
Longer he might have triumph'd – but alas!
In an unguarded hour it came to pass
He bray'd aloud; and show'd himself an ass!

The moral of this tale I could not guess
Till Mr Landor sent his works to press.

JOHN HOOKHAM FRERE

Although Dryden provides the form, it is clearly Walter Savage
Landor (1775–1864) who is the butt of the satire here.

T. S. ELIOT (1888–1965)

from Little Gidding

What we call the beginning is often the end
And to make an end is to make a beginning.
The end is where we start from . . .

from Gerontion

      Vacant shuttles
Weave the wind. I have no ghosts,
An old man in a draughty house
Under a windy knob . . .

from Ash Wednesday

If the lost word is lost, if the spent word is spent
If the unheard, unspoken
Word is unspoken, unheard;
Still is the unspoken word, the Word unheard,
The Word without a word, the Word within
The world and for the world;

from Choruses from 'The Rock'

I journeyed to the suburbs, and there I was told:
We toil for six days, on the seventh we must motor
To Hindhead, or Maidenhead.
If the weather is foul we stay at home and read the
   papers.

Chard Whitlow

(Mr Eliot's Sunday Evening Postscript)

As we get older we do not get any younger.
Seasons return, and to-day I am fifty-five,
And this time last year I was fifty-four,
And this time next year I shall be sixty-two.
And I cannot say I should like (to speak for myself)
To see my time over again – if you can call it time:
Fidgeting uneasily under a draughty stair,
Or counting sleepless nights in the crowded tube.

There are certain precautions – though none of them very reliable –
Against the blast from bombs and the flying splinter,
But not against the blast from heaven, *vento dei venti*,
The wind within a wind unable to speak for wind;
And the frigid burnings of purgatory will not be touched
By any emollient.
                    I think you will find this put,
Better than I could ever hope to express it,
In the words of Kharma: 'It is, we believe,
Idle to hope that the simple stirrup-pump
Will extinguish hell.'
                    Oh, listeners,
And you especially who have turned off the wireless,
And sit in Stoke or Basingstoke listening appreciatively to
    the silence,
(Which is also the silence of hell) pray, not for your skins,
    but your souls.

And pray for me also under the draughty stair.
As we get older we do not get any younger.

And pray for Kharma under the holy mountain.

HENRY REED

from The Love Song of J. Alfred Prufrock

   Let us go then, you and I,
When the evening is spread out against the sky
Like a patient etherised upon a table;
Let us go, through certain half-deserted streets,
The muttering retreats
Of restless nights in one-night cheap hotels
And sawdust restaurants with oyster-shells:
Streets that follow like a tedious argument
Of insidious intent
To lead you to an overwhelming question . . .
Oh, do not ask, 'What is it?'
Let us go and make our visit.

   In the room the women come and go
Talking of Michelangelo.

   The yellow fog that rubs its back upon the window-
      panes,
The yellow smoke that rubs its muzzle on the window-
      panes,
Licked its tongue into the corners of the evening,
Lingered upon the pools that stand in drains,
Let fall upon its back the soot that falls from chimneys,

This parody by a poet celebrated in his own right won a
competition in the *New Statesman*. Eliot himself commented: 'In
fact one is apt to think one could parody oneself much better. (As
a matter of fact some critics have said that I have done so.) But
there is one which deserves the success it has had, Henry Reed's
"Chard Whitlow".' There is no single poem to put beside Reed's
parody, which cleverly manages to summon echoes from almost all
Eliot's work, but a few examples are given here.

from *The Love Song of Tommo Frogley*

Comeahead then comeahead
When the skies round Birkie turn tomater red
Like some ould heartcase breathalysed in a copshop;
Comeahead past tellies on the blink
An bashed-in bins that stink:
Past playgrounds strewed with soupcans rubbers rocks
An offies gorrup like Fort Knox . . .
O comeahead I dare yer
An see ar NO GO area

In twos an twos the busies comes an goes
Chattin back ter their radios

The fog that hangs around the ferries
Squeezed out a sock near Fort Perch Rock
Squeezed out an udder one near Formby Light
Picked at its athlete's foot by Crosby baths
Towelled itself down against the floating roadway
Coughed up its lungs at Tranmere
Then crashed a lobbo job dead snug-an-tite

An there will be time
Fer me to go meet me peergroup in the dump;
Ter roll a drunk or give some cow a hump

Slipped by the terrace, made a sudden leap,
And seeing that it was a soft October night,
Curled once about the house, and fell asleep.

   And indeed there will be time
For the yellow smoke that slides along the street
Rubbing its back upon the window-panes;
There will be time, there will be time
To prepare a face to meet the faces that you meet;
There will be time to murder and create,
And time for all the works and days of hands
That lift and drop a question on your plate;
Time for you and time for me,
And time yet for a hundred indecisions,
And for a hundred visions and revisions,
Before the taking of a toast and tea.

   In the room the women come and go
Talking of Michelangelo.

from Macavity: The Mystery Cat

Macavity's a Mystery Cat: he's called the Hidden Paw —
For he's the master criminal who can defy the Law.
He's the bafflement of Scotland Yard, the Flying Squad's
   despair:
For when they reach the scene of crime — *Macavity's not
   there*!

Macavity, Macavity, there's no one like Macavity,
He's broken every human law, he breaks the law of gravity.
His powers of levitation would make a fakir stare,
And when you reach the scene of crime — *Macavity's not
   there*!
You may seek him in the basement, you may look up in
   the air —
But I tell you once and once again, *Macavity's not there*!

   *

An time ter wire another horseless carriage
Or have a gangshag in a broke-in garage
Time ter do what we goan ter do
Before we sit round sniffing bags of glue

In twos an twos the busies comes an goes
Chattin back ter their radios

ROGER CRAWFORD

This is a brilliant parody by a Liverpool man who specializes in
turning great poems into Scouse dialect and giving them a
Merseyside setting. 'Busies' are policemen.

The Accounting Cat

Liquidity's a mystery; it's very rarely seen,
It strikes and then is gone again, its getaway is clean,
And despite forensic evidence and great deductive flair,
The conclusion's inescapable, Liquidity's not there!

Liquidity, Liquidity, there's nothing like liquidity,
Its presence gives you confidence, its absence is timidity,
You own perhaps a property, you own perhaps a share,
But once you've lost your credit card, Liquidity's not
   there!
Your understated opulence inheres in what you wear,
But in the end you face the fact, Liquidity's not there!

Liquidity's a nifty term, it's business talk for cash,
It's money not tied up in things or hoovered in the crash,
Investments may return amounts of staggering obscenity,

Macavity, Macavity, there's no one like Macavity,
For he's a fiend in feline shape, a monster of depravity.
You may meet him in a by-street, you may see him in the
    square –
But when a crime's discovered, then *Macavity's not there*!

He's outwardly respectable. (They say he cheats at cards.)
And his footprints are not found in any file of Scotland
    Yard's.
And when the larder's looted, or the jewel-case is rifled,
Or when the milk is missing, or another Peke's been stifled,
Or the greenhouse glass is broken, and the trellis past repair –
Ay, there's the wonder of the thing! *Macavity's not there*!

And when the Foreign Office find a Treaty's gone astray,
Or the Admiralty lose some plans and drawings by the way,
There may be a scrap of paper in the hall or on the stair –
But it's useless to investigate – *Macavity's not there*!
And when the loss has been disclosed, the Secret Service say:
'It *must* have been Macavity!' – but he's a mile away.
You'll be sure to find him resting, or a-licking of his thumbs,
Or engaged in doing complicated long division sums.

Macavity, Macavity, there's no one like Macavity,
There never was a Cat of such deceitfulness and suavity.
He always has an alibi, and one or two to spare:
And whatever time the deed took place – MACAVITY
    WASN'T THERE!
And they say that all the Cats whose wicked deeds are
    widely known
(I might mention Mungojerrie, I might mention
    Griddlebone)
Are nothing more than agents for the Cat who all the time
Just controls their operations: the Napoleon of Crime!

The vastness of your holdings may explain your great serenity.
In publishing, to take the case of either of the Fabers,
A warehouse full of Larkin and The Bumper Book of
    Neighbours
Is very well, and when they sell, will satisfy the editors,
But not much use, in real terms, when dealing with the
    creditors.

Liquidity, Liquidity, there's nothing like Liquidity,
The glint of actual duckets brings respect and dipthelidity,
It's likely to self-immolate on contact with the air,
Say 'Raffle' in a crowded room; Liquidity's not there!

In the conduct of a company (proprietary limited)
There's always a suspicion that the system's maladministered,
In proper corporate planning you allow a little spare,
But when you need the wherewithal, Liquidity's not there!

Liquidity, Liquidity, there's nothing like Liquidity,
In purely economic terms it constitutes validity,
I wish I had a pound for every credit millionaire,
Who completely failed to register, LIQUIDITY WASN'T
    THERE!
When reputations tumble and the search is on for clues
(I might mention humpo-bumpo, I might mention drinkie-
    poos)
There's a suspect who can prove he was in Lima at the
    time,
They can't catch him, he's the brilliant Scarlet Pimpernel
    of crime!

JOHN CLARKE

RALPH WALDO EMERSON (1803–82)

Brahma

If the red slayer think he slays,
    Or if the slain think he is slain,
They know not well the subtle ways
    I keep, and pass, and turn again.

Far or forgot to me is near;
    Shadow and sunlight are the same;
The vanish'd gods to me appear;
    And one to me are shame and fame.

They reckon ill who leave me out;
    When me they fly, I am the wings;
I am the doubter and the doubt,
    And I the hymn the Brahmin sings.

The strong gods pine for my abode,
    And pine in vain the sacred Seven;
But thou, meek lover of the good!
    Find me, and turn thy back on heaven.

Brahma

If the wild bowler thinks he bowls,
    Or if the batsman thinks he's bowled,
They know not, poor misguided souls,
    They, too, shall perish unconsoled.

I am the batsman and the bat,
    I am the bowler and the ball,
The umpire, the pavilion cat,
    The roller, pitch, and stumps, and all.

ANDREW LANG

WILLIAM EMPSON (1906–84)

Villanelle

It is the pain, it is the pain, endures.
Your chemic beauty burned my muscles through.
Poise of my hands reminded me of yours.

What later purge from this deep toxin cures?
What kindness now could the old salve renew?
It is the pain, it is the pain, endures.

The infection slept (custom or change inures)
And when pain's secondary phase was due
Poise of my hands reminded me of yours.

How safe I felt, whom memory assures,
Rich that your grace safely by heart I knew.
It is the pain, it is the pain, endures.

My stare drank deep beauty that still allures.
My heart pumps yet the poison draught of you.
Poise of my hands reminded me of yours.

You are still kind whom the same shape immures.
Kind and beyond adieu. We miss our cue.
It is the pain, it is the pain, endures.
Poise of my hands reminded me of yours.

Request to Leda

Not your winged lust but his must now change suit.
The harp-waked Casanova rakes no range.
The worm is (pin-point) rational in the fruit.

Not girl for bird (gourd being man) breaks root.
Taking no plume for index in love's change
Not your winged lust but his must now change suit.

Desire is phosphorus: the chemic bruit
Lust bears like volts, who'll amplify, and strange
The worm is (pin-point) rational in the fruit.

DYLAN THOMAS *and* JOHN DAVENPORT

One of a number of parodies from *The Death of the King's Canary*, the satirical novel on which Thomas and Davenport began collaborating in 1940, but which was not published until long after both their deaths. Following the device of Owen Seaman's *The Battle of the Bays*, the plot of the novel concerns the search for a successor to the lately deceased Poet Laureate, and it gave a splendid opportunity for the authors to take off their most eminent contemporaries. According to Constantine Fitzgibbon, 'Dylan Thomas maintained that Davenport had written most of the verse parodies.' He adds: 'This may well be untrue, for if Dylan was not proud of them, he would not have given their authorship to John.' In Empson's case, as with the others, the whole style, rather than any single poem, is the target, but 'Villanelle' displays enough of Empson's quirkiness to show what his parodists were getting at.

EDWARD FITZGERALD (1809–83)

from The Rubáiyát of Omar Khayyám

1

Awake! for Morning in the Bowl of Night
Has flung the Stone that puts the Stars to Flight:
    And Lo! the Hunter of the East has caught
The Sultan's Turret in a Noose of Light.

7

Come, fill the Cup, and in the Fire of Spring
The Winter Garment of Repentance fling:
    The Bird of Time has but a little way
To fly – and Lo! the Bird is on the Wing.

11

Here with a Loaf of Bread beneath the Bough,
A Flask of Wine, a Book of Verse – and Thou
    Beside me singing in the Wilderness –
And Wilderness is Paradise enow.

12

'How sweet is mortal Sovranty!' – think some:
Others – 'How blest the Paradise to come!'
    Ah, take the Cash in hand and waive the Rest;
Oh, the brave Music of a distant Drum!

26

Oh, come with old Khayyám, and leave the Wise
To talk; one thing is certain, that Life flies;
    One thing is certain, and the Rest is Lies;
The Flower that once has blown for ever dies.

from *Strugnell's Rubáiyát*

1

Awake! for Morning on the Pitch of Night
Has whistled and has put the Stars to Flight.
The incandescent football in the East
Has brought the splendour of Tulse Hill to Light.

7

Another Pint! Come, loosen up, have Fun!
Fling off your Hang-Ups and enjoy the Sun:
Time's Spacecraft all too soon will carry you
Away – and Lo! the Countdown has begun.

11

Here with a Bag of Crisps beneath the Bough,
A Can of Beer, a Radio – and Thou
Beside me half asleep in Brockwell Park
And Brockwell Park is Paradise enow.

12

Some Men to everlasting Bliss aspire,
Their Lives, Auditions for the heavenly Choir:
Oh, use your Credit Card and waive the Rest –
Brave Music of a distant Amplifier!

26

Oh, come with Strugnell – Argument's no Tonic.
One thing's certain: Life flies supersonic.
One thing's certain, Man's Evasion chronic –
The Flower that's blown can never be bionic.

51
The Moving Finger writes; and, having writ,
Moves on: nor all thy Piety nor Wit
    Shall lure it back to cancel half a Line,
Nor all thy Tears wash out a Word of it.

51

The Moving Telex writes, and having writ,
Moves on; nor all thy Therapy nor Wit
Shall lure it back to cancel half a Line
Nor Tide nor Daz wash out a word of it.

WENDY COPE

One of the many poems attributed by Wendy Cope to the
impressionable South London poet, Jason Strugnell, whose
misfortune has been to fall under the all-too-obvious influence of
one great poet after another.

JAMES ELROY FLECKER (1884–1915)

Prologue to The Golden Journey to Samarkand

We who with songs beguile your pilgrimage
  And swear that Beauty lives though lilies die,
We Poets of the proud old lineage
  Who sing to find your hearts, we know not why, –

What shall we tell you? Tales, marvellous tales
  Of ships and stars and isles where good men rest,
Where nevermore the rose of sunset pales,
  And winds and shadows fall toward the West:

And there the world's first huge white-bearded kings
  In dim glades sleeping, murmur in their sleep,
And closer round their breasts the ivy clings,
  Cutting its pathway slow and red and deep.

And how beguile you? Death has no repose
  Warmer and deeper than that Orient sand
Which hides the beauty and bright faith of those
  Who made the Golden Journey to Samarkand.

And now they wait and whiten peaceably,
  Those conquerors, those poets, those so fair:
They know time comes, not only you and I,
  But the whole world shall whiten, here or there;

When those long caravans that cross the plain
  With dauntless feet and sound of silver bells
Put forth no more for glory or for gain,
  Take no more solace from the palm-girt wells.

When the great markets by the sea shut fast
  All that calm Sunday that goes on and on:
When even lovers find their peace at last,
  And Earth is but a star, that once had shone.

The Golden Road to Barcelona: 1992

We athletes who, with sternest discipline,
Still punish weary limbs that yearn for rest;
Who, hearts once pitched upon our high design,
Disdain all feats that fall below the best.

What drives us forward? Pride, consuming pride,
That scorns to bow to rigour, ache or strain;
That seeks those ecstasies we know abide
Beyond the bourn of puny-body's pain.

Down galleries of dedicated days,
One impulse thrusts us onward, one alone – a
Fierce desire to wear the victor's bays –
To Go for Gold – and Win! – in Barcelona.

To clutch the Bronze or Silver's splendid prize;
But, most of all, to grasp refulgent Gold,
The guerdon of a tireless enterprise –
A lifetime's bliss in one sweet rapture rolled!

And yet, of all those Knights who sought the Grail,
Most failed and died, albeit lion-hearted.
Our uttermost endeavours too may fail –
By sudden sickness, chance – or inches! – thwarted.

The winners are but few. To that great host
Of those who lose, this only can atone – a
Princely-proud ability to boast –
'We Took the Golden Road to Barcelona.'

MARTIN FAGG

ROBERT FROST (1874–1963)

from New Hampshire

If I must choose which I would elevate –
The people or the already lofty mountains,
I'd elevate the already lofty mountains.
The only fault I find with old New Hampshire
Is that her mountains aren't quite high enough.
I was not always so; I've come to be so.
How, to my sorrow, how have I attained
A height from which to look down critical
On mountains? What has given me assurance
To say what height becomes New Hampshire mountains,
Or any mountains? Can it be some strength
I feel, as of an earthquake in my back,
To heave them higher to the morning star?
Can it be foreign travel in the Alps?
Or having seen and credited a moment
The solid molding of vast peaks of cloud
Behind the pitiful reality
Of Lincoln, Lafayette, and Liberty?
Or some such sense as says how high shall jet
The fountain in proportion to the basin?
No, none of these has raised me to my throne
Of intellectual dissatisfaction . . .

Mr Frost Goes South to Boston

When I see buildings in a town together,
Stretching all around to touch the sky,
I like to know that they come down again
And so I go around the block to see,
And, sure enough, there is the downward side.
I say to myself these buildings never quite
Arrived at heaven although they went that way.
That's the way with buildings and with people.
The same applies to colts and cats and chickens
And cattle of all breeds and dogs and horses.
I think the buildings Boston has are high
Enough. I like to ride the elevator
Up to the top and then back I come again.
Now, don't get me wrong. I wouldn't want
A ticket to New York to ride up higher.
These buildings come as close to heaven now
As I myself would ever want to go.

FIRMAN HOUGHTON

The parodist begins by alluding to the opening lines of Frost's
poem 'Birches':

When I see birches bend to left and right
Across the lines of straighter darker trees,
I like to think . . .

But his clever mimicry of Frost's folksy manner seems to recall the
more garrulous and platitudinous side of the poet's personality,
well illustrated by almost any passage from 'New Hampshire'. I am
reminded of a competition for the most meaningless Russian
proverb, of which the winning entry was, 'The tallest trees are
closest to the sky.'

JOHN GALSWORTHY (1867–1933)

The Prayer

If on a Spring night I went by
And God were standing there,
What is the prayer I would cry
To Him? This is the prayer:

> 'O Lord of courage grave,
> O Master of this night of Spring.
> Make firm in me a heart too brave
> To ask Thee anything!'

A Prayer

If I popped in at Downing Street
And Eddie were at home,
What is the pome wherewith I'd greet
Him? I will write the pome:

> 'O, Eddie, dear old boy,
> O, C.M.G., C.B.,
> Make firm in me a heart too coy
> To write a pome for thee!'

MAX BEERBOHM

Sir Edward (alias Eddie) Marsh (1872–1953) was a celebrated
figure in political, literary and social circles during the 1920s and
1930s, being at one time private secretary to Winston Churchill.
He would ask famous poets to copy poems into a small black book
which Lady Diana Cooper had given him. Among those who did
so was John Galsworthy. Beerbohm put his 'Prayer' on the next
page but one.

W. S. GILBERT (1836–1911)

from The Yarn of the 'Nancy Bell'

'Twas on the shores that round our coast
  From Deal to Ramsgate span,
That I found alone, on a piece of stone,
  An elderly naval man.

His hair was weedy, his beard was long,
  And weedy and long was he,
And I heard this wight on the shore recite,
  In a singular minor key:

'Oh, I am a cook and a captain bold,
  And the mate of the *Nancy* brig,
And a bo'sun tight, and a midshipmite,
  And the crew of the captain's gig.'

And he shook his fists and he tore his hair,
  Till I really felt afraid;
For I couldn't help thinking the man had been drinking,
  And so I simply said:

'Oh, elderly man, it's little I know,
  Of the duties of men of the sea,
And I'll eat my hand if I understand
  How you can possibly be

'At once a cook, and a captain bold,
  And the mate of the *Nancy* brig,
And a bo'sun tight and a midshipmite,
  And the crew of the captain's gig.'

Then he gave a hitch to his trousers, which
  Is a trick all seamen larn,
And having got rid of a thumping quid,
  He spun this painful yarn:

Servant of the House

Surveying Britain's battled coast
As far as sight may scan,
On every hand the scene is planned
By an elderly youthful man.

His voice is ringing, his will is strong,
And hearty and strong is he;
Each day we hear his words of cheer
As he makes the sign of V.

'Oh, I am the captain of Britain's bark,
Home chief and war chief too,
And Ambassador to the zones of war
And the head of the Tory crew.'

And the Commons sit and tear their hair
For they simply cannot see,
With the weight he bears of home affairs,
How any man can be

At once the captain of Britain's bark,
Home chief *and* war chief too,
And Ambassador to the zones of war,
And head of the Tory crew.

The ship of State, *one* should navigate,
Another should run the war,
And they'll take their oath he can't do both
As well as a good deal more.

They wish he were Prime Minister
Or Minister of Defence –
But in either name he can always claim
Their vote of confidence.

''Twas in the good ship *Nancy Bell*
  That we sailed to the Indian sea,
And there on a reef we come to grief,
  Which has often occurred to me.

'And pretty nigh all o' the crew was drowned
  (There was seventy-seven o' soul),
And only ten of the *Nancy*'s men
  Said "Here!" to the muster roll.

'There was me and the cook and the captain bold,
  And the mate of the *Nancy* brig,
And the bo'sun tight and a midshipmite,
  And the crew of the captain's gig.

'For a month we'd neither wittles nor drink,
  Till a-hungry we did feel,
So, we drawed a lot, and, accordin' shot,
  The captain for our meal.

'The next lot fell to the *Nancy*'s mate,
  And a delicate dish he made;
Then our appetite with the midshipmite
  We seven survivors stayed.

'And then we murdered the bo'sun tight,
  And he much resembled pig;
Then we wittled free, did the cook and me,
  On the crew of the captain's gig.

    *

'And I never larf, and I never smile,
  And I never lark nor play,
But I sit and croak, and a single joke
  I have – which is to say:

'Oh, I am a cook and a captain bold,
  And the mate of the *Nancy* brig,
And a bo'sun tight, and a midshipmite,
  And the crew of the captain's gig!'

So in Britain's realm he takes the helm
However rough the sea,
And he'll eat his hat if he can't do that,
While making the sign of V.

Oh, he is the captain of Britain's bark,
Home chief and war chief too,
And Ambassador to the zones of war
And the head of the Tory crew.

SAGITTARIUS

In 1940, on becoming Prime Minister, Churchill appointed himself
Minister of Defence. This meant that he was in effect the war
supremo, and the Chiefs of Staff, who were not members of the
Cabinet, reported directly to him. In 1942, after the fall of
Singapore, there was a parliamentary vote of confidence in his
leadership, with 464 MPs supporting him, and only one, a pacifist
Independent Labour Party member, against. By the summer of
1942, however, the grumbling against Churchill had increased,
particularly among the Tories, and a second vote was taken, the
result being 476 to 25 in his favour, with 40 abstentions. As his
main critic had advocated that the Duke of Gloucester should be
appointed C-in-C, Churchill survived.

   'Sagittarius' was the pseudonym of Olga Katzin Miller (1896–
1987).

Gilbert's famous ballad was rejected by *Punch* as being
'too cannibalistic'.

from The Major-General's Song

I am the very pattern of a modern major-gineral:
I've information vegetable, animal, and mineral;
I know the kings of England, and I quote the fights historical,
From Marathon to Waterloo, in order categorical;
I'm very well acquainted, too, with matters mathematical;
I understand equations, both the simple and quadratical;
About binomial theorem I'm teeming with a lot of news –
(*Bothered for next rhyme.*) Lot o' news – lot o' news –
(*Struck with an idea.*) With many cheerful facts about the
   square of the hypotenuse;
(*Joyfully.*) With many cheerful facts about the square of the
   hypotenuse!

I'm very good at integral and differential calculus;
I know the scientific names of being animalculous;
In short, in matters vegetable, animal, and mineral
I am the very model of a modern major-gineral!

I know our mythic history, King Arthur's and Sir Caradoc's;
I answer hard acrostics; I've a pretty taste for paradox –
I quote in elegiacs all the crimes of Heliogabalus;
In conics I can floor peculiarities parabolous;
I can tell undoubted Raphaels from Gerard Dows and
   Zoffanies;
I know the croaking chorus from the *Frogs* of Aristophanes;
Then I can hum a fugue of which I've heard the music's
   din afore –
(*Bothered for next rhyme.*) Din afore? din afore? din afore? –
(*Struck with an idea.*) And whistle all the airs from that
   infernal nonsense, *Pinafore*,
(*Joyously.*) And whistle all the airs from that infernal
   nonsense, *Pinafore*.

Then I can write a washing-bill in Babylonic cuneiform,
And tell you every detail of Caractacus's uniform.
In short, in matters vegetable, animal, and mineral
I am the very pattern of a modern major-gineral!

The Elements

There's antimony, arsenic, aluminum, selenium,
And hydrogen and oxygen and nitrogen and rhenium,
And nickel, neodymium, neptunium, germanium,
And iron, americium, ruthenium, uranium,
Europium, zirconium, lutetium, vanadium,
And lanthanum and osmium and astatine and radium,
And gold and protactinium and indium and gallium,
And iodine and thorium and thulium and thallium.

There's yttrium, ytterbium, actinium, rubidium,
And boron, gadolinium, niobium, iridium,
And strontium and silicon and silver and samarium,
And bismuth, bromine, lithium, beryllium, and barium.

There's holmium and helium and hafnium and erbium,
And phosphorus and francium and fluorine and terbium,
And manganese and mercury, molybdenum, magnesium,
Dysprosium and scandium and cerium and cesium,
And lead, praseodymium and platinum, plutonium,
Palladium, promethium, potassium, polonium,
And tantalum, technetium, titanium, tellurium,
And cadmium and calcium and chromium and curium.

There's sulfur, californium, and fermium, berkelium,
And also mendelevium, einsteinium, nobelium,
And argon, krypton, neon, radon, xenon, zinc and
    rhodium,
And chlorine, carbon, cobalt, copper, tungsten, tin and
    sodium.

These are the only ones of which the news has come to
    Ha'vard,
And there may be many others, but they haven't been
    discavard.

TOM LEHRER

OLIVER GOLDSMITH (1730–74)

Song *from* The Vicar of Wakefield

When lovely woman stoops to folly
   And finds too late that men betray,
What charm can soothe her melancholy,
   What art can wash her guilt away?

The only art her guilt to cover,
   To hide her shame from every eye,
To give repentance to her lover,
   And wring his bosom – is to die.

from The Deserted Village

Ill fares the land, to hastening ills a prey,
Where wealth accumulates and men decay.

'When lovely woman'

When lovely woman wants a favour,
   And finds, too late, that man won't bend,
What earthly circumstance can save her
   From disappointment in the end?

The only way to bring him over,
   The last experiment to try,
Whether a husband or a lover,
   If he have feeling, is, to cry!

PHOEBE CARY

'When lovely woman'

When lovely woman stoops to folly
The evening can be awfully jolly.

MARY DEMETRIADIS

from *The Waste Land*

When lovely woman stoops to folly and
Paces about her room again, alone,
She smoothes her hair with automatic hand,
And puts a record on the gramophone.

T. S. ELIOT

'But how much more unfortunate are those'

But how much more unfortunate are those
Where wealth decays and population grows.

HILAIRE BELLOC

HARRY GRAHAM (1874–1936)

Three Ruthless Rhymes for Heartless Homes

Billy, in one of his nice new sashes,
Fell in the fire and was burnt to ashes;
Now, although the room grows chilly,
I haven't the heart to poke poor Billy.

*

'There's been an accident!' they said,
'Your servant's cut in half; he's dead!'
'Indeed!' said Mr Jones, 'and please
Send me the half that's got my keys.'

*

I had written to Aunt Maud,
Who was on a trip abroad,
When I heard she'd died of cramp,
Just too late to save the stamp.

Harry Graham was a son of the Establishment. After Eton,
Sandhurst and the Coldstream Guards, he was appointed ADC to
Canada's Governor-General and, in 1904, private secretary to Lord
Rosebery. However, he is known for other things. In 1899 he
published *Ruthless Rhymes for Heartless Homes*, inventing a new
style of humour and revealing untold depths of Edwardian cruelty
and cynicism. His poems were immensely popular.

' "It's three No Trumps," the soldier said'

'It's three No Trumps,' the soldier said;
A sniper's bullet struck him dead.
His cards bedecked the trench's bottom.
A comrade peered – 'Yes, he'd 'a' got 'em!'

GUY INNES

'Elaine, pretending it was salt'

Elaine, pretending it was salt,
Mixed powdered glass in Grandma's malt.
Her father cried, 'O child abhorred!' –
She used his cherished Waterford.

E. AITKEN

'Squire Squint, shooting at a pheasant'

Squire Squint, shooting at a pheasant,
Hit instead a sitting peasant.
'Well,' laughed Squire, 'sport can't be stopped
Just because an H is dropped.'

G. J. BLUNDELL

THOMAS GRAY (1716–71)

from Elegy Written in a Country Churchyard

The curfew tolls the knell of parting day,
The lowing herd wind slowly o'er the lea,
The ploughman homeward plods his weary way,
And leaves the world to darkness and to me.

Now fades the glimmering landscape on the sight,
And all the air a solemn stillness holds,
Save where the beetle wheels his droning flight,
And drowsy tinklings lull the distant folds;

Save that from yonder ivy-mantled tower
The moping owl does to the moon complain
Of such as, wandering near her secret bower,
Molest her ancient solitary reign.

Beneath those rugged elms, that yew-tree's shade,
Where heaves the turf in many a mouldering heap,
Each in his narrow cell for ever laid,
The rude forefathers of the hamlet sleep.

The breezy call of incense-breathing morn,
The swallow twittering from the straw-built shed,
The cock's shrill clarion or the echoing horn,
No more shall rouse them from their lowly bed.

For them no more the blazing hearth shall burn,
Or busy housewife ply her evening care:
No children run to lisp their sire's return,
Or climb his knees the envied kiss to share.

Oft did the harvest to their sickle yield,
Their furrow oft the stubborn glebe has broke;
How jocund did they drive their team afield!
How bowed the woods beneath their sturdy stroke!

*If Gray Had Had to Write His Elegy in the
Cemetery of Spoon River instead of in That of
Stoke Poges*

The curfew tolls the knell of parting day,
  The whippoorwill salutes the rising moon,
And wanly glimmer in her gentle ray
  The sinuous windings of the turbid Spoon.

Here where the flattering and mendacious swarm
  Of lying epitaphs their secrets keep,
At last incapable of further harm
  The lewd forefathers of the village sleep.

The earliest drug of half-awakened morn,
  Cocaine or hashish, strychnine, poppy-seeds
Or fiery produce of fermented corn
  No more shall start them on the day's misdeeds.

For them no more the whetstone's cheerful noise,
  No more the sun upon his daily course
Shall watch them savouring the genial joys
  Of murder, bigamy, arson and divorce.

Here they all lie; and, as the hour is late,
  O stranger, o'er their tombstones cease to stoop,
But bow thine ear to me and contemplate
  The unexpurgated annals of the group.

There are two hundred only: yet of these
  Some thirty died of drowning in the river,
Sixteen went mad, ten others had DT's.
  And twenty-eight cirrhosis of the liver.

Let not Ambition mock their useful toil,
Their homely joys and destiny obscure;
Nor Grandeur hear, with a disdainful smile,
The short and simple annals of the poor.

The boast of heraldry, the pomp of power,
And all that beauty, all that wealth e'er gave,
Awaits alike the inevitable hour.
The paths of glory lead but to the grave.

Nor you, ye Proud, impute to these the fault,
If Memory o'er their tomb no trophies raise,
Where through the long-drawn aisle and fretted vault
The pealing anthem swells the note of praise.

Can storied urn or animated bust
Back to its mansion call the fleeting breath?
Can Honour's voice provoke the silent dust,
Or Flattery soothe the dull cold ear of Death?

Perhaps in this neglected spot is laid
Some heart once pregnant with celestial fire;
Hands that the rod of empire might have swayed,
Or waked to ecstasy the living lyre.

But Knowledge to their eyes her ample page
Rich with the spoils of time did ne'er unroll;
Chill Penury repressed their noble rage,
And froze the genial current of the soul.

Full many a gem of purest ray serene
The dark unfathomed caves of ocean bear:
Full many a flower is born to blush unseen,
And waste its sweetness on the desert air.

Some village-Hampden that with dauntless breast
The little tyrant of his fields withstood;
Some mute inglorious Milton here may rest,
Some Cromwell guiltless of his country's blood.

Several by absent-minded friends were shot,
  Still more blew out their own exhausted brains,
One died of a mysterious inward rot,
  Three fell off roofs, and five were hit by trains.

One was harpooned, one gored by a bull-moose,
  Four on the Fourth fell victims to lock-jaw,
Ten in electric chair or hempen noose
  Suffered the last exaction of the law.

Stranger, you quail, and seem inclined to run;
  But, timid stranger, do not be unnerved;
I can assure you that there was not one
  Who got a tithe of what he had deserved.

Full many a vice is born to thrive unseen,
  Full many a crime the world does not discuss,
Full many a pervert lives to reach a green
  Replete old age, and so it was with us.

Here lies a parson who would often make
  Clandestine rendezvous with Claflin's Moll,
And 'neath the druggist's counter creep to take
  A sip of surreptitious alcohol.

And here a doctor, who had seven wives,
  And, fearing this *ménage* might seem grotesque,
Persuaded six of them to spend their lives
  Locked in a drawer of his private desk.

And others here there sleep who, given scope,
  Had writ their names large on the Scrolls of Crime,
Men who, with half a chance, might haply cope,
  With the first miscreants of recorded time.

Doubtless in this neglected spot is laid
  Some village Nero who has missed his due,
Some Bluebeard who dissected many a maid,
  And all for naught, since no one ever knew.

The applause of listening senates to command,
The threats of pain and ruin to despise,
To scatter plenty o'er a smiling land,
And read their history in a nation's eyes,

Their lot forbade: nor circumscribed alone
Their growing virtues, but their crimes confined;
Forbade to wade through slaughter to a throne,
And shut the gates of mercy on mankind,

The struggling pangs of conscious truth to hide,
To quench the blushes of ingenuous shame,
Or heap the shrine of Luxury and Pride
With incense kindled at the Muse's flame.

Far from the madding crowd's ignoble strife
Their sober wishes never learned to stray;
Along the cool sequestered vale of life
They kept the noiseless tenor of their way.

Yet even these bones from insult to protect
Some frail memorial still erected nigh,
With uncouth rhymes and shapeless sculpture decked,
Implores the passing tribute of a sigh.

Some poor bucolic Borgia here may rest
   Whose poisons sent whole families to their doom,
Some hayseed Herod who, within his breast,
   Concealed the sites of many an infant's tomb.

Types that the Muse of Masefield might have stirred,
   Or waked to ecstasy Gaboriau,
Each in his narrow cell at last interred,
   All, all are sleeping peacefully below.

*

Enough, enough! But, stranger, ere we part,
   Glancing farewell to each nefarious bier,
This warning I would beg you take to heart,
   'There is an end to even the worst career!'

J. C. SQUIRE

In 1916 the American writer, Edgar Lee Masters, published *The Spoon River Anthology*, a collection of versified confessions and revelations from beyond the grave by the former inhabitants of a Midwestern American village.

Elegy in Newgate

The Curfew tolls the hour of locking up,
   The grating bolts turn heavy on the key,
The turn-key hastens on beef-steaks to sup,
   And leaves the cell to treason and to me.

'THE SATIRIST'

Lines attributed to William Cobbett (1763–1835), who underwent imprisonment for his Radical views in the early 1800s and was once described as 'Undergraduate of Newgate'.

THOMAS HARDY (1840–1928)

Exeunt Omnes

Everybody else, then, going,
And I still left where the fair was? . . .
Much have I seen of neighbour loungers
Making a lusty showing,
Each now past all knowing.

There is an air of blankness
In the street and the littered spaces;
Thoroughfare, steeple, bridge and highway
Wizen themselves to lankness;
Kennels dribble dankness.

Folk all fade. And whither,
As I wait alone where the fair was?
Into the clammy and numbing night-fog
Whence they entered hither.
Soon one more goes thither!

A Luncheon (Thomas Hardy Entertains the Prince of Wales)

Lift latch, step in, be welcome, Sir,
Albeit to see you I'm unglad
And your face is fraught with a deathly shyness
Bleaching what pink it may have had,
Come in, come in, Your Royal Highness.

Beautiful weather? – Sir, that's true,
Though the farmers are casting rueful looks
At tilth's and pasture's dearth of spryness. –
Yes, Sir, I've written several books. –
A little more chicken, Your Royal Highness?

Lift latch, step out, your car is there,
To bear you hence from this antient vale.
We are both of us aged by our strange brief nighness,
But each of us lives to tell the tale.
Farewell, farewell, Your Royal Highness.

                              MAX BEERBOHM

On 20 July 1923 the Prince of Wales visited Thomas Hardy at his
home near Dorchester. When Mrs Hardy had inquired what the
Prince would like to eat, his secretary had cabled back, 'Chicken
and whisky'. The only detail recorded of this strange meeting was
that at one point the Prince retired to take off his waistcoat,
chucking it at his valet with the words, 'It's too damned hot! You
wear the bloody thing yourself.' In his heyday Hardy could have
made at least a short story out of that.

TONY HARRISON (1937–   )

Breaking the Chain

The mams, pig-sick of oilstains in the wash,
wished for their sons a better class of gear,
'wear their own clothes to work' but not go posh,
go up a rung or two but settle near.

This meant the 'drawing office' to the dads,
same place of work, but not blue-collar, white.
A box like a medal case went round the lads
as, one by one, their mams pushed them as 'bright'.

My dad bought it, from the last dad who still owed
the dad before, for a whole week's wage and drink.
I was brought down out of bed to have bestowed
the polished box wrapped in the Sporting Pink.

Looking at it now still breaks my heart!
The gap his gift acknowledged then's as wide as
eternity, but still I can't bear to part
with these never passed on, never used, dividers.

Pulling the Chain

When I were just a little lad, right small,
we had to share the lav wi' half the street.
Nights were the worst, you couldn't see at all.
Even in t'day, you had to mind yer feet.

I still have dreams about those great grey rats
– big as t'shoe-box where I like to keep
the family heirlooms, like me dad's flat 'ats
(I get 'em out occasional to weep

about the gap my culture interposed
between us, like). Any road, point being
I never went alone when indisposed;
I always took me mam when I went peeing.

I'd take the *Sporting Pink* to wipe me ass.
Me mam would stand outside, ay, even in t'rain
if it were raining. Why? I hear you ask.
Fact was, you see, *I* couldn't reach the chain.

                                        SIMON RAE

BRET HARTE (1836–1902)

Plain Language from Truthful James

Which I wish to remark,
  And my language is plain,
That for ways that are dark
  And for tricks that are vain,
The heathen Chinee is peculiar,
  Which the same I would rise to explain.

Ah Sin was his name;
  And I shall not deny
In regard to the same,
  What that name might imply;
But his smile it was pensive and childlike,
  As I frequent remarked to Bill Nye.

It was August the third;
  And quite soft was the skies;
Which it might be inferred
  That Ah Sin was likewise;
Yet he played it that day upon William
  And me in a way I despise.

Which we had a small game,
  And Ah Sin took a hand:
It was Euchre. The same
  He did not understand;
But he smiled as he sat by the table,
  With the smile that was childlike and bland.

The Heathen Pass-ee

Which I wish to remark,
   And my language is plain,
That for plots that are dark
   And not always in vain,
The Heathen Pass-ee is peculiar,
   And the same I would rise to explain.

I would also premise
   That the term of Pass-ee
Most fitly applies,
   As you probably see,
To one whose vocation is passing
   The 'ordinary B.A. degree'.

Tom Crib was his name,
   And I shall not deny
In regard to the same
   What that name might imply,
That his face it was trustful and childlike,
   And he had the most innocent eye.

Upon April the First
   The Little-Go fell,
And that was the worst
   Of the gentleman's sell,
For he fooled the Examining Body
   In a way I'm reluctant to tell.

The candidates came
   And Tom Crib soon appeared;
It was Euclid, the same
   Was 'the subject he feared';

Yet the cards they were stocked
  In a way that I grieve,
And my feelings were shocked
  At the state of Nye's sleeve:
Which was stuffed full of aces and bowers,
  And the same with intent to deceive.

But the hands that were played
  By that heathen Chinee,
And the points that he made,
  Were quite frightful to see, —
Till at last he put down a right bower,
  Which the same Nye had dealt unto me.

Then I looked up at Nye,
  And he gazed upon me;
And he rose with a sigh,
  And said, 'Can this be?
We are ruined by Chinese cheap labour, — '
  And he went for that heathen Chinee.

In the scene that ensued
  I did not take a hand,
But the floor it was strewed
  Like the leaves on the strand
With the cards that Ah Sin had been hiding,
  In the game 'he did not understand'.

In his sleeves, which were long,
  He had twenty-four packs, —
Which was coming it strong,
  Yet I state but the facts;
And we found on his nails, which were taper,
  What is frequent in tapers, — that's wax.

But he smiled as he sat by the table
  With a smile that was wary and weird.

Yet he did what he could,
  And the papers he showed
Were remarkably good,
  And his countenance glowed
With pride when I met him soon after
  As he walked down the Trumpington Road.

We did not find him out,
  Which I bitterly grieve,
For I've not the least doubt
  That he'd placed up his sleeve
Mr Todbunker's excellent Euclid,
  The same with intent to deceive.

But I shall not forget
  How the next day or two
A stiff paper was set
  By Examiner U—
On Euripides' tragedy, Bacchae,
  A subject Tom 'partially knew'

But the knowledge displayed
  By that Heathen Pass-ee,
And the answers he made
  Were quite frightful to see,
For he rapidly floored the whole paper
  By about twenty minutes to three.

Then I looked up at U—
  And he gazed upon me,
I observed, 'This won't do';
  He replied, 'Goodness me!
We are fooled by this artful young person.'
  And he sent for that Heathen Pass-ee.

Which is why I remark,
   And my language is plain,
That for ways that are dark,
   And for tricks that are vain,
The heathen Chinee is peculiar, –
   Which the same I am free to maintain.

The scene that ensued
  Was disgraceful to view,
For the floor it was strewed
  With a tolerable few
Of the 'tips' that Tom Crib had been hiding
  For the 'subject he partially knew'.

On the cuff of his shirt
  He had managed to get
What we hoped had been dirt,
  But which proved, I regret,
To be notes on the rise of the Drama,
  A question invariably set.

In his various coats
  We proceeded to seek,
Where we found sundry notes
  And – with sorrow I speak –
One of Bohn's publications, so useful
  To the student of Latin or Greek.

In the crown of his cap
  Were the Furies and Fates,
And a delicate map
  Of the Dorian States,
And we found in his palms, which were hollow,
  What are frequent in palms – that is, dates;

Which is why I remark,
  And my language is plain,
That for plots that are dark
  And not always in vain,
The Heathen Pass-ee is familiar,
  Which the same I am free to maintain.

                              A. C. HILTON

SEAMUS HEANEY (1939–)

Oysters

Our shells clacked on the plates.
My tongue was a filling estuary,
My palate hung with starlight:
As I tasted the salty Pleiades
Orion dipped his foot into the water.

Alive and violated
They lay on their beds of ice:
Bivalves: the split bulb
And philandering sigh of ocean.
Millions of them ripped and shucked and scattered.

We had driven to that coast
Through flowers and limestone
And there we were, toasting friendship,
Laying down a perfect memory
In the cool of thatch and crockery.

Over the Alps, packed deep in hay and snow,
The Romans hauled their oysters south to Rome:
I saw damp panniers disgorge
The frond-lipped, brine-stung
Glut of privilege

And was angry that my trust could not repose
In the clear light, like poetry or freedom
Leaning in from sea. I ate the day
Deliberately, that its tang
Might quicken me all into verb, pure verb.

Usquebaugh

Deft, practised, eager.
Your fingers twist the metal cap.
Late into the moth-infested night
We listen to soft scrapings
Of bottle-top on ridged glass,

The plash and glug of amber liquid
Streaming into tumblers, inches deep.
Life-water. Fire-tanged
Hard-stuff. Gallons of it,
Sipped and swigged and swallowed.

Whiskey: its terse vowels belie
The slow fuddling and mellowing,
Our guttural speech slurring
Into warm, thick blather,
The pie-eyed, slug-witted slump

Into soused oblivion –
And the awakening. I long
For pure, cold water as the pump
Creaks in the yard. A bucket
Clatters to the ground. Is agony.

                    WENDY COPE

Wendy Cope is a gifted parodist and I have included several of her
poems. She has herself been parodied by Kit Wright in the
following lines:

   I liked the project not one bit.
      I didn't think I had a hope,
   But got it done, and this is it:
      A parody of Wendy Cope!

FELICIA HEMANS (1793–1835)

from The Homes of England

The stately homes of England,
　How beautiful they stand,
Amidst their tall ancestral trees,
　O'er all the pleasant land!
The deer across their greensward bound,
　Through shade and sunny gleam;
And the swan glides past them with the sound
　Of some rejoicing stream.

The merry homes of England!
　Around their hearths by night,
What gladsome looks of household love
　Meet in the ruddy light!
There woman's voice flows forth in song,
　Or childhood's tale is told,
Or lips move tunefully along
　Some glorious page of old.

The blessed homes . . .

from *The Stately Homes of England*

The Stately Homes of England,
How beautiful they stand,
To prove the upper classes
Have still the upper hand;
Though the fact that they have to be rebuilt
And frequently mortgaged to the hilt
Is inclined to take the gilt
Off the gingerbread,
And certainly damps the fun
Of the eldest son –
But still we won't be beaten,
We'll scrimp and scrape and save,
The playing fields of Eton
Have made us frightfully brave –
And though if the Van Dycks have to go
And we pawn the Bechstein Grand,
We'll stand
By the Stately Homes of England.

*

The Stately Homes of England,
Although a trifle bleak,
Historically speaking,
Are more or less unique.

*

NOËL COWARD

GEORGE HERBERT (1593–1633)

from Longing

> With sick and famisht eyes,
> With doubling knees and weary bones,
>   To thee my cries,
>   To thee my grones,
> To thee my sighs, my tears ascend:
>   No end?
>
>   My throat, my soul is hoarse;
> My heart is wither'd like a ground
>   Which thou dost curse.
>   My thoughts turn round,
> And make me giddie; Lord, I fall,
>   Yet call.
>
>   From thee all pitie flows.
> Mothers are kinde, because thou art,
>   And dost dispose
>   To them a part:
> Their infants, them; and they suck thee
>   More free.
>
>   Bowels of pitie, heare!
> Lord of my soul, love of my minde,
>   Bow down thine eare!
>   Let not the winde
> Scatter my words, and in the same
>   Thy name!

Confusion

O how my mind
        Is gravell'd!
        Not a thought
That I can find
        But's ravel'd
        All to nought.
Short ends of threds,
        And narrow shreds
        Of lists,
Knot-snarl'd ruffs,
        Loose broken tufts
        Of twists,
Are my torn meditation's ragged clothing;
Which, wound and woven, shape a sute for nothing;
One while I think, and then I am in pain
To think how to unthink that thought again.

How can my soul
        But famish
        With this food?
Pleasure's full bowl
        Tastes rammish,
        Taints the blood;
Profit picks bones,
        And chews on stones
        That choak;
Honour climbs hills,
        Fats not, but fills
        With smoak.

Look on my sorrows round!
Mark well my furnace! O what flames,
   What heats abound!
   What griefs, what shames!
Consider, Lord; Lord, bow thine eare,
    And heare!

Lord Jesu, thou didst bow
Thy dying head upon the tree:
   O be not now
   More dead to me!
Lord heare! *Shall he that made the eare,*
    Not heare?

Behold, thy dust doth stirre,
It moves, it creeps, it aims at thee:
   Wilt thou deferre
   To succour me,
Thy pile of dust, wherein each crumme
    Sayes, Come?

And whilst my thoughts are greedy upon these,
They pass by pearls, and stoop to pick up pease.
Such wash and draff is fit for none but swine:
And such I am not, Lord, if I am Thine.
   Cloath me anew, and feed me then afresh;
   Else my soul dies famisht and starv'd with flesh.

CHRISTOPHER HARVEY

In his *Biographia Literaria* Coleridge quotes the first stanza of this
poem by Christopher Harvey (1597–1663) as an example of
'burlesque'. It was the custom until Victorian times for publishers
to include Harvey's *The Synagogue* in the same volume as
Herbert's *The Temple*. Harvey displays all the faults of the zealous
imitator, taking Herbert's intricate rhyming and abrupt breaking of
lines to an extreme. Although Harvey's purpose was certainly not
to mock, the stanza singled out by Coleridge found its way into
Dwight Macdonald's classic anthology, *Parodies*. In the absence of
any good intentional take-off of Herbert, the whole of 'Confusion'
is printed here to illustrate how close pious imitation can come to
parody. But this is not to answer the question of why Herbert has
so successfully foiled the parodists of later ages.

ROBERT HERRICK (1591–1674)

To the Virgins, to Make Much of Time

Gather ye rosebuds while ye may,
  Old Time is still a-flying:
And this same flower that smiles to-day
  To-morrow will be dying.

The glorious lamp of heaven, the sun,
  The higher he's a-getting,
The sooner will his race be run,
  And nearer he's to setting.

That age is best which is the first,
  When youth and blood are warmer;
But being spent, the worse, and worst
  Times still succeed the former.

Then be not coy, but use your time,
  And while ye may, go marry:
For having lost but once your prime,
  You may for ever tarry.

Upon Julia's Clothes

Whenas in silks my Julia goes,
Then, then (methinks) how sweetly flowes
That liquefaction of her clothes.

Next, when I cast mine eyes and see
That brave Vibration each way free;
O how that glittering taketh me!

Election Time

Gather ye bank-notes while ye may:
   The happy time is flitting;
The Member canvassing today
   Tomorrow will be sitting.

That glorious crib, the *Rising Sun*,
   Where patriots are glowing,
Too soon its brilliant course is run.
   Its beer will soon stop flowing.

ANONYMOUS

Upon Julia's Clothes

Whenas in furs my Julia goes,
Of slaughtered vermin goodness knows,
What tails depend upon her clothes!

Next, when I cast my eyes and see
The living whelp she lugs to tea,
Oh, how their likeness taketh me!

E. V. KNOX

E. V. Knox ('Evoe') was a tireless contributor to *Punch*, and its
Editor from 1932 to 1949.

THOMAS HOOD (1799–1845)

from Faithless Nelly Gray

A Pathetic Ballad

Ben Battle was a soldier bold,
   And used to war's alarms:
But a cannon-ball took off his legs,
   So he laid down his arms!

Now, as they bore him off the field,
   Said he, 'Let others shoot,
For here I leave my second leg,
   And the Forty-second Foot!'

The army-surgeons made him limbs:
   Said he, – 'They're only pegs:
But there's as wooden members quite
   As represent my legs!'

Now Ben he loved a pretty maid,
   Her name was Nelly Gray;
So he went to pay her his devours
   When he'd devoured his pay!

But when he called on Nelly Gray,
   She made him quite a scoff;
And when she saw his wooden legs,
   Began to take them off!

'O Nelly Gray! O Nelly Gray!
   Is this your love so warm?
The love that loves a scarlet coat,
   Should be more uniform!'

Said she, 'I loved a soldier once,
   For he was blithe and brave;

Ben Barley

Ben Barley was a barman stout
   Who drank both day and night,
Which made him heavy, dull and fat
   Though all he drank was Light.

He slowly drank himself to death,
   And at his wake so drear,
Although 'twas he who'd passed away,
   The guests laid on the beer.

His ghost came in and asked for gin
   In accents strange and far.
The landlord said, 'Clear off; we don't
   Serve spirits in this bar.'

GERARD BENSON

But I will never have a man
    With both legs in the grave!

'Before you had those timber toes,
    Your love I did allow,
But then, you know, you stand upon
    Another footing now!'

        *

Now when he went from Nelly Gray,
    His heart so heavy got —
And life was such a burthen grown,
    It made him take a knot!

So round his melancholy neck
    A rope he did entwine,
And, for his second time in life,
    Enlisted in the Line!

One end he tied around a beam,
    And then removed his pegs,
And, as his legs were off, — of course,
    He soon was off his legs!

And there he hung till he was dead
    As any nail in town, —
For though distress had cut him up,
    It could not cut him down!

A dozen men sat on his corpse,
    To find out why he died —
And they buried Ben in four cross-roads,
    With a *stake* in his inside!

Elegy on Thomas Hood

O spare a tear for poor Tom Hood,
Who, dazed by death, here lies;
His days abridged, he sighs across
The Bridge of Utmost Size.

His *penchant* was for punning rhymes
(Some lengthy, others – shorties);
But though his *forte* was his life,
He died within his forties.

The Muses cried: 'To you we give
The crown of rhymester's bay, Thos.'
Thos mused and thought that it might pay
To ladle out the pay-thos.

He spun the gold yet tangled yarn
Of sad Miss Kilmansegg;
And told how destiny contrived
To take her down a peg.

But now the weary toils of death
Have closed his rhyming toil,
And charged this very vital spark
To jump his mortal coil.

MARTIN FAGG

GERARD MANLEY HOPKINS (1844–89)

Pied Beauty

Glory be to God for dappled things –
  For skies of couple-colour as a brinded cow;
    For rose-moles all in stipple upon trout that swim;
Fresh firecoal chestnut-falls; finches' wings;
  Landscapes plotted and pieced – fold, fallow, and
      plough;
    And áll trádes, their gear and tackle and trim.

All things counter, original, spare, strange;
  Whatever is fickle, freckled (who knows how?)
    With swift, slow; sweet, sour; adazzle, dim;
He fathers-forth whose beauty is past change:
                Praise him.

Pied Beauty

(In addition to meaning 'dappled', pied is a printer's term for 'jumbled mixture')

Glory be to God for Hopkins' verse,
Which sprang sprung-rhythm on us; outraged syntax,
Hyphened and bracketed meaning in desperately-knotted
   stanzas,
Plotted and pieced together – tormentingly terse,
As though the uneasy author were sitting on tin-tacks,
While fathering-forth mind-blowing extravaganzas.

Oh, how he goes on (and on!), this tortured language-
   lover,
Whatever is bitter-sweet, contrariwise, he lauds,
Driven by God-only-knows what scourge, what whim;
For the sheer sharp shock of the way he puts it over,
            Praise him!

STANLEY J. SHARPLESS

A. E. HOUSMAN (1859–1936)

Bredon Hill

In summertime on Bredon
  The bells they sound so clear;
Round both the shires they ring them
  In steeples far and near,
  A happy noise to hear.

Here of a Sunday morning
  My love and I would lie,
And see the coloured counties,
  And hear the larks so high
  About us in the sky.

The bells would ring to call her
  In valleys miles away:
'Come all to church, good people;
  Good people, come and pray.'
  But here my love would stay.

Housman's reputation rests largely on a single collection of poems,
A Shropshire Lad. He was a lonely homosexual, writing his most
famous work at the time of the Oscar Wilde trial. He turned down
the offer of an Order of Merit from George V, who may have
found his letter of refusal a bit strange: 'I hope to escape the
reproach of thanklessness or churlish behaviour by borrowing
words with which an equally loyal servant, Admiral Cornwallis,
declined a similar mark of the Royal favour: "I am unhappily of a
turn of mind that would make my receiving that honour the most
unpleasant thing imaginable." ' Less charitable commentators held
that he had turned it down because Galsworthy was also an OM.

Summer Time on Bredon

'Tis Summer Time on Bredon,
    And now the farmers swear;
The cattle rise and listen
    In valleys far and near,
    And blush at what they hear.

But when the mists in autumn
    On Bredon tops are thick,
The happy hymns of farmers
    Go up from fold and rick,
    The cattle then are sick.

HUGH KINGSMILL

The Carpenter's Son

'Here the hangman stops his cart:
Now the best of friends must part.
Fare you well, for ill fare I:
Live, lads, and I will die.

'Oh, at home had I but stayed
'Prenticed to my father's trade,
Had I stuck to plane and adze,
I had not been lost, my lads.

'Then I might have built perhaps
Gallows-trees for other chaps,
Never dangled on my own,
Had I but left ill alone.

'Now, you see, they hang me high,
And the people passing by
Stop to shake their fists and curse;
So 'tis come from ill to worse.

'Here hang I, and right and left
Two poor fellows hang for theft:
All the same's the luck we prove,
Though the midmost hangs for love.

'Comrades all, that stand and gaze,
Walk henceforth in other ways;
See my neck and save your own:
Comrades all, leave ill alone.

'Make some day a decent end,
Shrewder fellows than your friend.
Fare you well, for ill fare I:
Live, lads, and I will die.'

A. E. Housman and a Few Friends

When lads have done with labour
   in Shropshire, one will cry,
'Let's go and kill a neighbour,'
   And t'other answers 'Aye!'

So this one kills his cousins,
   and that one kills his dad;
and, as they hang by dozens
   at Ludlow, lad by lad,

each of them one-and-twenty,
   all of them murderers,
the hangman mutters: 'Plenty
   even for Housman's verse.'

HUMBERT WOLFE

'What, still alive at twenty-two'

What, still alive at twenty-two,
A clean upstanding chap like you?
Sure, if your throat 'tis hard to slit,
Slit your girl's, and swing for it.

Like enough, you won't be glad,
When they come to hang you, lad:
But bacon's not the only thing
That's cured by hanging from a string.

So, when the spilt ink of the night
Spreads o'er the blotting pad of light,
Lads whose job is still to do
Shall whet their knives, and think of you.

HUGH KINGSMILL

MARY HOWITT (1799–1888)

from The Spider and the Fly

'Will you walk into my parlour?' said the Spider to the Fly,
''Tis the prettiest little parlour that ever you did spy;
The way into my parlour is up a winding stair,
And I have many curious things to show when you are
    there.'
'Oh no, no,' said the little Fly, 'to ask me is in vain;
For who goes up your winding stair can ne'er come down
    again.'

'I'm sure you must be weary, dear, with soaring up so high;
Will you rest upon my little bed?' said the Spider to the Fly.
'There are pretty curtains drawn around, the sheets are
    fine and thin;
And if you like to rest a while, I'll snugly tuck you in!'
'Oh no, no,' said the little Fly, 'for I've often heard it said
They never, never wake again, who sleep upon your bed!' . .

The Spider turned him round about, and went into his den
For well he knew the silly Fly would soon be back again;
So he wove a subtle web in little corner sky,
And set his table ready to dine upon the Fly.

Mary Howitt was the first English translator of Hans Christian
Andersen and a highly prolific poet and writer for children. Many
of her books were written in collaboration with her husband,
William. On his death, *The Times* summed up their achievement:
'Nothing that either of them wrote will live, but they were so
industrious, so disinterested, so amiable, so devoted to the work of
spreading good and innocent literature, that their names ought not
to disappear unmourned.'

The Lobster Quadrille

'Will you walk a little faster?' said a whiting to a snail,
'There's a porpoise close behind us, and he's treading on
    my tail.
See how eagerly the lobsters and the turtles all advance!

'They are waiting on the shingle – will you come and join
    the dance?
  Will you, won't you, will you, won't you, will you join
    the dance?
  Will you, won't you, will you, won't you, won't you
  join the dance?

'You can really have no notion how delightful it will be
When they take us up and throw us, with the lobsters, out
    to sea!'
But the snail replied 'Too far, too far!' and gave a look
    askance –
Said he thanked the whiting kindly, but he would not join
    the dance.
  Would not, could not, would not, could not, would not
  join the dance.
  Would not, could not, would not, could not, could not
  join the dance.

'What matters it how far we go?' his scaly friend replied.
'There is another shore, you know, upon the other side.
The further off from England the nearer is to France –
Then turn not pale, beloved snail, but come and join the
    dance.
  Will you, won't you, will you, won't you, will you join
    the dance?
  Will you, won't you, will you, won't you, won't you
  join the dance?'

                                    LEWIS CARROLL

TED HUGHES (1930–   )

That Moment

When the pistol muzzle oozing blue vapour
Was lifted away
Like a cigarette lifted from an ashtray

And the only face left in the world
Lay broken
Between hands that relaxed, being too late

And the trees closed forever
And the streets closed forever

And the body lay on the gravel
Of the abandoned world
Among abandoned utilities
Exposed to infinity forever

Crow had to start searching for something to eat.

Budgie Finds His Voice

from The Life and Songs of the Budgie *by Jake Strugnell*

God decided he was tired
Of his spinning toys.
They wobbled and grew still.

When the sun was lifted away
Like an orange lifted from a fruit-bowl

And darkness, blacker
Than an oil-slick
Covered everything forever

And the last ear left on earth
Lay on the beach,
Deaf as a shell

And the land froze
And the sea froze

'Who's a pretty boy then?' Budgie cried.

WENDY COPE

LEIGH HUNT (1784–1859)

Jenny Kissed Me

Jenny kissed me when we met,
  Jumping from the chair she sat in;
Time, you thief, who love to get
  Sweets into your list, put that in!
Say I'm weary, say I'm sad,
  Say that health and wealth have missed me,
Say I'm growing old, but add,
  Jenny kissed me.

'Jenny' was Jane Welsh Carlyle, Thomas Carlyle's wife. She had expressed concern for Leigh Hunt when he was ill for some weeks during an influenza epidemic. On recovery, he went to give her the good news himself and she jumped up and kissed him. 'I never heard of Mrs Carlyle kissing any other man,' said a later favourite; 'not even me.'

'Time, you thief, who love to get'

Time, you thief, who love to get
Sweets within your pipe, put *that* in!
Say I'm weary, say I'm sad,
Say I'm growing old – but add,
G. M. Trevelyan wanted me to deliver a Clark Lecture.

Yours sincerely, and with deep regret, MAX BEERBOHM

During the Second World War, when Max Beerbohm was staying
in England, at Abinger in Surrey, he was invited to give the Clark
Lecture by the eminent historian G. M. Trevelyan. He declined in a
very Maxian way: 'I have views on a great number of subjects, but
no great co-ordinated body of views on any subject. I have been
rather a lightweight; and mature years have not remedied this
defect.'

Jenny Hit Me

Jenny hit me when we met,
  Leaping from the knee she sat on;
Fate, you clown, who love to get
  Medals on your chest, pin that on!
Say I'm ancient, say I'm mad,
  Say the costume doesn't fit me,
Say that Santa drinks, but add,
  Jenny hit me.

JOHN CLARKE

John Clarke is the author of *The Complete Book of Australian
Verse*, in which many of the great English and American poets are
revealed to have been Australians.

SAMUEL JOHNSON (1709–84)

from The Vanity of Human Wishes

Let Observation with extensive View,
Survey Mankind, from *China* to *Peru*;
Remark each anxious Toil, each eager Strife,
And watch the busy Scenes of crouded Life;
Then say how Hope and Fear, Desire and Hate,
O'erspread with Snares the clouded Maze of Fate,
Where wav'ring Man, betray'd by vent'rous Pride,
To tread the dreary Paths without a guide,
As treach'rous Phantoms in the Mist delude,
Shuns fancied Ills, or chases airy Good.
How rarely Reason guides the stubborn Choice,
Rules the bold Hand, or prompts the suppliant Voice,
How Nations sink, by darling Schemes oppres'd,
When Vengeance listens to the Fool's Request.

'Let Observation, shuddering the While'

Let Observation, shuddering the While,
Direct her Gaze on this demented Isle,
Where Vice and Folly reign as ne'er before:
There struts a Punk, and here parades a Whore.
Permissive Britons, quite bereft of Shame,
Applaud 'the Love that dares not speak its Name'.
The Youth, intent upon erotic Pleasure,
Marry in Haste, and soon divorce at Leisure.
The Barren, spurning the Decree of Fate,
Rush off and hire themselves a Surrogate.
Plays, Films and Books, fast swimming with the Tide,
Poor Chastity and Modesty deride.
A new-made Bishop (oh, for Peter's Sword!)
Denies the Resurrection of the Lord . . .
'Enough!' cries Observation to the Skies,
Sinks to the Ground – and puts out both her Eyes.

F. MULLEN

The winner of a *Spectator* competition calling for poems by
Dr Johnson commenting upon the modern scene.

'I put my hat upon my head'

I put my hat upon my head
  And walk'd into the Strand,
And there I met another man
  Whose hat was in his hand.

Johnson improvised this quatrain to show the inanity of *The Hermit of Warkworth*, a lengthy poem in the same metre by Thomas Percy (1729–1811), the antiquarian. George Steevens, who records a slightly different version, says that Percy himself was present. In time, ironically, the origin of the lines has been forgotten and they have become associated entirely with Johnson, prompting such exercises as the one opposite, written more in continuation than in a spirit of parody.

'I took him by the arm and said'

I took him by the arm and said,
  'Pray, Sir, what do you mean?
The snow is falling thick and fast,
  The winter wind blows keen!'

He fixed me with an outraged eye
  And said, 'Hast thou forgot
That on this day the martyr Charles
  Was slain hard by this spot?'

I doffed my hat and home returned,
  My soul within me quailing,
And, in atonement for my sin,
  Touched not a single railing.

F. MULLEN

BEN JONSON (1573–1637)

Song: To Celia

Drink to me only with thine eyes,
   And I will pledge with mine;
Or leave a kiss but in the cup,
   And I'll not look for wine.
The thirst that from the soul doth rise
   Doth ask a drink divine:
But might I of Jove's nectar sup,
   I would not change for thine.

I sent thee late a rosy wreath,
   Not so much honouring thee,
As giving it a hope that there
   It could not withered be.
But thou thereon didst only breathe,
   And sent'st it back to me:
Since when it grows, and smells, I swear,
   Not of itself, but thee.

To the Wine Treasurer of the Circuit Mess

Wink at it only with thine eyes,
    Nor taste it while we dine;
Or pour the liquor in my cup,
    But do not call it wine.
The thirst that from the Courts doth rise
    Doth ask a drink divine;
But might I of ditch water sup
    I would not change for thine.

I sent thee late three guineas, net,
    Not so much trusting thee,
As hoping that in small sound beer
    It might expended be;
But thou therewith didst only get
    An odd job lot for me;
Since when I daily growl and swear
    Both at thy wine and thee.

                    HORACE SMITH

JOHN KEATS (1795–1821)

On First Looking into Chapman's Homer

Much have I travelled in the realms of gold,
    And many goodly states and kingdoms seen;
    Round many western islands have I been
Which bards in fealty to Apollo hold.
Oft of one wide expanse had I been told
    That deep-browed Homer ruled as his demesne:
    Yet did I never breathe its pure serene
Till I heard Chapman speak out loud and bold:
Then felt I like some watcher of the skies
    When a new planet swims into his ken;
Or like stout Cortez, when with eagle eyes
    He stared at the Pacific – and all his men
Looked at each other with a wild surmise –
    Silent, upon a peak in Darien.

On First Looking through Krafft-Ebing's Psychopathia Sexualis

Much have I travelled in those realms of old
Where many a whore in hall-doors could be seen
Of many a bonnie brothel or shebeen
Which bawds connived at by policemen hold.
I too have listened when the Quay was coaled,
But never did I taste the Pure Obscene –
Much less imagine that my past was clean –
Till this Krafft-Ebing out his story told.
Then felt I rather taken by surprise
As on the evening when I met Macran,
And retrospective thoughts and doubts did rise –
Was I quite normal when my life began
With love that leans towards rural sympathies
Potent behind a cart with Mary Ann?

OLIVER ST JOHN GOGARTY

from La Belle Dame Sans Merci

'O what can ail thee, knight-at-arms,
   Alone and palely loitering?
The sedge has withered from the lake,
    And no birds sing.

'O what can ail thee, knight-at-arms,
   So haggard and so woe-begone?
The squirrel's granary is full,
    And the harvest's done.

'I see a lily on thy brow
   With anguish moist and fever dew;
And on thy cheek a fading rose
    Fast withereth too.'

Answer to a Kind Enquiry

O, what can ail thee, knight at arms,
   Alone and palely loitering?
– I suffer intestinal qualms
   And heartburn's sting.

These haggard cheeks, this fevered brow
   My inner turbulence proclaim,
And antiperistalsis now
   'S my only aim.

Last night my military mates
   And I made merry in the Mess;
Ah, he who so participates
   Should shun excess!

The blushful Hippocrene flowed on,
   I leapt the chairs a shade too quick –
And that is why I look so wan
   And feel so sick.

MARY HOLTBY

FRANCIS SCOTT KEY (1779–1843)

from Final Curtain

O say, can you see,
By the dawn's early light,
What so proudly we hailed
At the twilight's last gleaming,
Whose broad stripes and bright stars,
Through the perilous fight,
O'er the ramparts we watched
Were so gallantly streaming?
And the rockets' red glare
The bombs bursting in air,
Gave proof through the night
That our flag was still there.
O say, does that Star-
Spangled Banner yet wave
O'er the land of the free
And the home of the brave?

     *

O thus be it ever
When free men shall stand
Between their loved homes
And war's desolation!
Blest with vict'ry and peace,
May the heav'n-rescued land
Praise the Power that hath made
And preserved us a nation.
Then conquer we must,
For our cause it is just,
And this be our motto:
'In God is our trust.'
And the Star-Spangled Banner
In triumph shall wave
O'er the land of the free
And the home of the brave.

Final Curtain

Oh, say can you hear
On the Watergate tapes
That I gave to the Judge
How I lied like a trooper?
When the chips are all down
I guess no one escapes;
I've a date at high noon,
And I'm no Gary Cooper.
If they're going to impeach
There's no gun I can reach,
So I may as well quit
With a heart-rending speech.
Oh, say does that flag
That I've dirtied still wave?
If I play my cards right,
There's some loot I can save.

Oh, this is the crunch,
I may have to resign,
But those bums are dead wrong
If they think I'm defeated.
When they pension me off
At the end of the line
And my taxes are paid,
They can (passage deleted).
I'm not out of the woods,
But I've still got the goods,
Though I may go to jail
With the rest of the hoods.
George Washington's dead,
Like the pledge that I gave,
But if he were alive
He would turn in his grave.

                    ROGER WODDIS

JOYCE KILMER (1888–1918)

Trees

I think that I shall never see
A poem lovely as a tree.

A tree whose hungry mouth is prest
Against the earth's sweet flowing breast;

A tree that looks at God all day,
And lifts her leafy arms to pray;

A tree that may in Summer wear
A nest of robins in her hair;

Upon whose bosom snow has lain;
Who intimately lives with rain.

Poems are made by fools like me,
But only God can make a tree.

Kilmer's full name was Arthur Joyce Kilmer. He was also the author of a spiteful tirade against women poets that includes the lines,

> Your tiny voices mock God's wrath,
> You snails that crawl along his path!

> Why, what has God or man to do
> With wet, amorphous things like you?

and ends with the advice:

> Take up your needles, drop your pen,
> And leave the poet's craft to men.

There is some poetic justice in the fact that Kilmer is now remembered solely for a weak and sentimental poem that lends itself to parody.

Poems

I think that I shall never read
A tree of any shape or breed —
For all its xylem and its phloem —
As fascinating as a poem.
Trees must make themselves and so
They tend to seem a little slow
To those accustomed to the pace
Of poems that speed through time and space
As fast as thought. We shouldn't blame
The trees, of course: we'd be the same
If we had roots instead of brains.
While trees just grow, a poem explains,
By precept and example, how
Leaves develop on the bough
And new ideas in the mind.
A sensibility refined
By reading many poems will be
More able to admire a tree
Than lumberjacks and nesting birds
Who lack a poet's way with words
And tend to look at any tree
In terms of its utility.
And so before we give our praise
To pines and oaks and laurels and bays,
We ought to celebrate the poems
That made our human hearts their homes.

TOM DISCH

RUDYARD KIPLING (1865–1936)

If –

If you can keep your head when all about you
   Are losing theirs and blaming it on you,
If you can trust yourself when all men doubt you,
   But make allowance for their doubting too;
If you can wait and not be tired by waiting,
   Or being lied about, don't deal in lies,
Or being hated don't give way to hating,
   And yet don't look too good, nor talk too wise:

If you can dream – and not make dreams your master;
   If you can think – and not make thoughts your aim,
If you can meet with Triumph and Disaster
   And treat those two impostors just the same;
If you can bear to hear the truth you've spoken
   Twisted by knaves to make a trap for fools,
Or watch the things you gave your life to, broken,
   And stoop and build 'em up with worn-out tools:

If you can make one heap of all your winnings
   And risk it on one turn of pitch-and-toss,
And lose, and start again at your beginnings
   And never breathe a word about your loss;
If you can force your heart and nerve and sinew
   To serve your turn long after they are gone,
And so hold on when there is nothing in you
   Except the Will which says to them: 'Hold on!'

If you can talk with crowds and keep your virtue,
   Or walk with Kings – nor lose the common touch,
If neither foes nor loving friends can hurt you,
   If all men count with you, but none too much;

Recruiting Song

If you can keep your head when all about you
Are losing theirs and aiming things at you;
If you can leave a class to work without you
And guarantee they'll keep hard at it, too;
If you can mark and not grow tired of marking,
Of counting money, writing your Reports;
If you can stand the end-of-term sky-larking,
And still have spirit left to watch the Sports;

If you can talk, nor lose your voice with talking,
Give punishments without a biased mind;
If you can stop an idle mob from squawking
At every doubtful meaning they can find;
If you can dream – and not make dreams your master;
Or talk with Heads – nor lose the common touch;
If you can save your subject from disaster
By tactfully not plugging it too much;

If you can bear to hear the truth you've spoken
Twisted and laughed at by moronic fools;
If you're prepared to watch equipment broken
By 'scholars' who have scant regard for rules;
If you can fill the unforgiving minute
With ninety seconds' worth of distance run,
Teaching's for you, and everything that's in it,
And – which is more – you're welcome to it, son!

MICHAEL FOSTER

If you can fill the unforgiving minute
    With sixty seconds' worth of distance run,
Yours is the Earth and everything that's in it,
    And – which is more – you'll be a Man, my son!

In 1989 a certain Martin Seymour-Smith published a biography of
Kipling which was only noticed because he claimed that his subject
was a homosexual. There is no convincing evidence for this,
though Seymour-Smith defended his views in these terms: 'I came
to the conclusion that Kipling was a homosexual after carrying out
a great deal of serious research. He did, after all, go to a public
school.' Roger Woddis dashed off his superbly dismissive parody,
using the title of one of Kipling's short-story collections.

from La Nuit Blanche

I had seen, as dawn was breaking
    And I staggered to my rest,
Tara Devi softly shaking
    From the Cart Road to the crest.
I had seen the spurs of Jakko
    Heave and quiver, swell and sink.
Was it Earthquake or tobacco,
    Day of Doom or Night of Drink?

Rewards and Fairies

If you can sleep when those who write about you
    Are buried deep in serious research,
If scholars who proclaim your work and spout you
    Ascribe it to the slipper and the birch;
If you are drawn to men with muscles rippling,
    And fancy brawn, according to the myth,
You might, when all is said, think more of Kipling,
    And rather less of Martin Seymour-Smith.

If you can bear to wallow in a mudyard,
    And pig it there with academic fools,
If you can snigger, when you rubbish Rudyard,
    At what goes on in English public schools;
If you can prove a saint is made of plaster,
    Or dare to claim an honoured name undone,
Your work of art will make the heart beat faster,
    And – which is more – you'll make a mint, my son!

ROGER WODDIS

To R. K.

Will there never come a season
Which shall rid us from the curse
Of a prose which knows no reason
And an unmelodious verse:
When the world shall cease to wonder
At the genius of an Ass,
And a boy's eccentric blunder
Shall not bring success to pass:

In the full, fresh fragrant morning
  I observed a camel crawl,
Laws of gravitation scorning,
  On the ceiling and the wall.
Then I watched a fender walking,
  And I heard grey leeches sing,
And a red-hot monkey talking
  Did not seem the proper thing.

Then a Creature, skinned and crimson,
  Ran about the floor and cried,
And they said I had the 'jims' on,
  And they dosed me with bromide,
And they locked me in my bedroom –
  Me and one wee Blood Red Mouse –
Though I said: – 'To give my head room
  You had best unroof the house.'

    *

Half the night I watched the Heavens
  Fizz like '81 champagne –
Fly to sixes and to sevens,
  Wheel and thunder back again;
And when all was peace and order
  Save one planet nailed askew,
Much I wept because my warder
  Would not let me set it true . . .

When mankind shall be delivered
From the clash of magazines,
And the inkstand shall be shivered
Into countless smithereens:
When there stands a muzzled stripling,
Mute, beside a muzzled bore:
When the Rudyards cease from kipling
And the Haggards Ride no more.

J. K. STEPHEN

J. K. Stephen (1859–92) was one of the cleverest Victorian
parodists. He loved both Eton and King's College, Cambridge, and
contributed to their magazines long after he had left the places
themselves. Some of his best and most enduring poems appeared in
Granta. He gave up law for journalism, but suffered a bad accident
in 1886 when his head was gashed by the sails of a windmill, and
he never really got over it. He died not long after the publication of
his book of parodies, *Lapsus Calami* – 'slips of the pen'. He
probably had no single poem of Kipling's in mind when he wrote
his celebrated lines 'To R. K.', but, apart from being in the same
metre, 'La Nuit Blanche' shows its author at his most strenuous
and will do to illustrate Stephen's point.

Recessional

1897

God of our fathers, known of old,
   Lord of our far-flung battle-line,
Beneath Whose awful Hand we hold
   Dominion over palm and pine —
Lord God of Hosts, be with us yet,
Lest we forget — lest we forget!

The tumult and the shouting dies;
   The Captains and the Kings depart:
Still stands Thine ancient sacrifice,
   An humble and a contrite heart.
Lord God of Hosts, be with us yet,
Lest we forget — lest we forget!

Far-called, our navies melt away.
   On dune and headland sinks the fire.
Lo, all our pomp of yesterday
   Is one with Nineveh and Tyre!
Judge of the Nations, spare us yet,
Lest we forget — lest we forget!

If, drunk with sight of power, we loose
   Wild tongues that have not Thee in awe,
Such boastings as the Gentiles use,
   Or lesser breeds without the Law —
Lord God of Hosts, be with us yet,
Lest we forget — lest we forget!

For heathen heart that puts her trust
   In reeking tube and iron shard,
All valiant dust that builds on dust,
   And guarding, calls not Thee to guard,
For frantic boast and foolish word —
Thy mercy on Thy People, Lord!

Post-Recessional

God of your fathers, known of old,
  For patience with man's swaggering line,
He did not answer you when told
  About you and your palm and pine,
Though you deployed your far-flung host
And boasted that you did not boast.

Though drunk with sight of power and blind,
  Even as you bowed your head in awe,
You kicked up both your heels behind
  At lesser breeds without the law;
Lest they forget, lest they forget,
That yours was the exclusive set.

We fancied heaven preferring much,
  Your rowdiest song, your slangiest sentence,
Your honest banjo banged, to such
  Very recessional repentance;
Now if your native land be dear,
Whisper (or shout) and we shall hear.

Cut down, our navies melt away.
  From ode and war-song fades the fire,
We are a jolly sight to-day
  Too near to Sidon and to Tyre
To make it sound so very nice
To offer ancient sacrifice.

Rise up and bid the trumpets blow
  When it is gallant to be gay,
Tell the wide world it shall not know
  Our face until we turn to bay.
Bless you, you shall be blameless yet,
For God forgives and men forget.

                                    G. K. CHESTERTON

from Tommy

I went into a public-'ouse to get a pint o' beer,
The publican 'e up an' sez, 'We serve no red-coats here.'
The girls be'ind the bar they laughed an' giggled fit to
    die,
I outs into the street again an' to myself sez I:
  O it's Tommy this, an' Tommy that, an' 'Tommy, go
    away';
  But it's 'Thank you, Mister Atkins,' when the band
    begins to play –
  The band begins to play, my boys, the band begins to
    play,
  O it's 'Thank you, Mister Atkins,' when the band
    begins to play.

I went into a theatre as sober as could be,
They gave a drunk civilian room, but 'adn't none for me;
They sent me to the gallery or round the music-'alls,
But when it comes to fightin', Lord! they'll shove me in
    the stalls!
  For it's Tommy this, an' Tommy that, an' 'Tommy,
    wait outside';
  But it's 'Special train for Atkins' when the trooper's on
    the tide –
  The troopship's on the tide, my boys, the troopship's
    on the tide,
  O it's 'Special train for Atkins' when the trooper's on
    the tide . . .

from *Harold Wilson's Selected Poems*

I went out of the conf'rence to get a pint of beer,
But the lads inside the tap-room didn't even give a cheer;
Long faces in the Long Bar, and inquests in the loos,
Some lads, who's lost their seats, give me boos instead of
    booze.

  It was Harold this and Harold that, wi' a proper
    genuflection,
  Now it's 'Eff you, Harold Wilson, who lost us the
    Election.'
  In nineteen sixty-four, my lads, you sang a different song:
  It was 'God save Harold Wilson, who can never do no
    wrong.'

It serves you right, you union boys, that you've now got
    Carr, the bleeder!
If you'd have played along o' me, I'd still be Britain's leader.
We'd have give the same ol' med'cine to all trade union men,
But it'd have been much better, wi' *me* at Number Ten.

  Oh, it's Harold this and Harold that, as they sups their
    bitter down,
  A-mutt'ring and a-waiting for them memoirs by George
    Brown.
  Though I don't give an effing damn, for each sidelong
    effing look,
  I thinks they might have waited for my own effing
    book.

M. K. CHEESEMAN

In 1970 Mary Wilson published a selection of her poems. In this
parody, her husband is imagined as turning to the style of Kipling
to reflect upon the change in his fortunes after his defeat in the
general election that year. It was all the more bitter as he had been
expected to win, but the trade unions had turned upon him after he
tried to reform them.

from Loot

(*Chorus*): Loo! loo! Lulu! lulu! Loo! loo! Loot! loot!
     loot!
        Ow the loot!
        Bloomin' loot!
      That's the thing to make the boys git up an' shoot!
        It's the same with dogs an' men,
        If you'd make 'em come again
      Clap 'em forward with a Loo! loo! Lulu! Loot!
(*ff*)   Whoopee! Tear 'im, puppy! Loo! loo! Lulu!
        Loot! loot! loot!

When Earth's Last Picture is Painted

When Earth's last picture is painted, and the tubes are
   twisted and dried,
When the oldest colours have faded, and the youngest
   critic has died,
We shall rest, and, faith, we shall need it – lie down for
   an æon or two,
Till the Master of All Good Workmen shall put us to
   work anew.

And those that were good shall be happy: they shall sit in
   a golden chair;
They shall splash at a ten-league canvas with brushes of
   comets' hair.
They shall find real saints to draw from – Magdalene,
   Peter, and Paul;
They shall work for an age at a sitting and never be tired
   at all!

P.C., X, 36

Then it's collar 'im tight,
  In the name o' the Lawd!
'Ustle 'im, shake 'im till 'e's sick,
  Wot, 'e *would*, would 'e? Well,
  Then yer've got ter give 'im 'Ell,
An' it's trunch, trunch, truncheon does the trick.

                    MAX BEERBOHM

Beerbohm used this chorus as an epigraph to his devastating
parody of Kipling's short-story style in *A Christmas Garland*,
attributing it to the mythical *Police Station Ditties*.

Freedom is in Peril

When the last newspaper is printed and the ink is faded
  and dried,
And the oldest critic is muzzled and the youngest croaker
  has died,
We shall pass to a tranquil era of government by decree,
When every voice shall be silenced but the voice of the
  B.B.C.

We shall hearken to Government spokesmen, we shall
  listen to Government news;
And no one will doubt or question, and none shall express
  their views.
And only the good shall be favoured, and only the killjoy
  shall fall,
And the murmur of opposition will never be heard at all.

And only the Master shall praise us, and only the Master
    shall blame;
And no one shall work for money, and no one shall work
    for fame,
But each for the joy of the working, and each, in his
    separate star,
Shall draw the Thing as he sees It for the God of Things
    as They are!

And only the Leader shall praise us and only the Leader
  shall blame,
And Parliament will be sitting, but Parliament will be
  tame,
And the star of freedom will vanish; we shall steer by the
  Fascist star,
And no one will then remember the sort of people we are.

SAGITTARIUS

Prompted by the statement of Lloyd George on 24 March 1942:
'We are fighting the battle of freedom in the world against great
odds. Do not add to these odds by deeds which cast a doubt on the
sincerity of our aims.'

WALTER SAVAGE LANDOR (1775–1864)

'I strove with none'

I strove with none; for none were worth my strife;
　　Nature I loved, and, next to Nature, Art;
I warmed both hands before the fire of life;
　　It sinks, and I am ready to depart.

'I strove with none'

I strove with none for none was worth my strife;
  Reason I loved, and next to reason, doubt;
I warmed both hands before the fire of life
  And put it out.

E. M. FORSTER

G. W. LANGFORD (dates unknown)

from 'Speak gently; it is better far'

Speak gently; it is better far
To rule by love than fear;
Speak gently; let no harsh word mar
The good we may do here.

Speak gently to the little child;
Its love be sure to gain;
Teach it in accents soft and mild;
It may not long remain.

'Speak roughly to your little boy'

Speak roughly to your little boy,
    And beat him when he sneezes;
He only does it to annoy,
    Because he knows it teases.

I speak severely to my boy,
    I beat him when he sneezes;
For he can thoroughly enjoy
    The pepper when he pleases!

LEWIS CARROLL

PHILIP LARKIN (1922–85)

Mr Bleaney

'This was Mr Bleaney's room. He stayed
The whole time he was at the Bodies, till
They moved him.' Flowered curtains, thin and frayed,
Fall to within five inches of the sill,

Whose window shows a strip of building land,
Tussocky, littered. 'Mr Bleaney took
My bit of garden properly in hand.'
Bed, upright chair, sixty-watt bulb, no hook

Behind the door, no room for books or bags –
'I'll take it.' So it happens that I lie
Where Mr Bleaney lay, and stub my fags
On the same saucer-souvenir, and try

Stuffing my ears with cotton-wool, to drown
The jabbering set he egged her on to buy.
I know his habits – what time he came down,
His preference for sauce to gravy, why

He kept on plugging at the four aways –
Likewise their yearly frame: the Frinton folk
Who put him up for summer holidays,
And Christmas at his sister's house in Stoke.

But if he stood and watched the frigid wind
Tousling the clouds, lay on the fusty bed
Telling himself that this was home, and grinned,
And shivered, without shaking off the dread

That how we live measures our own nature,
And at his age having no more to show
Than one hired box should make him pretty sure
He warranted no better, I don't know.

Mr Strugnell

'This was Mr Strugnell's room,' she'll say –
And look down at the lumpy, single bed.
'He stayed here up until he went away
And kept his bicycle out in that shed.

'He had a job in Norwood library –
He was a quiet sort who liked to read –
Dick Francis mostly, and some poetry –
He liked John Betjeman very much indeed

'But not Pam Ayres or even Patience Strong –
He'd change the subject if I mentioned them,
Or say, "It's time for me to run along –
Your taste's too highbrow for me, Mrs M."

'And up he'd go and listen to that jazz.
I don't mind telling you it was a bore –
Few things in this house have been tiresome as
The sound of his foot tapping on the floor.

'He didn't seem the sort for being free
With girls or going out and having fun.
He had a funny turn in 'sixty-three
And ran round shouting "Yippee! It's begun!"

'I don't know what he meant, but after that
He had a different look, much more relaxed.
Some nights he'd come in late, too tired to chat,
As if he had been somewhat overtaxed.

'And now he's gone. He said he found Tulse Hill
Too stimulating – wanted somewhere dull.
At last he's found a place that fits the bill –
Enjoying perfect boredom up in Hull.'

                                    WENDY COPE

D. H. LAWRENCE (1885–1930)

from Snake

A snake came to my water-trough
On a hot, hot day, and I in pyjamas for the heat,
To drink there.

In the deep, strange-scented shade of the great dark
    carob-tree
I came down the steps with my pitcher
And must wait, must stand and wait, for there he was at
    the trough before me.

He reached down from a fissure in the earth-wall in the
    gloom
And trailed his yellow-brown slackness soft-bellied down,
    over the edge of the stone trough
And rested his throat upon the stone bottom,
And where the water had dripped from the tap, in a
    small clearness,
He sipped with his straight mouth,
Softly drank through his straight gums, into his slack
    long body,
Silently.

Someone was before me at my water-trough,
And I, like a second comer, waiting.

He lifted his head from his drinking, as cattle do,
And looked at me vaguely, as drinking cattle do,
And flickered his two-forked tongue from his lips, and
    mused a moment,
And stooped and drank a little more,
Being earth-brown, earth-golden from the burning bowels
    of the earth
On the day of Sicilian July, with Etna smoking.

*

The Snake *on D. H. Lawrence*

Some creep came to my water trough
And stood there, hopping from foot to foot,
In his pyjamas.
I knew his sort – a poet.
The dark-haired ones are all right, mild drinkers perhaps,
But the red-heads are liable to fly off the handle.
He put the whole length of my back up, standing there
Like a stick of rock.
I could tell what he was thinking – 'They're all the same'.
I reminded him of his penis.
So I thought, right mate, you can just wait till I've had my
    fill.
What a nerve! To think that the whole poem of my
    existence
Is just to be a piece of his foetid imagery!
I was just framing in my mind some neat metaphor for
    him,
When he hurled a lump of wood at me.
Therefore I relieved myself in the trough and left.

N. J. WARBURTON

Competitors were asked for poems in which animals replied to
poets who had written about them.

EDWARD LEAR (1812–88)

from 'How pleasant to know Mr Lear!'

How pleasant to know Mr Lear!
　Who has written such volumes of stuff!
Some think him ill-tempered and queer,
　But a few think him pleasant enough.

His mind is concrete and fastidious,
　His nose is remarkably big;
His visage is more or less hideous,
　His beard it resembles a wig.

He has ears, and two eyes, and ten fingers,
　Leastways if you reckon two thumbs;
Long ago he was one of the singers,
　But now he is one of the dumbs.

He sits in a beautiful parlour,
　With hundreds of books on the wall;
He drinks a great deal of Marsala,
　But never gets tipsy at all.

He has many friends, laymen and clerical;
　Old Foss is the name of his cat;
His body is perfectly spherical,
　He weareth a runcible hat . . .

'There was an Old Man with a beard'

There was an Old Man with a beard,
Who said, 'It is just as I feared! –
Two Owls and a Hen, four Larks and a Wren,
Have all built their nests in my beard!'

Lines for Cuscuscaraway and
Mirza Murad Ali Beg

How unpleasant to meet Mr Eliot!
With his features of clerical cut,
And his brow so grim
And his mouth so prim
And his conversation, so nicely
Restricted to What Precisely
And If and Perhaps and But.
How unpleasant to meet Mr Eliot!
With a bobtail cur
In a coat of fur
And a porpentine cat
And a wopsical hat:
How unpleasant to meet Mr Eliot!
     (Whether his mouth be open or shut).

                              T. S. ELIOT

'There was an old man with a beard'

There was an old man with a beard,
A funny old man with a beard,
   He had a big beard,
   A great big old beard,
That amusing old man with a beard.

                    JOHN CLARKE

from The Jumblies

They went to sea in a Sieve, they did,
  In a Sieve they went to sea:
In spite of all their friends could say,
On a winter's morn, on a stormy day,
  In a Sieve they went to sea!
And when the Sieve turned round and round,
And every one cried, 'You'll all be drowned!'
They called aloud, 'Our Sieve ain't big,
But we don't care a button! we don't care a fig!
  In a Sieve we'll go to sea!'
    Far and few, far and few,
      Are the lands where the Jumblies live;
    Their heads are green, and their hands are blue,
      And they went to sea in a Sieve.

They sailed away in a Sieve, they did,
  In a Sieve they sailed so fast,
With only a beautiful pea-green veil
Tied with a riband by way of a sail,
  To a small tobacco-pipe mast;
And every one said, who saw them go,
'O won't they be soon upset, you know!
For the sky is dark, and the voyage is long,
And happen what may, it's extremely wrong
  In a Sieve to sail so fast!'
    Far and few, far and few,
      Are the lands where the Jumblies live;
    Their heads are green, and their hands are blue,
      And they went to sea in a Sieve . . .

In the spring of 1989 the Labour Party tried to abandon its long-held policy of unilateral disarmament. But its new policy was a fudge. Nuclear weapons were to be left as bargaining counters. The key question that Neil Kinnock would not answer was whether he would treat them as a deterrent and be prepared to use them by pressing the button. This policy pleased no one: the left of the party felt betrayed, while the right knew they were being conned.

Eat Your Heart Out, Edward Lear!

'We will negotiate with Trident and with the policy line that comes
with all that operational weaponry, the policy line that never says yes
or no to the question, "Will you press the button?" ' – *Neil Kinnock*

They went to sea in a Sieve, they did,
    In a Sieve they went to sea:
In spite of sickness among the crew,
And half the passengers wanting to spew,
    In a Sieve they went to sea!
And when the Sieve turned round and round,
Everyone feared they'd all be drowned,
And cried as they veered from left to right,
'We won't press the button, then again we might!
    In a Sieve we'll go to sea!'

Far and few, far and few,
Are the lands where the Fumblies live;
Their heads are pink, and their hearts are blue,
And they went to sea in a Sieve.

They sailed away in a Sieve, they did,
    With a compass made of brass;
They tacked in a zigzag policy line,
The course they plotted you could only define
    As that of a Whitehall farce.
And everyone said who saw them go,
'They won't say yes, and they won't say no.'
And Neptune said, as he rose from the sea,
'If you like my Trident, please feel free
    To stick it up your arse!'

Far and few, far and few,
Are the lands where the Fumblies live;
Their heads are pink, and their hearts are blue,
. And they went to sea in a Sieve.

ROGER WODDIS

CHRISTOPHER LOGUE (1926–   )

I Shall Vote Labour

I shall vote Labour because
   God votes Labour.
I shall vote Labour in order to protect
   the sacred institution of The Family.
I shall vote Labour because
   I am a dog.
I shall vote Labour because Ringo votes Labour.
I shall vote Labour because
upper-class hoorays annoy me in expensive
   restaurants
I shall vote Labour because
   I am on a diet.
I shall vote Labour because if I don't
   somebody else will:
   AND
I shall vote Labour because if one person does it
   everybody will be wanting to do it.
I shall vote Labour because
   my husband looks like Anthony Wedgwood Benn.
I shall vote Labour because I am obedient.
I shall vote Labour because if I do not vote Labour
   my balls will drop off.
I shall vote Labour because
   there are too few cars on the road.
I shall vote Labour because
   Mrs Wilson promised me £5 if I did.
I shall vote Labour because I love
   Look at Life films.
I shall vote Labour because I am
   a hopeless drug addict.

I Shall Vote Centre

I shall vote Centre because
    the opinion-polls say I ought to vote Centre.
I shall vote Centre in order to protect
    the sacred institution of *Any Questions?*
I shall vote Centre because the Centre
    has got it just about Right.
I shall vote Centre because
    I am fond of claret.
I shall vote Centre because Janet Suzman
    will vote Centre.
I shall vote Centre because if I don't
    Benn will put me to work in the salt-mines.
    AND
I shall vote Centre because
    Shirley has been through a gruelling time.
I shall vote Centre because my wife
    had her breasts fondled by a man on the Underground.
I shall vote Centre because if I do not vote Centre
    I shall become impotent.
I shall vote Centre because I know
    how to pronounce Lech Walesa.
I shall vote Centre because
    my dentist is a member of CND.
I shall vote Centre because I want to see
    the Fire Service handed back to private enterprise.
I shall vote Centre because
    there isn't enough sport on television.
I shall vote Centre because I want to stop
    bus-conductors calling me 'squire'.
I shall vote Centre because the Queen
    has a very difficult job and she does it superbly.

I shall vote Labour because
   I failed to be a dollar millionaire aged three.
I shall vote Labour because Labour will build
   more maximum-security prisons.
I shall vote Labour because I want to shop
   in an all-weather precinct stretching from Yeovil to
   Glasgow.
I shall vote Labour because I want to rape an air-
   hostess.
I shall vote Labour because I am a hairdresser.
I shall vote Labour because
   the Queen's stamp collection is the best in the world.
I shall vote Labour because
   deep in my heart
I am a Conservative.

I shall vote Centre because,
    deep down,
I am very shallow.

ROGER WODDIS

Christopher Logue's poem was written in 1966. Roger Woddis's parody followed twenty years later.

HENRY WADSWORTH LONGFELLOW (1807–82)

from Evangeline: A Tale of Acadie

This is the forest primeval. The murmuring pines and the
　　hemlocks,
Bearded with moss, and in garments green, indistinct in
　　the twilight,
Stand like Druids of eld, with voices sad and prophetic,
Stand like harpers hoar, with beards that rest on their
　　bosoms.
Loud from its rocky caverns, the deep-voiced
　　neighbouring ocean
Speaks, and in accents disconsolate answers the wail of
　　the forest.

This is the forest primeval; but where are the hearts that
　　beneath it
Leaped like the roe, when he hears in the woodland the
　　voice of the huntsman?
Where is the thatch-roofed village, the home of Acadian
　　farmers, –
Men whose lives glided on like rivers that water the
　　woodlands,
Darkened by shadows of earth, but reflecting an image of
　　heaven?
Waste are those pleasant farms, and the farmers for ever
　　departed,
Scattered like dust and leaves, when the mighty blasts of
　　October
Seize them, and whirl them aloft, and sprinkle them far
　　over the ocean,
Naught but tradition remains of the beautiful village of
　　Grand-Pré . . .

The Metre Columbian

This is the metre Columbian. The soft-flowing trochees
  and dactyls,
Blended with fragments spondaic, and here and there an
  iambus,
Syllables often sixteen, or more or less, as it happens,
Difficult always to scan, and depending greatly on accent,
Being a close imitation, in English, of Latin hexameters –
Fluent in sound and avoiding the stiffness of blank verse,
Having the grandeur and flow of America's mountains
  and rivers,
Such as no bard could achieve in a mean little island like
  England;
Oft, at the end of a line, the sentence dividing abruptly
Breaks, and in accents mellifluous, follows the thoughts of
  the author.

                                        ANONYMOUS

from Excelsior

The shades of night were falling fast,
As through an Alpine village passed
A youth, who bore, 'mid snow and ice,
A banner, with the strange device,
       Excelsior!

His brow was sad; his eye beneath
Flashed like a falchion from its sheath,
And like a silver clarion rung
The accents of that unknown tongue,
       Excelsior!

In happy homes he saw the light
Of household fires gleam warm and bright;
Above, the spectral glaciers shone,
And from his lips escaped a groan,
       Excelsior!

'Try not the Pass!' the old man said;
'Dark lowers the tempest overhead,
The roaring torrent is deep and wide!'
And loud that clarion voice replied,
       Excelsior!

'O stay,' the maiden said, 'and rest
Thy weary head upon this breast!'
A tear stood in his bright blue eye,
But still he answered with a sigh,
       Excelsior!

The Shades of Night

The shades of night were falling fast,
   And the rain was falling faster,
When through an Alpine village passed
   An Alpine village pastor:
A youth who bore mid snow and ice
   A bird that wouldn't chirrup,
And a banner with the strange device –
   'Mrs Winslow's soothing syrup.'

'Beware the pass,' the old man said,
   'My bold, my desperate fellah;
Dark lowers the tempest overhead,
   And you'll want your umbrella;
And the roaring torrent is deep and wide –
   You may hear how loud it washes.'
But still that clarion voice replied:
   'I've got my old goloshes.'

'Oh, stay,' the maiden said, 'and rest
   (For the wind blows from the nor'ward)
Thy weary head upon my breast –
   And please don't think I'm forward.'
A tear stood in his bright blue eye,
   And he gladly would have tarried;
But still he answered with a sigh:
   'Unhappily I'm married.'

A. E. HOUSMAN

from The Village Blacksmith

Under a spreading chestnut-tree
    The village smithy stands;
The smith, a mighty man is he,
    With large and sinewy hands;
And the muscles of his brawny arms
    Are strong as iron bands.

His hair is crisp, and black, and long,
    His face is like the tan;
His brow is wet with honest sweat,
    He earns whate'er he can,
And looks the whole world in the face,
    For he owes not any man.

Week in, week out, from morn till night,
    You can hear his bellows blow;
You can hear him swing his heavy sledge,
    With measured beat and slow,
Like a sexton ringing the village bell,
    When the evening sun is low.

And children coming home from school
    Look in at the open door;
They love to see the flaming forge,
    And hear the bellows roar,
And catch the burning sparks that fly
    Like chaff from a threshing-floor.

He goes on Sunday to the church,
    And sits among his boys;
He hears the parson pray and preach,
    He hears his daughter's voice,
Singing in the village choir,
    And it makes his heart rejoice.

        *

The Splendid Bankrupt

Being a hint to our legislators and a reminder to the official receiver

Under its spreading bankruptcy
  The village mansion stands;
Its lord, a mighty man is he,
  With large, broad-acred lands;
And the laws that baulk his creditors
  Are strong as iron bands.

His laugh is free and loud and long,
  His dress is spick-and-span;
He pays no debt with honest sweat,
  He keeps whate'er he can,
And stares the whole world in the face,
  For he fears not any man.

Week in, week out, from morn till night,
  Prince-like he runs the show;
And a round of social gaieties
  Keeps things from getting slow –
As the *agent* of his wife, of course,
  His credit is never low.

His children, coming back from school,
  Bless their progenitor,
Who's ruffling at the yearly rate
  Of fifteen thou. or more,
Nor care they how his victims fly
  To the workhouse open door.

He goes on Sunday to the church
  With all whom he employs,
To hear the parson pray and preach,
  Condemning stolen joys;
It falls like water off his back –
  His conscience ne'er annoys.

Toiling – rejoicing – sorrowing,
    Onward through life he goes;
Each morning sees some task begin,
    Each evening sees it close;
Something attempted, something done,
    Has earned a night's repose.

Thanks, thanks to thee, my worthy friend,
    For the lesson thou hast taught!
Thus at the flaming forge of life
    Our fortunes must be wrought;
Thus on its sounding anvil shaped
    Each burning deed and thought.

from The Song of Hiawatha

'Honour be to Mudjekeewis!'
Cried the warriors, cried the old men,
When he came in triumph homeward
With the sacred Belt of Wampum,
From the regions of the North-Wind,
From the kingdom of Wabasso,
From the land of the White Rabbit.
    He had stolen the Belt of Wampum,
From the neck of Mishe-Mokwa,
From the Great Bear of the mountains,
From the terror of the nations,
As he lay asleep and cumbrous
On the summit of the mountains,
Like a rock with mosses on it,
Spotted brown and grey with mosses . . .

Scheming, promoting, squandering,
  Onward through life he goes;
Each morning sees some 'deal' begun,
  Each evening sees it close;
Some *coup* attempted, some one 'done',
  Has earned a night's repose.

Thanks, thanks, to thee, my worthy friend,
  For the lesson thou hast taught!
Thus in the busy City life
  Our fortunes must be wrought;
Thus does the Splendid Bankrupt thrive
  While honest fools get nought!

ARTHUR A. SYKES

The Modern Hiawatha

He killed the noble Mudjokivis.
Of the skin he made him mittens,
Made them with the fur side inside,
Made them with the skin side outside.
He, to get the warm side inside,
Put the inside skin side outside;
He, to get the cold side outside,
Put the warm side fur side inside,
That's why he put the fur side inside,
Why he put the skin side outside,
Why he turned them inside outside.

GEORGE A. STRONG

The Arrow and the Song

I shot an arrow into the air,
It fell to earth, I know not where;
For, so swiftly it flew, the sight
Could not follow it in its flight.

I breathed a song into the air,
It fell to earth, I know not where;
For who has sight so keen and strong
That it can follow the flight of song?

Long, long afterward, in an oak
I found the arrow, still unbroke;
And the song, from beginning to end,
I found again in the heart of a friend.

A Shot at Random

I shot an arrow into the air:
I don't know how it fell or where;
But strangely enough, at my journey's end,
I found it again in the neck of a friend.

D. B. WYNDHAM LEWIS

RICHARD LOVELACE (1618–57/8)

To Lucasta, Going to the Wars

Tell me not, Sweet, I am unkind,
  That from the nunnery
Of thy chaste breast and quiet mind
  To war and arms I fly.

True, a new mistress now I chase,
  The first foe in the field;
And with a stronger faith embrace
  A sword, a horse, a shield.

Yet this inconstancy is such
  As thou too shalt adore;
I could not love thee, Dear, so much,
  Loved I not Honour more.

Lucasta Replies to Lovelace

Tell me not, friend, you are unkind,
    If ink and books laid by,
You turn up in a uniform
    Looking all smart and spry.

I thought your ink one horrid smudge,
    Your books one pile of trash,
And with less fear of smear embrace
    A sword, a belt, a sash.

Yet this inconstancy forgive,
    Though gold lace I adore,
I could not love the lace so much
    Loved I not Lovelace more.

G. K. CHESTERTON

Cavalier Lyric

I sometimes sleep with other girls
in boudoir or cheap joint,
with energy and tenderness
trying not to disappoint.
So do not think of helpful whores
as aberrational blots;
I could not love you half so well
without my practice shots.

JAMES SIMMONS

WILLIAM MCGONAGALL (1825–1902)

from The Tay Bridge Disaster

Beautiful Railway Bridge of the Silv'ry Tay!
Alas! I am very sorry to say
That ninety lives have been taken away
On the last Sabbath day of 1879,
Which will be remember'd for a very long time.

'Twas about seven o'clock at night,
And the wind it blew with all its might,
And the rain came pouring down,
And the dark clouds seem'd to frown,
And the Demon of the air seem'd to say –
'I'll blow down the Bridge of Tay.'

When the train left Edinburgh
The passengers' hearts were light and felt no sorrow,
But Boreas blew a terrific gale,
Which made their hearts for to quail,
And many of the passengers with fear did say –
'I hope God will send us safe across the Bridge of Tay.'

But when the train came near to Wormit Bay,
Boreas he did loud and angry bray,
And shook the central girders of the Bridge of Tay
On the last Sabbath day of 1879,
Which will be remember'd for a very long time.

So the train sped on with all its might,
And Bonnie Dundee soon hove in sight,
And the passengers' hearts felt light,
Thinking they would enjoy themselves on the New Year,
With their friends at home they lov'd most dear,
And wish them all a happy New Year.

'It was in the Spring of 1825'

It was in the Spring of 1825
That poet McGonagall commenced to be alive.
He spent his youth in various Scottish towns,
Where his father laboured for meagre half-crowns.
William had a gift for tragic recitation
Which later became famous throughout the nation,
But it was in bonnie Dundee city
That he composed his first poetic ditty.
This was in Dundee holiday week, June 1877,
When a voice commanding him to write came from
      Heaven.
Though William as a poet had developed late,
His flood-gates were open wide by July 1878,
When he presented himself at fair Balmoral's gate
To offer his poetry to the Queen sitting in state,
In hope of one day becoming Poet Laureate.
His sharp rebuff on that sad day
Did not cause him undue dismay,
And he continued on his poetic way
With his famous *Beautiful Railway Bridge of the Silvery
      Tay*,
Followed by another on that bridge's sad demise
Amid the passengers' woeful cries
On the last Sabbath day of 1879
(Which will be remembered for a very long time).
In March, 1887, he set out in search of further fame
To far New York, but finding that none came,
He returned to Dundee without delay
Just in time for the opening of the New Railway Bridge
      across the Tay.

So the train mov'd slowly along the Bridge of Tay,
Until it was about midway,
Then the central girders with a crash gave way,
And down went the train and passengers into the Tay!
The Storm Field did loudly bray,
Because ninety lives had been taken away,
On the last Sabbath day of 1879,
Which will be remember'd for a very long time.

*

I must now conclude my lay
By telling the world fearlessly without the least dismay,
That your central girders would not have given way,
At least many sensible men do say,
Had they been supported on each side with buttresses,
At least many sensible men confesses,
For the stronger we our houses do build,
The less chance we have of being killed.

Verses on all state occasions now poured from his pen,
Together with a strong line in all disasters known to men.
He survived long enough Edward VII's coronation to
    review,
Which was on August 9th 1902,
But the poet's sad death soon after unfortunately
    occurred,
To be precise on August 23rd.

NOËL PETTY

LOUIS MACNEICE (1907–63)

from Bagpipe Music

It's no go the merrygoround, it's no go the rickshaw,
All we want is a limousine and a ticket for the peepshow.
Their knickers are made of crêpe-de-chine, their shoes are
    made of python,
Their halls are lined with tiger rugs and their walls with
    heads of bison.

John MacDonald found a corpse, put it under the sofa,
Waited till it came to life and hit it with a poker,
Sold its eyes for souvenirs, sold its blood for whisky,
Kept its bones for dumb-bells to use when he was fifty.

It's no go the Yogi-Man, it's no go Blavatsky,
All we want is a bank balance and a bit of skirt in a taxi.

*

It's no go my honey love, it's no go my poppet;
Work your hands from day to day, the winds will blow
    the profit.
The glass is falling hour by hour, the glass will fall for
    ever,
But if you break the bloody glass you won't hold up the
    weather.

More Bagpipe Music

It's all go to Claridges, it's all go the champers,
The Glyndebourne music's such a drag, but there's always
the Fortnum hampers;
We've a town and a country place, of course, where we
keep our gees and doggies,
And we often weekend on the Continent in spite of the
Krauts and Froggies.

Enoch Powell has got it right: deport the nigs and Pakkis,
The TUC's a bunch of Trots, and their leaders Moscow
lackeys.
We'd give no dole to the unemployed, if they won't work
they're lazy,
We've lots of City directorships, but of what we're rather
hazy.

It's all go to hunt with the Quorn, it's all go to Ascot,
We've a brand-new Rolls we got as a perk, with our
family crest as a mascot.
The Socialists tax us too much, we've always voted Tory
But we'll not say how we made our pile, for that's another
story.

E. O. PARROTT

CHRISTOPHER MARLOWE (1564–93)

'Come live with me and be my love'

Come live with me and be my love,
And we will all the pleasures prove,
That hills and valleys, dales and fields,
And all the craggy mountains yields.

There we will sit upon the rocks,
And see the shepherds feed their flocks,
By shallow rivers to whose falls
Melodious birds sing madrigals.

And I will make thee beds of roses
With a thousand fragrant posies,
A cap of flowers, and a kirtle
Embroider'd all with leaves of myrtle;

A gown made of the finest wool
Which from our pretty lambs we pull;
Fair lined slippers for the cold;
With buckles of the purest gold;

A belt of straw and ivy buds,
With coral clasps and amber studs:
And if these pleasures may thee move,
Come live with me and be my love.

The shepherd-swains shall dance and sing
For thy delight each May morning:
If these delights thy mind may move,
Then live with me and be my love.

'If all the world and love were young'

If all the world and love were young,
And truth in every shepherd's tongue,
These pretty pleasures might we move
To live with thee and be thy love.

Time drives the flocks from field to fold,
When rivers rage and rocks grow cold,
And Philomel becometh dumb;
The rest complain of cares to come.

The flowers do fade, and wanton fields
To wayward winter reckoning yields;
A honey tongue, a heart of gall,
Is fancy's spring, but sorrow's fall.

Thy gowns, thy shoes, thy beds of roses,
Thy cap, thy kirtle, and thy posies
Soon break, soon wither, soon forgotten,
In folly ripe, in reason rotten.

Thy belt of straw and ivy buds,
Thy coral clasps and amber studs,
All these in me no means can move
To come to thee and be thy love.

But could youth last and love still breed,
Had joys no date no age no need,
Then these delights my mind might move
To live with thee and be thy love.

WALTER RALEGH

Using the same style and verse form, Ralegh's poem replies to
Marlowe's and presents a rather different view of silvan bliss.

ANDREW MARVELL (1621–78)

from To His Coy Mistress

Had we but world enough, and time,
This coyness, Lady, were no crime.
We would sit down and think which way
To walk and pass our long love's day.
Thou by the Indian Ganges' side
Shouldst rubies find: I by the tide
Of Humber would complain. I would
Love you ten years before the Flood,
And you should, if you please, refuse
Till the conversion of the Jews.
My vegetable love should grow
Vaster than empires, and more slow;
An hundred years should go to praise
Thine eyes and on thy forehead gaze;
Two hundred to adore each breast;
But thirty thousand to the rest;
An age at least to every part,
And the last age should show your heart;
For, Lady, you deserve this state,
Nor would I love at lower rate.
   But at my back I always hear
Time's winged Chariot hurrying near:
And yonder all before us lie
Deserts of vast Eternity . . .

To His Importunate Mistress

Were there no limits to my lust,
Lady, I would deserve your trust;
Our rituals would never cease
Till jealous death compelled release;
For generations you would hear
My grateful grunting at your ear,
And on your pleasures I would feast
Daily a hundred times at least.

Yet, lady, there are chasms still
Twixt my potential and my will;
Though I appreciate your state,
I cannot love at higher rate.

But round my back I always feel
Your quick, imploring fingers steal;
Though now for Women's Rights you weep,
Grant me one Male Right . . . to sleep.

                        PAUL GRIFFIN

JOHN MASEFIELD (1878–1967)

Sea-Fever

I must go down to the seas again, to the lonely sea and
    the sky,
And all I ask is a tall ship and a star to steer her by,
And the wheel's kick and the wind's song and the white
    sail's shaking,
And a grey mist on the sea's face and a grey dawn
    breaking.

I must go down to the seas again, for the call of the
    running tide
Is a wild call and a clear call that may not be denied;
And all I ask is a windy day with the white clouds flying,
And the flung spray and the blown spume, and the sea-
    gulls crying.

I must go down to the seas again to the vagrant gypsy
    life,
To the gull's way and the whale's way where the wind's
    like a whetted knife;
And all I ask is a merry yarn from a laughing fellow-
    rover,
And quiet sleep and a sweet dream when the long trick's
    over.

Sea-Chill

I must go down to the seas again, where the billows romp
  and reel.
So all I ask is a large ship that rides on an even keel,
And a mild breeze and a broad deck with a slight list to
  leeward,
And a clean chair in a snug nook and a nice, kind steward.

I must go down to the seas again, the sport of wind and
  tide,
As the gray wave and the green wave play leapfrog over
  the side.
And all I want is a glassy calm with a bone-dry scupper,
A good book and a warm rug and a light, plain supper.

I must go down to the seas again, though there I'm a total
  loss,
And can't say which is worst, the pitch, the plunge, the
  roll, the toss.
But all I ask is a safe retreat in a bar well tended,
And a soft berth and a smooth course till the long trip's
  ended.

ARTHUR GUITERMAN

Written in response to a news report that, after crossing the
Atlantic by liner, the poet's wife had announced: 'It was too uppy-
downy and Mr Masefield was ill.'

from 'No man takes the farm'

No man takes the farm,
Nothing grows there;
The ivy's arm
Strangles the rose there.

Old Farmer Kyrle
Farmed there the last;
He beat his girl
(It's seven years past).

After market it was
He beat his girl;
He liked his glass,
Old Farmer Kyrle.

Old Kyrle's son
Said to his father:
'Now, dad, you ha' done,
I'll kill you rather!

'Stop beating sister,
Or by God I'll kill you!'
Kyrle was full of liquor –
Old Kyrle said: 'Will you?'

Kyrle took his cobb'd stick
And beat his daughter;
He said: 'I'll teach my chick
As a father oughter.'

Young Will, the son,
Heard his sister shriek;
He took his gun
Quick as a streak.

He said: 'Now, dad,
Stop, once for all!'

Pastoral

'The lumpish trollop!
Let 'er bleed;
I'll gie 'er a wallop,'
Said Farmer Seed.

The black old man
As he went past
Knifed his girl Nan,
Muttering 'Blast!'

From the chimney corner
Ironing clothes
Old Grandma Horner
Spat out oaths.

'D—n you, Pa!'
Roared Seed's son Fred;
Caught up a crowbar,
Stunned him dead.

'Ha' done, you swine!'
'You gorbling trull!'
'Gorm you, it's mine!'
'By Zookers, you shull!'

Old Uncle Twitchen
Choked and blue;
Ned in the kitchen
Strangling Sue.

They hanged Seed soon
In Gloucester Jail;
In the full moon
From a nail.

George and Fred
Killed each other;

He was a good lad,
Good at kicking the ball.

His father clubbed
The girl on the head.
Young Will upped
And shot him dead.

'Now, sister,' said Will,
'I've a-killed father,
As I said I'd kill.
O my love, I'd rather

'A-kill him again
Than see you suffer.
O my little Jane,
Kiss good-bye to your brother.

'I won't see you again,
Nor the cows homing,
Nor the mice in the grain,
Nor the primrose coming,

    *

'For I'll be hung
In Gloucester prison
When the bell's rung
And the sun's risen.'

    *

They hanged Will
As Will said;
With one thrill
They choked him dead . . .

All are dead
Save their mother.

From Starvegoose Farm
She wandered raving,
Biting her arm
And gnawing the paving.

In Bristol Moll —

D. B. WYNDHAM LEWIS

A. A. MILNE (1882–1956)

from The King's Breakfast

The King asked
The Queen, and
The Queen asked
The Dairymaid:
'Could we have some butter for
The Royal slice of bread?'
The Queen asked
The Dairymaid,
The Dairymaid
Said, 'Certainly,
I'll go and tell
The cow
Now
Before she goes to bed.'

The Dairymaid
She curtsied,
And went and told
The Alderney;
'Don't forget the butter for
The Royal slice of bread.'
The Alderney
Said sleepily:
'You'd better tell
His Majesty
That many people nowadays
Like marmalade
Instead.'

Someone Asked the Publisher

Someone asked
The publisher,
Who went and asked
The agent:
'Could we have some writing for
The woolly folk to read?'
The agent asked
His partner,
His partner
Said: 'Certainly.
I'll go and tell
The author
Now
The kind of stuff we need.'

The partner
He curtsied,
And went and told
The author:
'Don't forget the writing that
The woolly folk need.'
The author
Said wearily:
'You'd better tell
The publisher
That many people nowadays
Like hugaboo
To read.'

J. B. MORTON

from Vespers

Hush! Hush! Whisper who dares!
Christopher Robin is saying his prayers . . .

In 1924 A. A. Milne published one of the most popular books of
poems of the first half of the century, *When We Were Very Young*.
This appeared just two years after *The Waste Land*, appealing to a
rather different audience. He depicted a dream-world of happy
middle-class children surrounded by nannies, gardeners and
chauffeurs. Milne was deeply anxious about money, and penned a
new version of the National Anthem.

O Lord our God arise,
Guard our securities;
   Don't let them fall.
Confound all party hacks,
Save those my party backs,
And let the income tax
   Be optional –
God save the Queen.

from Disobedience

James James
Morrison Morrison
Weatherby George Dupree
Took great
Care of his Mother,
Though he was only three.
James James
Said to his Mother,
'Mother,' he said, said he;
'You must never go down to the end of the town, if you
  don't go down with me.'

'Hush, hush'

Hush, hush,
Nobody cares!
Christopher Robin
Has
    Fallen
        Down-
            Stairs.

J. B. MORTON

'John Percy'

John Percy
Said to his nursy:
    'Nursy,' he said, said he,
'Tell father
I'd much rather
    He didn't write books about me.'
'Lawkamercy!'
Shouted nursy,
    'John Percy,' said she,
'If dad stopped it,
If dad dropped it,
    We shouldn't have honey for tea!'

J. B. MORTON

John Campbell Audrieu Bingham Michael Morton was known to
the literary world as J. B. Morton and to a wider public as
'Beachcomber' of the *Daily Express*. He wrote his famous
humorous column from the 1920s to the 1950s, creating a host of
perennially funny characters like Mr Justice Cocklecarrot, Mrs
McGurgle and Captain Foulenough. Evelyn Waugh's verdict on
him was that 'he had the greatest comic fertility of any
Englishman.'

JOHN MILTON (1608–74)

On His Blindness

When I consider how my light is spent,
　Ere half my days, in this dark world and wide,
　And that one talent which is death to hide
　Lodged with me useless, though my soul more bent
To serve therewith my Maker, and present
　My true account, lest he returning chide,
　'Doth God exact day-labour, light denied?'
　I fondly ask. But Patience, to prevent
That murmur, soon replies: 'God doth not need
　Either man's work or his own gifts; who best
　Bear his mild yoke, they serve him best. His state
Is kingly: thousands at his bidding speed,
　And post o'er land and ocean without rest;
　They also serve who only stand and wait.'

from Paradise Lost, Book IV

With thee conversing I forget all time,
All seasons and their change, all please alike.
Sweet is the breath of morn, her rising sweet,
With charm of earliest birds; pleasant the sun,
When first on this delightful land he spreads
His orient beams, on herb, tree, fruit, and flow'r,
Glist'ring with dew; fragrant the fertile earth
After soft showers; and sweet the coming on
Of grateful ev'ning mild, then silent night
With this her solemn bird and this fair moon,

Lament of a Subwayite

When I consider the many hours spent
  As suff'ring on the Subway trains I ride,
  And stand, and hang, and vainly seek to hide
My feet beneath the cross seats to prevent
The colored lady tall and corpulent
  Who wheezes with exhaustion at my side
  From crushing them beneath her massive stride
And maiming me before her swift descent –

Great words of fury sputter in my brain
  And I am tempted to cry out in heat
'A seat! A seat! My kingdom for a seat!
  Why should I bend and break beneath the strain?'
Methinks I hear the song the harsh wheels sang:
'They also pay who only stand and hang.'

EUGENE O'NEILL

Paradise Lost, Book IV, lines 639–654

It's all the same to me what time it is
When I'm with you; I don't care if it snows.
It's nice to get up early in the morning
And listen to the birds that beat you to it.
It gives you quite a kick to see the sun
Light up the landscape, chasing off the dew.
And then again there's nothing like the smell
Of fresh, damp earth after a spot of rain.
I like the way that twilight settles down,
And all at once it's night; there goes an owl,

And these the gems of Heav'n, her starry train:
But neither breath of morn, when she ascends
With charm of earliest birds, nor rising sun
On this delightful land; nor herb, fruit, flow'r,
Glist'ring with dew, nor fragrance after showers,
Nor grateful ev'ning mild, nor silent night
With this her solemn bird, nor walk by moon
Or glittering starlight without thee is sweet.

And there's the moon, with all the blinking stars.
Yet somehow, honey, the soft morning air,
The dew, the birdies singing fit to bust,
Sunshine and shower, morning, noon and night –
To cut it short, the programme as before,
When you are not around, just leaves me flat.

LESLIE JOHNSON

This is not so much a parody as an ingenious paraphrase, in more
colloquial terms, of Eve's expression of love for Adam. Milton
wins.

THOMAS MOORE (1779–1852)

from Lalla Rookh

Oh! ever thus from childhood's hour,
I've seen my fondest hopes decay;
I never loved a tree or flower,
But 'twas the first to fade away.
I never nursed a dear gazelle,
To glad me with its soft black eye,
But when it came to know me well,
And love me, it was sure to die!

'Twas Ever Thus

I never rear'd a young gazelle,
(Because, you see, I never tried);
But had it known and loved me well,
No doubt the creature would have died.

My rich and aged Uncle John
Has known me long and loves me well,
But still persists in living on —
I would he were a young gazelle.

H. S. LEIGH

WILLIAM MORRIS (1834–96)

Two Red Roses across the Moon

There was a lady lived in a hall,
Large in the eyes, and slim and tall;
And ever she sung from noon to noon,
Two red roses across the moon.

There was a knight came riding by
In early spring, when the roads were dry;
And he heard that lady sing at the noon,
Two red roses across the moon.

Yet none the more he stopp'd at all,
But he rode a-gallop past the hall;
And left that lady singing at noon,
Two red roses across the moon.

Because, forsooth, the battle was set,
And the scarlet and blue had got to be met,
He rode on the spur till the next warm noon: –
Two red roses across the moon.

But the battle was scatter'd from hill to hill,
From the windmill to the watermill;
And he said to himself, as it near'd the noon,
Two red roses across the moon.

You scarce could see for the scarlet and blue,
A golden helm or a golden shoe;
So he cried, as the fight grew thick at the noon,
Two red roses across the moon!

Verily then the gold bore through
The huddled spears of the scarlet and blue;
And they cried, as they cut them down at the noon,
Two red roses across the moon!

Ballad

The auld wife sat at her ivied door,
  (*Butter and eggs and a pound of cheese*)
A thing she had frequently done before;
  And her spectacles lay on her apron'd knees.

The piper he piped on the hill-top high,
  (*Butter and eggs and a pound of cheese*)
Till the cow said 'I die,' and the goose ask'd 'Why?'
  And the dog said nothing, but search'd for fleas.

The farmer he strode through the square farmyard;
  (*Butter and eggs and a pound of cheese*)
His last brew of ale was a trifle hard –
  The connexion of which with the plot one sees.

The farmer's daughter hath frank blue eyes;
  (*Butter and eggs and a pound of cheese*)
She hears the rooks caw in the windy skies,
  As she sits at her lattice and shells her peas.

The farmer's daughter hath ripe red lips;
  (*Butter and eggs and a pound of cheese*)
If you try to approach her, away she skips
  Over tables and chairs with apparent ease.

The farmer's daughter hath soft brown hair;
  (*Butter and eggs and a pound of cheese*)
And I met with a ballad, I can't say where,
  Which wholly consisted of lines like these.

PART II

She sat with her hands 'neath her dimpled cheeks,
  (*Butter and eggs and a pound of cheese*)

I trow he stopp'd when he rode again
By the hall, though draggled sore with the rain;
And his lips were pinch'd to kiss at the noon
Two red roses across the moon.

Under the may she stoop'd to the crown,
All was gold, there was nothing of brown;
And the horns blew up in the hall at noon,
Two red roses across the moon.

William Morris was a Victorian all-rounder – poet, essayist, designer of textiles and wallpaper, early conservationist, active socialist and publisher of fine books. He exhausted his contemporaries, and Max Beerbohm remarked of him, 'Of course, he was a wonderful all-rounder, but walking round him always tired me.'

And spake not a word. While a lady speaks
  There is hope, but she didn't even sneeze.

She sat, with her hands 'neath her crimson cheeks;
  (*Butter and eggs and a pound of cheese*)
She gave up mending her father's breeks,
  And let the cat roll in her new chemise.

She sat, with her hands 'neath her burning cheeks,
  (*Butter and eggs and a pound of cheese*)
And gazed at the piper for thirteen weeks;
  Then she follow'd him out o'er the misty leas.

Her sheep follow'd her, as their tails did them.
  (*Butter and eggs and a pound of cheese*)
And this song is consider'd a perfect gem,
  And as to the meaning, it's what you please.

                                        C. S. CALVERLEY

HENRY NEWBOLT (1862–1938)

Vitaï Lampada

There's a breathless hush in the Close tonight –
  Ten to make and the match to win –
A bumping pitch and a blinding light,
  An hour to play and the last man in.
And it's not for the sake of a ribboned coat,
  Or the selfish hope of a season's fame,
But his Captain's hand on his shoulder smote –
  'Play up! play up! and play the game!'

The sand of the desert is sodden red, –
  Red with the wreck of a square that broke; –
The Gatling's jammed and the Colonel dead,
  And the regiment blind with dust and smoke.
The river of death has brimmed his banks,
  And England's far, and Honour a name,
But the voice of a schoolboy rallies the ranks:
  'Play up! play up! and play the game!'

This is the word that year by year,
  While in her place the School is set,
Every one of her sons must hear,
  And none that hears it dare forget.
This they all with a joyful mind
  Bear through life like a torch in flame,
And falling fling to the host behind –
  'Play up! play up! and play the game!'

There's a Breathless Hush

There's a breathless hush in the Close tonight –
  Ten to make and the match to win
As our number eleven squared up for the fight.
  The first ball reared and grazed his chin,
And the second one jumped and split his thumb,
  But little he cared for life's hard knocks
Till the third ball beat him and struck him plumb
  In a place where wiser men wear a box.

He thought of his honour and thought of the School
  And thought of the threat to his manly twitch,
And a voice inside said to him, 'Don't be a fool',
  So 'Sod this!' he muttered, and limped from the pitch.
There's a breathless hush in the Close tonight –
  Harrow won't play us again, they say.
'What bounder was that?' hissed the Head, death-white.
  Matron blushed: 'It was Bond, sir, J.'

NOËL PETTY

'There's a breathless hush on the Centre Court'

There's a breathless hush on the Centre Court,
It's match point, and the champion's serve:
For hours the finalists have fought
A battle of wits and guts and nerve;
Bang! Wham! Zonc! They smash and volley,
It's in . . . it's out . . . and tempers flame,
Honour's at stake (not to mention lolly),
'Hey, Mister Umpire, what's the game?'

Drake's Drum

Drake he's in his hammock an' a thousand mile away,
  (Capten, art tha sleepin' there below?),
Slung atween the round shot in Nombre Dios Bay,
  An' dreamin' arl the time o' Plymouth Hoe.
Yarnder lumes the Island, yarnder lie the ships,
  Wi' sailor lads a dancin' heel-an'-toe,
An' the shore-lights flashin', an' the night-tide dashin',
  He sees et art so plainly as he saw et long ago.

Drake he was a Devon man, an' rüled the Devon seas,
  (Capten, art tha sleepin' there below?),
Rovin' tho' his death fell, he went wi' heart at ease,
  An' dreamin' arl the time o' Plymouth Hoe.
'Take my drum to England, hang et by the shore,
  Strike et when your powder's runnin' low;
If the Dons sight Devon, I'll quit the port o' Heaven,
  An' drum them up the Channel as we drummed them
    long ago.'

Drake he's in his hammock till the great Armadas come,
  (Capten, art tha sleepin' there below?),

When earthly trophies have turned to dust,
And all his rackets lie unstrung,
And the winner has gone to join the just,
And stride the heavenly hosts among,
Up in that Wimbledon on high
He'll fling the challenge just the same,
And greet the Lord with a fearless cry:
'Hey, Mister Umpire, what's the game?'

STANLEY J. SHARPLESS

The Great Poll-Tax Victory of '88

The Duke was in his hammock and a thousand miles
    away
    ('*London on the line, your Grace; for you*')
Slung between the beech trees, one limpid day in May
    ('*Bertie here – we're rather in a stew . . .*')
Yonder lay Westminster, yonder lay the House
With politicians, oily through and through,
And the endless gabbin' and the old back-stabbin';
But he saw his duty plainly as he'd always used to do.

The Duke is a backwoodsman, and keeps his backwoods
    ground,
    ('*London on the line, your Grace; for you*')
Doesn't study politics, but knows which side is sound
    ('*Bertie here – we're rather in a stew*')
Call him from the grouse-moor, call him from the hunt,
Call him when you need a vote or two.
If you need ammunition to kill the opposition,
He'll drum 'em through the lobbies as he's always used to
    do.

NOËL PETTY

Slung atween the round shot, listenin' for the drum,
    An' dreamin' arl the time o' Plymouth Hoe.
Call him on the deep sea, call him up the Sound,
    Call him when ye sail to meet the foe;
Where the old trade's plyin' an' the old flag flyin'
    They shall find him ware an' wakin', as they found him
        long ago!

The two major measures carried through in the first year of the 1987 Parliament were the Great Education Reform Bill and the Community Charge Bill. In the Commons, a Tory rebellion led by Sir George Young and Michael Mates attempted to ensure that the Community Charge related to a person's income – his or her ability to pay. It failed there, and so hope was transferred to the Lords. The Conservative Chief Whip was Bertie Denham, the Captain Gentleman-at-Arms, also a novelist, and a keen huntsman who once turned up to a meeting I attended in full riding kit. But above all, he was the most successful whipper-in of Tory peers in recent memory: many came to the debate and the Government won by a sizeable majority.

DOROTHY PARKER (1893–1967)

Résumé

Razors pain you;
Rivers are damp;
Acids stain you;
And drugs cause cramp.
Guns aren't lawful;
Nooses give;
Gas smells awful;
You might as well live.

The Story So Far

Poland works nicely,
Chad's going well,
Burma's precisely
Successful as hell,
Haiti is lovely,
This time of year,
Sudan is just darling,
Thank God for Zaire,
Chile's a dish,
Brazil is a dream,
South Africa's bliss,
And Iran is a scream.
Go lease a car,
Go purchase a suit,
Everything's ducky,
And I'm King Canute.

JOHN CLARKE

AMBROSE PHILIPS (1675–1749)

To Miss Margaret Pulteney, Daughter of Daniel Pulteney Esq., in the Nursery

Dimply Damsel, sweetly smiling,
All caressing, none beguiling;
Bud of beauty fairly blowing,
Ev'ry charm to Nature owing,
This and that new thing admiring,
Much of this and that inquiring,
Knowledge by degrees attaining,
Day by day some virtue gaining,
Ten years hence when I leave chiming
Beardless poets fondly rhyming
(Fescu'd now perhaps in spelling)
On thy riper beauties dwelling,
Shall accuse each killing feature
Of the cruel charming creature,
Whom I knew complying, willing,
Tender, and averse to killing.

from *Namby-Pamby*

All ye poets of the age,
All ye witlings of the stage,
Learn your jingles to reform,
Crop your numbers and conform.
Let your little verses flow
Gently, sweetly, row by row;
Let the verse the subject fit,
Little subject, little wit.
Namby-Pamby is your guide,
Albion's joy, Hibernia's pride.
Namby-Pamby, pilly-piss,
Rhimy-pim'd on Missy Miss
Tartaretta Tartaree,
From the navel to the knee;
That her father's gracy grace
Might give him a placy place.

     *

As an actor does his part,
So the nurses get by heart
Namby-Pamby's little rhimes,
Little jingle, little chimes,
To repeat to Missy-miss,
Piddling ponds of pissy-piss;
Cracking-packing like a lady,
Or bye-bying in the crady.
Namby-Pamby ne'er will die
While the nurse sings lullaby.

HENRY CAREY

EDGAR ALLAN POE (1809–49)

from The Raven

Once upon a midnight dreary, while I pondered, weak
  and weary,
Over many a quaint and curious volume of forgotten
  lore, –
While I nodded, nearly napping, suddenly there came a
  tapping,
As of some one gently rapping, rapping at my chamber
  door.
''Tis some visitor,' I muttered, 'tapping at my chamber
  door;
      Only this and nothing more.'

        *

Open here I flung the shutter, when, with many a flirt
  and flutter,
In there stepped a stately Raven of the saintly days of
  yore.
Not the least obeisance made he; not a minute stopped or
  stayed he;
But, with mien of lord or lady, perched above my
  chamber door,
Perched upon a bust of Pallas just above my chamber
  door:
      Perched, and sat, and nothing more.

Then this ebony bird beguiling my sad fancy into smiling
By the grave and stern decorum of the countenance it
  wore, –
'Though thy crest be shorn and shaven, thou,' I said, 'art
  sure no craven,
Ghastly grim and ancient Raven wandering from the
  Nightly shore:

Croaked the Eagle: 'Nevermore'

While the bombers, southward flocking, set Italian cities
   rocking,
Suddenly there came a knocking at Il Duce's office door.
He with fiery decision opened to admit a vision,
An expected apparition who had often called before –
   Destiny at hand once more.

Into that apartment regal slunk instead a Roman eagle,
Moping, moulting and bedraggled and extremely sick and
   sore,
With its plumage torn and tattered, beak and talons badly
   battered
And morale completely shattered, flapped and flopped
   upon the floor –
     Only that and nothing more.

'Answer!' cried the Fascist showman, 'emblem of the
   conquering Roman,
Fowl of Fate, and bird of omen, winging from the Libyan
   shore!
When shall my Imperial legions drive the Allies from those
   regions,
When shall I through Alexandria lead the Axis desert
   Korps?'
     Croaked the eagle 'Nevermore!'

'When will rebel Abyssinians yield up their usurped
   dominions?
When will Suez and Tunisia fall as spoils of glorious war?
When will Africa surrender to Islam's ordained defender?
When shall I sweep Mare Nostrum, undisputed
   conqueror?'
     Croaked the eagle 'Nevermore!'

Tell me what thy lordly name is on the Night's Plutonian
   shore!'
      Quoth the Raven, 'Nevermore.'

                    *

Then, methought, the air grew denser, perfumed from an
   unseen censer
Swung by seraphim whose foot-falls tinkled on the tufted
   floor.
'Wretch,' I cried, 'thy God hath lent thee — by these
   angels he hath sent thee
Respite — respite and nepenthe from thy memories of
   Lenore!
Quaff, oh quaff this kind nepenthe, and forget this lost
   Lenore!'
      Quoth the Raven, 'Nevermore.'

                    *

'Be that word our sign of parting, bird or fiend!' I
   shrieked up-starting
'Get thee back into the tempest and the Night's Plutonian
   shore!
Leave no black plume as a token of that lie thy soul hath
   spoken!
Leave my loneliness unbroken! quit the bust above my
   door!
Take thy beak from out my heart, and take thy form
   from off my door!'
      Quoth the Raven, 'Nevermore.'

'When with Fascist ceremonial entering my realms
   colonial,
Shall I reign from captive Hellas to the forfeited Côte
   d'Or?
When shall my resolve tenacious lead to conquests still
   more spacious,
When shall I Rome's world wide empire of antiquity
   restore?'
      Croaked the eagle 'Definitely, positively,
unequivocally,
categorically, irretrievably, inexorably, irrevocably and
finally – Nevermore!'

                                        SAGITTARIUS

ALEXANDER POPE (1688–1744)

from The Rape of the Lock

   For lo! the board with cups and spoons is crown'd,
The berries crackle, and the mill turns round;
On shining altars of Japan they raise
The silver lamp; the fiery spirits blaze:
From silver spouts the grateful liquors glide,
While China's earth receives the smoking tide:
At once they gratify their sense and taste,
And frequent cups prolong the rich repast.

Straight hover round the Fair her airy band;
Some, as she sipp'd, the fuming liquor fann'd,
Some o'er her lap their careful plumes display'd,
Trembling, and conscious of the rich brocade.
Coffee (which makes the politician wise,
And see through all things with his half-shut eyes)
Sent up in vapours to the Baron's brain
New stratagems, the radiant Lock to gain.
Ah cease, rash youth! desist ere 'tis too late,
Fear the just Gods, and think of Scylla's Fate!
Chang'd to a bird, and sent to flit in air,
She dearly pays for Nisus' injur'd hair!

from *A Pipe of Tobacco*

Blest leaf! whose aromatic gales dispense
To Templars modesty, to parsons sense:
So raptur'd priests, at fam'd Dodona's shrine
Drank inspiration from the steam divine.
Poison that cures, a vapour that affords
Content, more solid than the smile of lords:
Rest to the weary, to the hungry food,
The last kind refuge of the wise and good:
Inspir'd by thee, dull cits adjust the scale
Of Europe's peace, when other statesmen fail.

By thee protected, and thy sister, beer,
Poets rejoice, nor think the bailiff near.
Nor less, the critic owns thy genial aid,
While supperless he plies the piddling trade.
What tho' to love and soft delights a foe,
By ladies hated, hated by the beau,
Yet social freedom, long to courts unknown,
Fair health, fair truth, and virtue are thy own.
Come to thy poet, come with healing wings,
And let me taste thee unexcis'd by kings.

ISAAC HAWKINS BROWNE

This eulogy to tobacco is from a set of parodies that appeared in 1736.
Philips, Thomson and Swift are among the other poets whose styles
are imitated. Pope admired the parody of his own work, declaring:
'Browne is an excellent copyist, and those who take it ill of him are
very much in the wrong.' Its reputation persisted, and in *Mansfield
Park* Mary Crawford asks, 'Do you remember Hawkins Browne's
"Address to Tobacco" in imitation of Pope?' Hawkins Browne sat in
the House of Commons for two terms, but, according to Johnson, he
never spoke.

from The Odyssey, Book XI

With many a weary step, and many a groan,
Up a high hill he heaves a huge round stone;
The huge round stone, resulting with a bound,
Thunders impetuous down, and smoaks along the
    ground.

Samuel Johnson quotes these lines in his *Life of Pope* as a rare
example of the ability of verse to embody the action described.
'Who does not perceive the stone to move slowly upward, and roll
violently back?' he asks, but then immediately offers his own
parody to show the looseness of any connection between sound
and sense.

'While many a merry tale'

While many a merry tale, and many a song,
Chear'd the rough road, we wish'd the rough road long,
The rough road then, returning in a round,
Mock'd our impatient steps, for all was fairy ground.

SAMUEL JOHNSON

COLE PORTER (1891–1964)

from Let's Do It

When the little Bluebird,
Who has never said a word,
Starts to sing: 'Spring, spring';
When the little Bluebell,
In the bottom of the dell,
Starts to ring: 'Ding, ding';
When the little blue clerk,
In the middle of his work,
Starts a tune to the moon up above, –
It is nature, that's all,
Simply telling us to fall in love.

And that's why birds do it, bees do it,
Even educated fleas do it,
Let's do it, let's fall in love.
In Spain the best upper sets do it,
Lithuanians and Letts do it,
Let's do it, let's fall in love.
The Dutch in old Amsterdam do it,
Not to mention the Finns.
Folks in Siam do it, –
Think of Siamese twins.
Some Argentines, without means, do it,
People say, in Boston even beans do it,
Let's do it, let's fall in love.

Sponges, they say, do it,
Oysters down in Oyster Bay do it,
Let's do it, let's fall in love.
Cold Cape Cod clams, 'gainst their wish, do it,
Even lazy jellyfish do it,
Let's do it, let's fall in love.

from *Let's Do It*

Mr Irving Berlin
Often emphasizes sin
In a charming way.
Mr Coward we know
Wrote a song or two to show
Sex was here to stay.
Richard Rodgers it's true
Takes a more romantic view
Of that sly biological urge.
But it really was Cole
Who contrived to make the whole
Thing merge.

He said that Belgians and Dutch do it,
Even Hildegarde and Hutch do it,
Let's do it, let's fall in love.
Monkeys whenever you look do it,
Aly Khan and King Farouk do it,
Let's do it, let's fall in love.
The most recherché cocottes do it
In a luxury flat,
Locks, Dunns and Scotts do it
At the drop of a hat,
Excited spinsters in spas do it,
Duchesses when opening bazaars do it,
Let's do it, let's fall in love.

Our leading writers in swarms do it,
Somerset and all the Maughams do it,
Let's do it, let's fall in love.
The Brontës felt that they must do it,
Mrs Humphry Ward could just do it,

Electric eels, I might add, do it,
Though it shocks them, I know.
Why ask if shad do it?
Waiter, bring me shad roe.
In shallow shoals, English soles do it,
Goldfish, in the privacy of bowls, do it,
Let's do it, let's fall in love.

*

The chimpanzees in the zoos do it,
Some courageous kangaroos do it,
Let's do it, let's fall in love.
I'm sure giraffes, on the sly, do it,
Heavy hippopotami do it,
Let's do it, let's fall in love.
Old sloths who hang down from twigs do it,
Though the effort is great,
Sweet guinea pigs do it,
Buy a couple and wait.
The world admits bears in pits do it,
Even Pekineses in the Ritz do it,
Let's do it, let's fall in love.

Let's do it, let's fall in love.
Anouilh and Sartre – God knows why – do it,
As a sort of a curse
Eliot and Fry do it,
But they do it in verse.
Some mystics, as a routine do it,
Even Evelyn Waugh and Graham Greene do it,
Let's do it, let's fall in love.

*

The House of Commons en bloc do it,
Civil Servants by the clock do it,
Let's do it, let's fall in love.
Deacons who've done it before do it,
Minor canons with a roar do it,
Let's do it, let's fall in love.
Some rather rorty old rips do it
When they get a bit tight,
Government Whips do it
If it takes them all night,
Old mountain goats in ravines do it,
Probably we'll live to see machines do it,
Let's do it, let's fall in love.

                                        NOËL COWARD

EZRA POUND (1885–1972)

from Mœurs Contemporaines

They will come no more,
The old men with beautiful manners.

Il était comme un tout petit garçon
With his blouse full of apples
And sticking out all the way round;
Blagueur! 'Con gli occhi onesti e tardi' . . .

Another Canto

Monsieur Ezra Pound croit que
By using foreign words
He will persuade the little freaks
Who call themselves intellectuals
To believe that he is saying
Quelque chose très deep, ma foi!

J. B. MORTON

ADELAIDE A. PROCTOR (1825–64)

from The Lost Chord

Seated one day at the organ,
I was weary and ill at ease,
And my fingers wandered idly
Over the noisy keys.
I knew not what I was playing,
Or what I was dreaming then,
But I struck one chord of music
Like the sound of a great Amen.

The Lost Chord

Seated one day at the organ
  I jumped as if I'd been shot,
For the Dean was upon me, snarling
  'Stainer – and *make it hot.*'

All week I swung Stainer and Barnby,
  Bach, Gounod, and Bunnett in A;
I said, 'Gosh, the old bus is a wonder!'
  The Dean, with a nod, said 'Okay'.

              D. B. WYNDHAM LEWIS

CRAIG RAINE (1944–   )

The Gardener

Up and down the lawn he walks with cycling hands
that tremble on the mower's stethoscope.

Creases blink behind his knees.
He stares at a prance of spray

and wrestles with Leviathan alone. Victorious,
he bangs the grass box empty like a clog . . .

The shears are a Y that wants to be an X –
he holds them like a water diviner,

and hangs them upside down, a wish-bone.
His hands row gently on the plunger

and detonate the earth. He smacks the clods
and dandles weeds on trembling prongs.

They lie, a heap of dusters softly shaken out.
At night he plays a pattering hose, fanned

like a drummer's brush. His aim is to grow
the Kremlin – the roses' tight pink cupolas

ring bells . . . For this he stands in weariness,
tired as a teapot, feeling the small of his back.

The Lavatory Attendant

I counted two and seventy stenches
All well defined and several stinks!
                    Coleridge

Slumped on a chair, his body is an S
That wants to be a minus sign.

His face is overripe Wensleydale
Going blue at the edges.

In overalls of sacerdotal white
He guards a row of fonts

With lids like eye-patches. Snapped shut
They are castanets. All day he hears

Short-lived Niagaras, the clank
And gurgle of canescent cisterns.

When evening comes he sluices a thin tide
Across sand-coloured lino.

Turns Medusa on her head
And wipes the floor with her.

                              WENDY COPE

HENRY REED (1914–86)

Naming of Parts

To-day we have naming of parts. Yesterday,
We had daily cleaning. And to-morrow morning,
We shall have what to do after firing. But to-day,
To-day we have naming of parts. Japonica
Glistens like coral in all of the neighbouring gardens,
    And to-day we have naming of parts.

This is the lower sling swivel. And this
Is the upper sling swivel, whose use you will see,
When you are given your slings. And this is the piling
   swivel,
Which in your case you have not got. The branches
Hold in the gardens their silent, eloquent gestures,
    Which in our case we have not got.

This is the safety-catch, which is always released
With an easy flick of the thumb. And please do not let me
See anyone using his finger. You can do it quite easy
If you have any strength in your thumb. The blossoms
Are fragile and motionless, never letting anyone see
    Any of them using their finger.

And this you can see is the bolt. The purpose of this
Is to open the breech, as you see. We can slide it
Rapidly backwards and forwards: we call this
Easing the spring. And rapidly backwards and forwards
The early bees are assaulting and fumbling the flowers:
    They call it easing the Spring.

Marking of Folders

Today we have marking of folders. Yesterday
We had assessments. And tomorrow morning
We shall have what to do after GCSE. But today
Today we have marking of folders. Daffodils
Dance in their jocund glee around my garden,
    And today we have marking of folders.

This is the replacement mark-scheme. And this
Is the official mark sheet, whose use you will see,
When you have read the grade descriptions. And
This is the green book,
Which in your case you have not got. The tulips
Hold in the garden their silent, eloquent gestures,
    Which in our case we often also make.

These are the objectives, which are always to be observed
In setting all the assignments. And please do not let me
See anyone fiddling his marks. You can do it quite easy
If you have any brains in your head. The flowers
Are fragile and motionless, never letting anyone see
    Any of them fiddling their marks.

And these you can see are the grade divisions. The
Purpose of these
Is to sort out the candidates. We can slide these
Rapidly backwards and forwards; we call this
Marking the units. And rapidly backwards and forwards
The early bees are assaulting and fumbling the flowers;
    They call it marking the work.

They call it easing the Spring: it is perfectly easy
If you have any strength in your thumb: like the bolt,
And the breech, and the cocking-piece, and the point of
  balance,
Which in our case we have not got; and the almond-
  blossom
Silent in all of the gardens and the bees going backwards
  and forwards,
    For to-day we have naming of parts.

They call it marking the work: it is perfectly easy
If you have any brains in your head; like the scheme
And the sheets and the syllabus and the new green book,
Which in our case we have not got; and the cherry
   blossom
Silent in all of the gardens and the bees going
Backwards and forwards,
      For today we have marking of folders.

ANNE ANDERTON

In 1988, the O level and CSE exams for fifteen- and sixteen-year-olds were replaced in British schools by the GCSE. This exam had been planned for more than ten years and proved a great success, but it had teething troubles. It includes, as well as written papers, an assessment of the pupil's work over a period of two years. Many teachers had to learn a new system that involved more practical work and regular assessment, and it is to their credit that they did it so well.

Anne Anderton teaches at a school in Newcastle under Lyme.

CHRISTINA ROSSETTI (1830–94)

A Birthday

My heart is like a singing bird
  Whose nest is in a watered shoot:
My heart is like an apple-tree
  Whose boughs are bent with thickset fruit;
My heart is like a rainbow shell
  That paddles in a halcyon sea;
My heart is gladder than all these
  Because my love is come to me.

Raise me a dais of silk and down;
  Hang it with vair and purple dyes;
Carve it in doves and pomegranates,
  And peacocks with a hundred eyes;
Work it in gold and silver grapes,
  In leaves and silver fleurs-de-lys;
Because the birthday of my life
  Is come, my love is come to me.

An Unexpected Pleasure

My heart is like one asked to dine
Whose evening dress is up the spout;
My heart is like a man would be
Whose raging tooth is half pulled out.
My heart is like a howling swell
Who boggles on his upper C;
My heart is madder than all these –
My wife's mamma has come to tea.

Raise me a bump upon my crown,
Bang it till green in purple dies;
Feed me on bombs and fulminates,
And turncocks of a medium size.
Work me a suit in crimson apes
And sky-blue beetles on the spree;
Because the mother of my wife
Has come – and means to stay with me.

                                   ANONYMOUS

DANTE GABRIEL ROSSETTI (1828–82)

For 'The Wine of Circe'

by Edward Burne Jones

Dusk-haired and gold-robed o'er the golden wine
  She stoops, wherein, distilled of death and shame,
  Sink the black drops; while, lit with fragrant flame,
Round her spread board the golden sunflowers shine.
Doth Helios here with Hecatè combine
  (O Circe, thou their votaress!) to proclaim
  For these thy guests all rapture in Love's name,
Till pitiless Night gave Day the countersign?

Lords of their hour, they come. And by her knee
  Those cowering beasts, their equals heretofore,
Wait; who with them in new equality
  To-night shall echo back the sea's dull roar
  With a vain wail from passion's tide-strown shore
Where the dishevelled seaweed hates the sea.

Sonnet for a Picture

That nose is out of drawing. With a gasp,
  She pants upon the passionate lips that ache
  With the red drain of her own mouth, and make
A monochord of colour. Like an asp,
One lithe lock wriggles in his rutilant grasp.
  Her bosom is an oven of myrrh, to bake
  Love's white warm shewbread to a browner cake.
The lock his fingers clench has burst its hasp.
The legs are absolutely abominable.
  Ah! what keen overgust of wild-eyed woes
  Flags in that bosom, flushes in that nose?
Nay! Death sets riddles for desire to spell,
  Responsive. What red hem earth's passion sews,
But may be ravenously unripped in hell?

A. C. SWINBURNE

Rossetti was first and foremost a painter, being a founder, with
Millais, Holman Hunt and others, of the Pre-Raphaelite
Brotherhood. He was also a prolific minor poet, and here, using
the form and style of Rossetti's 'Sonnets for Pictures', Swinburne
hits out at both poet and painter in one swipe.

JAMES M. SAYLES (dates unknown)

from Star of the Evening

Beau—ti—ful star in heav'n so bright,
Soft—ly falls thy sil—v'ry light,
As thou mov—est from earth a—far,
Star of the eve—ning, beauti—ful star,
Star of the eve—ning, beau—ti—ful star.

CHORUS:
   Beau—ti—ful star, —
   Beau—ti—ful star, —
   Star—of the eve—ning,
Beau—ti—ful, beau—ti—ful star . . .

The Song of the Mock Turtle

Beautiful soup, so rich and green,
Waiting in a hot tureen!
Who for such dainties would not stoop?
Soup of the evening, beautiful Soup!
Soup of the evening, beautiful Soup!
   Beau—ootiful Soo—oop!
   Beau—ootiful Soo—oop!
Soo—oop of the e—e—evening,
   Beautiful, beautiful Soup!

Beautiful Soup! who cares for fish,
Game, or any other dish?
Who would not give all else for two p
ennyworth only of beautiful Soup?
Pennyworth only of beautiful Soup?
   Beau—ootiful Soo—oop!
   Beau—ootiful Soo—oop!
Soo—oop of the e—e—evening,
   Beautiful, beauti—FUL SOUP!

LEWIS CARROLL

WALTER SCOTT (1771–1832)

from Bonnie Dundee

To the Lords of Convention 'twas Claver'se who spoke,
'Ere the King's crown shall fall, there are crowns to be
  broke;
So let each cavalier who loves honour and me
Come follow the bonnet of Bonnie Dundee:

> 'Come fill up my cup, come fill up my can,
> Come saddle your horses, and call up your men,
> Come open the West Port and let me gang free,
> And its room for the bonnets of Bonnie Dundee!'

    *

'Away to the hills, to the caves, to the rocks, –
Ere I own an usurper, I'll couch with the fox;
And tremble, false Whigs in the midst of your glee,
You have not seen the last of my bonnet and me!

> 'Come fill up my cup . . .'

'To *the Looking-Glass world it was*
Alice *that said*'

To the Looking-Glass world it was Alice that said
'I've a sceptre in hand I've a crown on my head.
Let the Looking-Glass creatures, whatever they be,
Come and dine with the Red Queen, the White Queen,
and me!'

Then fill up the glasses as quick as you can,
And sprinkle the table with buttons and bran:
Put cats in the coffee, and mice in the tea –
And welcome Queen Alice with thirty-times-three!

'O Looking-Glass creatures,' quoth Alice, 'draw near!
'Tis an honour to see me, a favour to hear:
'Tis a privilege high to have dinner and tea
Along with the Red Queen, the White Queen, and me!'

Then fill up the glasses with treacle and ink,
Or anything else that is pleasant to drink:
Mix sand with the cider, and wool with the wine –
And welcome Queen Alice with ninety-times-nine!

LEWIS CARROLL

ROBERT W. SERVICE (1874–1958)

from The Shooting of Dan McGrew

A bunch of the boys were whooping it up in the
    Malamute Saloon,
  The kid that handles the music box was hitting a rag-
    time tune;
Back of the bar, in a solo game, sat Dangerous Dan
    McGrew,
  And watching his luck was his light o' love, the lady
    that's known as Lou.
When out of the night, which was fifty below, and into
    the din and the glare,
  There stumbled a miner fresh from the creeks, dog-
    dirty and loaded for bear.
He looked like a man with a foot in the grave, and
    scarcely the strength of a louse.
  Yet he tilted a poke of dust on the bar, and he called
    for drinks for the house.
There was none could place the stranger's face though we
    searched ourselves for a clue:
  But we drank his health, and the last to drink was
    Dangerous Dan McGrew.
There's men that somehow just grip your eyes, and hold
    them hard like a spell,
  And such was he, and he looked at me like a man who
    had lived in hell;
With a face most hair, and the dreary stare of a dog
    whose day is done,
  As he watered the green stuff in his glass, and the
    drops fell one by one.
Then I got to figgering who he was, and wondering what
    he'd do,

The Outcast

A Tale of a Ladies' Cricket Match

Out in the silent Rockies,
    Tracking the Teddy-bears,
There's a man whose brow is furrowed,
    Whose hairs are silvered hairs.
Folks in that far-off region
    Know him as 'Jaundiced Jim';
And now I'll tell you his story,
    How do I know it? I'm him!

Once I was gay and mirthful,
    Ready with quip and jest,
Strong men shook at the stories
    That I would get off my chest.
I knew no doubts nor sorrows;
    I was filled with the joy of youth.
But I dished my life in one second
    Through a morbid passion for truth.

Angela Grace Maguffin
    Was the belle of the county then.
Suitors? Including me – well,
    There must have been nine or ten.
But I put in some tricky work, and
    Cut out the entire batch
Till the fatal day that undid me –
    The day of the Ladies' Match.

Cricket was not my forte.
    I never won a match
With a fifty made against time, or

And I turned my head and there watching him was the
    lady that's known as Lou.
His eyes went rubbering round the room, and he seemed
    in a kind of daze
    Till at last that old piano fell in the way of his
    wandering gaze.
The rag-time kid was having a drink, there was no one
    else on the stool,
    So the stranger stumbled across the room, and flops
    down there like a fool.
In a buckskin shirt that was glazed with dirt he sat, and I
    saw him sway.
    Then he clutched the keys with his talon hands – my
    God but that man could play!

    *

Then on a sudden the music changed, so soft that you
    scarce could hear,
    But you felt that your life had been looted clean of all
    that it once held dear.
That some one had stolen the woman you loved, that her
    love was a devil's lie;
    That your guts were gone, and the best for you was to
    crawl away and die.
'Twas the crowning cry of a heart's despair, and it
    thrilled you thro' and thro',
    And it found its goal in the blackened soul of the lady
    that's known as Lou.
Then the stranger turned and his eyes they burned in a
    most peculiar way,
    In a buckskin shirt that was glazed with dirt he sat,
    and I saw him sway.
Then his lips went in, in a kind of grin, and he spoke and
    his voice was calm,
    And 'Boys,' says he, 'you don't know me, and none of
    you care a damn,

A wonderful one-hand catch.
Rude men called me a rabbit;
  So I thought it were best that day,
Lest Grace should have cause to despise me,
  To umpire and not to play.

(Why did no guardian angel
  Down to my rescue swoop,
And hiss in my ear: 'You juggins!
  Desist, or you're in the soup!'
Why did the Fates permit me
  To tackle that evil job?
Why did I offer to umpire?
  Why did – excuse this sob.)

Everything went like clockwork;
  The sky was a gentle blue;
The sun was shining above us,
  As the sun is so apt to do.
Everything went, as stated,
  Like wheels of some well-made clock:
There wasn't a sign of disaster
  Till Grace came in for her knock.

Nature seemed tense, expectant,
  All round was a solemn hush,
She murmured: 'What's this, please, umpire?'
  I said: 'Two leg,' with a blush.
Down to the crease moved the bowler . . .
  Ah! Fate, 'twas a scurvy trick.
My Grace swiped out – and I heard it . . .
  Yes, an unmistakable click.

''S that?' cried the cad of a bowler.
  'How *was* it?' yelled slip, the brute.
For a moment I stood there breathless –
  Breathless, and dazed, and mute.

But I want to state, and my words are straight and I'll bet
   my poke they're true,
  That one of you here is a hound of hell and that one is
   Dan McGrew.'
Then I ducked my head, and the lights went out and two
   guns blazed in the dark
  And a woman screamed, and the lights went up, and
   two men lay stiff and stark:
Pitched on his head, and pumped full of lead was
   Dangerous Dan McGrew
  While the man from the creeks lay clutched to the
   breast of the lady that's known as Lou.

'*How* was it?' All creation
   Seemed filled with a hideous shout,
I wavered an instant, gulping . . .
   Then hoarsely I muttered: 'Out!'

Down where the grizzly grizzles;
   Out where the possums poss;
Where the boulders fall from the hill-side,
   And, rolling, gather no moss;
Where the wild cat sits in the sunshine,
   Chewing a human limb,
There's a thin, sad, pale, grey hermit:
   Folks know him as 'Jaundiced Jim'.

P. G. WODEHOUSE

P. G. Wodehouse wrote a number of poems before the First World
War. Some of them appeared on the front page of the *Daily
Express*, under the name of 'Mr Parrot'. This bird proved to be an
eloquent advocate of Jo Chamberlain's policy of Imperial
Preference for goods from the Empire. In the poem above,
however, Wodehouse turns his attention to ladies' cricket. Women
had played a bit in the nineteenth century: the first team, called
White Heather, was formed in 1887, and the first championship
took place the following year. Soon there were teams in Australia
and New Zealand, and in 1900 even Kenya boasted a Ladies'
Eleven. It is one of the anomalous features of English history that
women were allowed to go to the crease, but not to the polling
station.

WILLIAM SHAKESPEARE (1564–1616)

from Much Ado about Nothing

Sigh no more, ladies, sigh no more,
    Men were deceivers ever;
One foot in sea, and one on shore,
    To one thing constant never.
            Then sigh not so,
            But let them go,
        And be you blithe and bonny,
    Converting all your sounds of woe
        Into Hey nonny, nonny.

Sing no more ditties, sing no moe
    Of dumps so dull and heavy;
The fraud of men was ever so,
    Since summer first was leavy.
            Then sigh not so,
            But let them go,
        And be you blithe and bonny,
    Converting all your sounds of woe
        Into Hey nonny, nonny.

from As You Like It

            All the world's a stage,
And all the men and women merely players:
They have their exits and their entrances;
And one man in his time plays many parts,
His acts being seven ages. At first the infant,
Mewling and puking in the nurse's arms.
And then the whining schoolboy, with his satchel,
And shining morning face, creeping like snail

Much Ado about Nothing in the City

Sigh no more, dealers, sigh no more,
   Shares were unstable ever,
They often have been down before,
   At high rates constant never.
      Then sigh not so,
      Soon up they'll go,
And you'll be blithe and funny,
   Converting all your notes of woe
Into hey money, money.

Write no more letters, write no mo
   On stocks so dull and heavy.
At times on 'Change 'tis always so,
   When bears a tribute levy.
      Then sigh not so,
      And don't be low,
In sunshine you'll make honey,
   Converting all your notes of woe
Into hey money, money.

ANONYMOUS

The Patriot's Progress

      St Stephen's is a stage,
And half the opposition are but players:
For clap-traps, and deceptions, and effects,
Fill up their thoughts throughout their many parts,
Their acts being sev'n. At first the Demagogue,
Railing and mouthing at the hustings' front:
And then the cogging Candidate, with beer,
Fibs, cringes, and cockades, giving to voters

Unwillingly to school. And then the lover,
Sighing like furnace, with a woful ballad
Made to his mistress' eyebrow. Then a soldier,
Full of strange oaths, and bearded like the pard,
Jealous in honour, sudden and quick in quarrel,
Seeking the bubble reputation
Even in the cannon's mouth. And then the justice,
In fair round belly with good capon lin'd,
With eyes severe, and beard of formal cut,
Full of wise saws and modern instances;
And so he plays his part. The sixth age shifts
Into the lean and slipper'd pantaloon,
With spectacles on nose and pouch on side,
His youthful hose well sav'd a world too wide
For his shrunk shank; and his big manly voice,
Turning again towards childish treble, pipes
And whistles in his sound. Last scene of all,
That ends this strange eventful history,
Is second childishness, and mere oblivion,
Sans teeth, sans eyes, sans taste, sans everything.

Unwillingly a pledge. And then the Member,
Crackling like furnace, with a flaming story
Made on the country's fall. Then he turns Courtier,
Full of smooth words, and secret as a midwife,
Pleas'd with all rulers, zealous for the church,
Seeking the useful fame of orthodoxy,
Ev'n from the *Canon's* mouth. And then a Secretary,
In fair white waistcoat, with boil'd chicken lin'd,
With placid smile, and speech of ready answer,
Lib'ral of promises and army contracts,
And so he rules the state. The sixth act brings him
To be a snug retired old baronet,
With ribband red on breast, and star on side:
His early zeal for change a world too hot
For his cool age: and his big eloquence,
Turning to gentler sounds, obedient pipes –
And we must pay the piper. Scene the last,
That ends this comfortable history,
Is a fat pension and a pompous peerage,
With cash, with coronet – with all but conscience.

HORACE TWISS

Horace Twiss (1787–1849) pursued an intermittent parliamentary
career and his manner in the House of Commons was described by
one observer as 'very flippant, facetious and unbusinesslike'. But he
is notable for having initiated parliamentary reports in *The Times*,
and his quick wit and hospitality earned him a high reputation in
London society.

from The Winter's Tale

When daffodils begin to peer,
　　With heigh! the doxy over the dale,
Why, then comes in the sweet o' the year;
　　For the red blood reigns in the winter's pale.

　　*

The lark, that tirra-lirra chaunts,
　　With heigh! with heigh! the thrust and the jay,
Are summer songs for me and my aunts
　　While we lie tumbling in the hay.

from Cymbeline

Hark! hark! the lark at heaven's gate sings,
　　And Phoebus 'gins arise,
His steeds to water at those springs
　　On chalic'd flowers that lies;
And winking Mary-buds begin
　　To ope their golden eyes:
With every thing that pretty is,
　　My lady sweet, arise:
　　　　Arise, arise!

from *'Savonarola' Brown*

When pears hang green on the garden wall
  With a nid, and a nod, and a niddy-niddy-o,
Then prank you, lads and lasses all,
    With a yea and a nay and a niddy-o.

But when the thrush flies out o' the frost
  With a nid, [*etc.*]
'Tis time for loons to count the cost,
    With a yea [*etc.*]

MAX BEERBOHM

In Beerbohm's story ' "Savonarola" Brown', Brown is a constant
playgoer of the narrator's acquaintance who, on his death, turns
out to be the author of an unfinished dramatic work entitled
'Savonarola'. This play, with its Italian setting, bafflingly unfunny
clown, drunken porter and whimsical songs, shows every possible
sign of Shakespearian influence.

Dawn Chorus

Hark, hark, the bark as Fido springs
  And at the postman flies!
With well-adjusted teeth he clings,
  Extracting frantic cries;
And rattling milkcarts now begin
  To crash-land their supplies –
Mayst hear, my love, the merry din,
  Then ope unwilling eyes:
        Arise, arise!
  And bang the pan that fries.

MARY HOLTBY

from Hamlet

To be, or not to be: that is the question:
Whether 'tis nobler in the mind to suffer
The slings and arrows of outrageous fortune,
Or to take arms against a sea of troubles,
And by opposing end them? To die: to sleep;
No more; and, by a sleep to say we end
The heart-ache and the thousand natural shocks
That flesh is heir to, 'tis a consummation
Devoutly to be wish'd. To die, to sleep;
To sleep: perchance to dream: ay, there's the rub;
For in that sleep of death what dreams may come
When we have shuffled off this mortal coil,
Must give us pause. There's the respect
That makes calamity of so long life;
For who would bear the whips and scorns of time,
The oppressor's wrong, the proud man's contumely,
The pangs of dispriz'd love, the law's delay,
The insolence of office, and the spurns
That patient merit of the unworthy takes,
When he himself might his quietus make
With a bare bodkin? Who would fardels bear,
To grunt and sweat under a weary life,
But that the dread of something after death,
The undiscover'd country from whose bourn
No traveller returns, puzzles the will,
And makes us rather bear those ills we have,
Than fly to others that we know not of?
Thus conscience doth make cowards of us all;
And thus the native hue of resolution
Is sicklied o'er with the pale cast of thought,
And enterprises of great pith and moment
With this regard their currents turn awry,
And lose the name of action.

Toothache

To have it out or not? that is the question –
Whether 'tis better for the jaws to suffer
The pangs and torments of an aching tooth,
Or to take steel against a host of troubles,
And, by extracting, end them? To pull – to tug! –
No more: and by a tug to say we end
The tooth-ache, and a thousand natural ills
The jaw is heir to. 'Tis a consummation
Devoutly to be wished! To pull – to tug! –
To tug – perchance to break! Ay, there's the rub,
For in that wrench what agonies may come,
When we have half-dislodged the stubborn foe,
Must give us pause. There's the respect
That makes an aching tooth of so long life,
For who would bear the whips and stings of pain,
The old wife's nostrum, dentist's contumely;
The pangs of hope deferred, kind sleep's delay;
The insolence of pity, and the spurns,
That patient sickness of the healthy takes,
When he himself might his quietus make
For one poor shilling? Who would fardels bear,
To groan and sink beneath a load of pain? –
But that the dread of something lodged within
The linen-twisted forceps, from whose pangs
No jaw at ease returns, puzzles the will,
And makes it rather bear the ills it has
Than fly to others that it knows not of.
Thus dentists do make cowards of us all,
And thus the native hue of resolution
Is sicklied o'er with the pale cast of fear;
And many a one, whose courage seeks the door,
With this regard his footsteps turns away,
Scared at the name of dentist.

                         ANONYMOUS

from Macbeth

THIRD WITCH: Scale of dragon, tooth of wolf,
Witches' mummy, maw and gulf
Of the ravin'd salt-sea shark,
Root of hemlock digg'd i' the dark,
Liver of blaspheming Jew,
Gall of goat, and slips of yew
Sliver'd in the moon's eclipse,
Nose of Turk, and Tartar's lips,
Finger of birth-strangled babe
Ditch-deliver'd by a drab,
Make the gruel thick and slab:
Add thereto a tiger's chaudron,
For the ingredients of our cauldron.
ALL: Double, double toil and trouble;
Fire burn and cauldron bubble.
SECOND WITCH: Cool it with a baboon's blood,
Then the charm is firm and good.

from Richard II

This royal throne of kings, this scepter'd isle,
This earth of majesty, this seat of Mars,
This other Eden, demi-paradise,
This fortress built by Nature for herself
Against infection and the hand of war,
This happy breed of men, this little world,
This precious stone set in the silver sea,
Which serves it in the office of a wall,
Or as a moat defensive to a house,
Against the envy of less happier lands,
This blessed plot, this earth, this realm, this England.

'Into concrete mixer throw'

Into concrete mixer throw
Brick from shoddy bungalow,
Thrice three chunks of orange peel
Gathered from the beach at Deal,
Foot of hare untimely slain
On the outer traffic lane,
Cast-off paper from a toffee,
Cup of instantaneous coffee,
Then, with fag-end torn from lip,
Sexy film and comic strip,
Nucleus of hydrogen,
Thousandth egg of battery hen,
Paint-brush used for marking wall,
Thoroughly compound them all.
This charm, once set and left to stand,
Will cast a blight on any land.

BARBARA ROE

This Railway Station

This squalid dome of soot-obscuréd glass,
This larger lavatory or spittoon,
This vault of echoes, rudely amplified,
This meeting-place of draughts, whose smut-filled air
Strikes chill upon the stoutest traveller's chest,
This worried trippers' haunt, this dunghill world
Whence porter-cocks crow false civilities,
This traffic jam, stirred in a thousand jars,
Which serves as hypodermic for the times,
Inoculating tourists 'gainst the press
Of progress and the piercing shrieks of speed,
This dark and dank depression of the soul,
This builder's blot, this curse, this Railway Station.

ALLAN M. LAING

PERCY BYSSHE SHELLEY (1792–1822)

Ozymandias

I met a traveller from an antique land
Who said: Two vast and trunkless legs of stone
Stand in the desert . . . Near them, on the sand,
Half sunk, a shattered visage lies, whose frown,
And wrinkled lip, and sneer of cold command,
Tell that its sculptor well those passions read
Which yet survive, stamped on these lifeless things,
The hand that mocked them, and the heart that fed:
And on the pedestal these words appear:
'My name is Ozymandias, king of kings:
Look on my works, ye Mighty, and despair!'
Nothing beside remains. Round the decay
Of that colossal wreck, boundless and bare
The lone and level sands stretch far away.

Ozymandias Revisited

I met a traveller from an antique land
Who said: Two vast and trunkless legs of stone
Stand in the desert . . . Near them on the sand
Half sunk, a shatter'd visage lies, whose frown
And wrinkled lip and sneer of cold command
Tell that its sculptor well those passions read
Which still survive, stamp'd on these lifeless things,
The hand that mocked them and the heart that fed;
And on the pedestal these words appear:
'My name is Ozymandias, king of kings!
Look on my works, ye Mighty and despair!'
Also the names of Emory P. Gray,
Mr and Mrs Dukes, and Oscar Baer,
Of 17 West 4th Street, Oyster Bay.

MORRIS BISHOP

PHILIP SIDNEY (1554–86)

The Bargain

My true love hath my heart, and I have his,
   By just exchange, one for the other given.
I hold his dear, and mine he cannot miss,
   There never was a better bargain driven.
His heart in me keeps me and him in one,
   My heart in him his thoughts and senses guides;
He loves my heart, for once it was his own,
   I cherish his, because in me it bides.
His heart his wound receivèd from my sight,
   My heart was wounded with his wounded heart;
For as from me on him his hurt did light,
   So still methought in me his hurt did smart.
     Both equal hurt, in this change sought our bliss:
     My true love hath my heart and I have his.

Strugnell's Bargain

My true love hath my heart and I have hers:
We swapped last Tuesday and felt quite elated
But now, whenever one of us refers
To 'my heart', things get rather complicated.
Just now, when she complained 'My heart is racing',
'You mean *my* heart is racing,' I replied.
'That's what I said.' 'You mean the heart replacing
Your heart, my love.' 'Oh piss off, Jake!' she cried.
I ask you, do you think Sir Philip Sidney
Got spoken to like that? And I suspect
If I threw in my liver and a kidney,
She'd still address me with as scant respect.
Therefore do I revoke my opening line:
My love can keep her heart and I'll have mine.

WENDY COPE

'My *true* love *hath my heart and I have his*'

My true love hath my heart and I have his;
What clever stuff this transplant business is!

PATRICIA STOCKBRIDGE

GEORGE R. SIMS (1847–1922)

from Two Women

To-night is a midnight meeting, and the Earl is in the chair;
There's food and a little sermon for all who enter there,
For all of our erring sisters who, finding their trade is slack,
Have time to sit down and listen to the holy men in black.

To-night is a midnight meeting, and in from the filthy street
They are bringing the wretched wantons who sin for a
    crust to eat;
There's cake to be had, and coffee, as well as the
    brimstone tracts
That paint in such flaming colours the end of their evil acts.

To-night is a midnight meeting, and out of the rain and
    dirt
There creeps in a sinful woman – drenched is her
    draggled skirt,
Drenched are the gaudy feathers that droop in her
    shapeless hat,
And her hair hangs over her shoulders in a wet, untidy mat.

She hears of the fiery furnace that waits for the wicked
    dead;
Of the torture in store for the outcast who sins for her
    daily bread;
She hears that a God of mercy has built, on a sunlit shore,
A haven of rest eternal for those who shall sin no more.

Anon by the silent waters she kneels, with her eyes upcast,
And whispers her Heavenly Father, 'O God, I have
    sinned my last.
Here, in this cruel city, to live I must sin the sin;
Save me from that, O Father! – pity, and take me in.'

The Ballad of George R. Sims

It's an easy game, this reviewin' – the editor sends yer a
  book,
Yer puts it down on yer table and yer gives it a 'asty look,
An' then, Sir, yer writes about it as though yer 'ad read it
  all through,
And if ye're a pal o' the author yer gives it a good review.

But if the author's a wrong 'un – and *some* are, as I've
  'eard tell –
Or if 'e's a stranger to yer, why then yer can give him 'ell.
So what would yer 'ave me do, Sir, to humour an editor's
  whims,
When I'm pally with Calder-Marshall, and never knew
  George R. Sims?

It is easy for you to deride me and brush me off with a
  laugh
And say 'Well, the answer's potty – yer review it just 'arf
  and 'arf' –
For I fear I must change my tune, Sir, and pump the
  bellows of praise
And say that both 'alves are good, Sir, in utterly different
  ways.

I'm forgettin' my cockney lingo – for I lapse in my style
  now and then
As Sims used to do in his ballads when he wrote of the
  Upper Ten –
'Round in the sensuous galop the high-born maids are
  swung
Clasped in the arms of *roués* whose vice is on every
  tongue'.

A plunge in the muddy river, a cry on the chill night air,
And the waters upon their bosom a pilgrim sister bear;
She has laved the stain of the city from her soul in the
    river slime,
She has sought for the promised haven through the door
    of a deadly crime.

*

To-night is a midnight meeting — a ball in a Western
    square —
And rank and fashion and beauty, and a Prince of the
    blood are there;
In the light of a thousand tapers the jewelled bosoms gleam,
And the cheeks of the men are flushing, and the eyes of
    the women beam.

Round in the sensuous galop the high-born maids are
    swung,
Clasped in the arms of *roués* whose vice is on ev'ry tongue;
And the stately Norman mothers look on the scene with
    pride
If the *roué* is only wealthy and in search of a youthful bride.

But fair above all the women is the beautiful Countess
    May,
And wealthy and great and titled yield to her queenly
    sway;
Her they delight to honour, her they are proud to know,
For wherever the Countess visits, a Prince of the blood
    will go.

The story is common gossip; there isn't a noble dame
That bows to the reigning beauty but knows of her evil
    fame.
She is married — had sons and daughters when she
    humoured a Prince's whim;
But her husband is proud of her conquest — the Prince is
    a friend to *him*.

'It was Christmas Day in the workhouse' is his best
    known line of all,
And this is his usual metre, which comes, as you may
    recall,
Through Tennyson, Gordon, Kipling and on to the
    Sergeants' Mess,
A rhythm that's made to recite in, be it mufti or evening
    dress.

Now Arthur shows in his intro that George R. Sims was a
    bloke
Who didn't compose his ballads as a sort of caustic joke;
He cared about social justice but he didn't aim very high
Though he knew how to lay on the sobstuff and make his
    audience cry.

The village church on the back-drop is painted over for
    good,
The village concerts are done for where the Young Reciter
    stood,
The magic-lantern is broken and we laugh at the mission
    hymns –
We laugh and we well might weep with the Ballads of
    George R. Sims.

JOHN BETJEMAN

This poem appeared in the *New Statesman* on 25 October 1968 as
a review of a collection of ballads by George R. Sims. Sims was a
popular journalist who wrote a column under the heading
'Mustard and Cress' for the *Sunday Referee*, where he championed
the underdog. Two series of articles by him, called 'How the Poor
Live', shocked the middle classes of late Victorian England and
acted as a popular version of Disraeli's *The Two Nations*. In the
1870s Sims published his ballads, including his most famous, 'It
was Christmas Day in the Workhouse'. These ballads, intended for
public recitation, were mawkish and melodramatic, which no

The bishop who christens her babies, the coachman who
  drives her pair,
The maid who carries her letters, the footman behind her
  chair,
The Marquis, her white-haired father, her brothers, so
  gossips say –
All know of the guilty passion of the Prince and the
  Countess May.

The doors of the Court are open, and the great Lord
  Chamberlain bows,
Though he knows that the titled wanton has broken her
  marriage vows;
And all of the courtiers flatter, and strive for a friendly
  glance –
On her whom the Prince delights in who dares to look
  askance?

She is crowned with the world's fresh roses; no tongue
  has a word of blame;
But the woman who falls from hunger is a thing too foul
  to name.
She is blessed who barters her honour just for a prince's
  smile;
The vice of the Court is *charming*, and the vice of the
  alley *vile*.

So, world, shall it be for ever – this hunting the street girl
  down,
While you honour the titled Phryne, and hold her in high
  renown;
But when, at the great uprising, they meet for the
  Judgment Day,
I'd rather be that drowned harlot than the beautiful
  Countess May.

doubt accounted for their wide appeal, and they kept their author living in state in Regent's Park. His poetic muse seems to have diminished, however, when he switched from alcohol to lemon juice. Sims also wrote plays, which did well, although they were described by the theatre critic William Archer as 'Zola diluted at the Aldgate Pump'.

EDITH SITWELL (1887–1964)

Said King Pompey

Said King Pompey, the emperor's ape,
Shuddering black in his temporal cape
Of dust: 'The dust is everything –
The heart to love and the voice to sing,
Indianapolis,
And the Acropolis,
Also the hairy sky that we
Take for a coverlet comfortably.' . . .
Said the Bishop
Eating his ketchup –
'There still remains Eternity
(Swelling the diocese) –
That elephantiasis,
The flunkeyed and trumpeting Sea!'

Contours

Round – oblong – like jam –
Terse as virulent hermaphrodites;
Calling across the sodden twisted ends of Time.
Edifices of importunity
Sway like Parmesan before the half-tones
Of Episcopalian Michaelmas;
Bodies are so impossible to see in retrospect –
And yet I know the well of truth
Is gutted like pratchful Unicorn.
Sog, sog, sog – why is my mind amphibious?
That's what it is.

NOËL COWARD

In 1923 Noël Coward lampooned Edith Sitwell and her two
brothers, Osbert and Sacheverell, in some sketches which he called
'The Swiss Family Whittlebot'. This was in the wake of the first
performance of Edith's avant-garde poems for recitation through a
loud-speaker with musical accompaniment, *Façade*. She was
furious and nursed her grievance against Coward for many years.
It was only aggravated by Coward's description of the eccentric
behaviour of Miss Hernia Whittlebot, 'who was busy preparing for
publication her new books, "Gilded Sluts" and "Garbage". She
breakfasts on onions and Vichy water.'

CHRISTOPHER SMART (1722–71)

from Jubilate Deo

For I will consider my Cat Jeoffry.

For he is the servant of the Living God duly and daily
serving him.

For at the first glance of the glory of God in the East he
worships in his way.

For is this done by wreathing his body seven times round
with elegant quickness.

For then he leaps up to catch the musk, which is the
blessing of God upon his prayer.

For he rolls upon prank to work it in.

For having done duty and received blessing he begins to
consider himself.

For this he performs in ten degrees.

For first he looks upon his fore-paws to see if they are
clean.

For secondly he kicks up behind to clear away there.

For thirdly he works it upon stretch with the fore-paws
extended.

For fourthly he sharpens his paws by wood.

For fifthly he washes himself.

For Sixthly he rolls upon wash.

For Seventhly he fleas himself, that he may not be
interrupted upon the beat.

For Eighthly he rubs himself against a post.

For Ninthly he looks up for his instructions.

For Tenthly he goes in quest of food.

For having consider'd God and himself he will consider
his neighbour.

For if he meets another cat he will kiss her in kindness.

For when he takes his prey he plays with it to give it
chance.

Jubilate Matteo

For I rejoice in my cat Matty.

For his coat is variegated in black and brown, with white undersides.

For in every way his whiskers are marvellous.

For he resists the Devil and is completely neuter.

For he sleeps and washes himself and walks warily in the ways of Putney.

For he is at home in the whole district of SW15.

For in this district the great Yorkshire Murderer ate his last meal before he entered into captivity.

For in the Book of Crime there is no name like John Reginald Halliday Christie.

For Yorkshire indeed excels in all things, as Geoffrey Boycott is the best Batsman.

For the Yorkshire Ripper and the Hull Arsonist have their horns exalted in glory.

For Yorkshire is therefore acknowledged the greatest County.

For Hull was once of the company, that is now of Humberside.

For Sir Leonard Hutton once scored 364 runs in a Test Match.

For Fred Trueman too is a flagrant glory to Yorkshire.

For my cat wanders in the ways of the angels of Yorkshire.

For in his soul God has shown him a remarkable vision of Putney.

For he has also trodden in the paths of the newly fashionable.

For those who live in Gwendolen Avenue cry 'Drop dead, darling!'

For one mouse in seven escapes by his dallying.

For when his day's work is done his business more
   properly begins.

For he keeps the Lord's watch in the night against the
   adversary.

For he counteracts the powers of darkness by his
   electrical skin and glaring eyes.

For he counteracts the Devil, who is death, by brisking
   about the life

For in his morning orisons he loves the sun and the sun
   loves him.

For he is of the tribe of Tiger.

For the Cherub Cat is a term of the Angel Tiger.

For he has the subtlety and hissing of a serpent, which in
   goodness he suppresses.

For he will not do destruction, if he is well-fed, neither
   will he spit without provocation.

For he purrs in thankfulness, when God tells him he's a
   good Cat.

For he is an instrument for the children to learn
   benevolence upon.

For every house is incompleat without him and a blessing
   is lacking in the spirit.

For the Lord commanded Moses concerning the cats at
   the departure of the Children of Israel from Egypt.

For every family had one cat at least in the bag.

For the English Cats are the best in Europe.

For in Cambalt Road and Dealtry Road where the Vet
  lives there are professional people.
For Erpingham Road and Danemere Street and Dryburgh
  Road include the intelligentsia.
For in Clarendon Drive the British Broadcasting
  Corporation is rampant.
For the glory of God has deserted the simple.
For the old who gossiped in Bangalore Road are unknown
  to the dayspring.
For there is a shortage of the old people who adorned the
  novels of William Trevor.
For in the knowledge of this I cling to the old folkways of
  Gwalior Road and Olivette Street.
For I rejoice in my cat, who has the true spirit of Putney.

GAVIN EWART

from A Song to David

Strong is the horse upon his speed;
Strong in pursuit the rapid glede,
   Which makes at once his game:
Strong the tall ostrich on the ground;
Strong through the turbulent profound
   Shoots xiphias to his aim.

Strong is the lion – like a coal
His eye-ball – like a bastion's mole
   His chest against the foes:
Strong, the gier-eagle on his sail,
Strong against tide, the enormous whale
   Emerges as he goes.

Kit Smart went to Cambridge where he acquired the habit of
getting into debt. At the age of thirty he started to go mad,
developing a religious mania, and for a time he was confined to an
asylum, though when Johnson visited him there he declared him
sane. It was there that he wrote *A Song to David*. Smart was
clearly a kind and gentle person and, when he went bankrupt and
was obliged to live within the rules of King's Bench, a few loyal
friends rallied to support him.

Christopher Smart

Mad is the poet men call Kit;
Mad is his thought, and mad his wit,
   And madness, sure, he writes;
Mad as the pig when he is stuck;
Mad as the bull that runs amuck,
   Or rabid dog that bites.

Mad as his eyes are rimmed with black;
Mad as his stare is lustre-lack;
   Mad as his prayers are long:
Mad as his wig is shrunk and torn;
Mad as his shoes are long outworn;
   Mad as his faith is strong.

STANLEY SHAW

This poem won a competition in the *Spectator*, when readers were
asked to compose a poem in the style of a well-known poet
describing his own condition in a light-hearted manner.

STEVIE SMITH (1902–71)

Not Waving but Drowning

Nobody heard him, the dead man,
But still he lay moaning:
I was much further out than you thought
And not waving but drowning.

Poor chap, he always loved larking
And now he's dead
It must have been too cold for him his heart gave way,
They said.

Oh, no no no, it was too cold always
(Still the dead one lay moaning)
I was much too far out all my life
And not waving but drowning.

Not Wavell but Browning

Nobody read him, the poor sod,
He was always moaning:
I am much more way out than you think
And not Wavell but Browning.

Poor chap, he always loved Larkin
And now he's dead,
The critics were too cold for him, his art gave way
They said.

Oh, no no no, they were too cold always
(He still never stopped moaning)
I was obscene and avant-garde and obscure
And not Wavell but Browning.

GAVIN EWART

Field Marshal Lord Wavell commanded the British army in Egypt
at the time when it was faced with Rommel's thrusting attacks.
Churchill then became impatient for a more offensive campaign
and removed Wavell to the command in India. History has shown
greater understanding, however, for Wavell has now been credited
with laying the foundations of Montgomery's later victories. In
Delhi, in 1943, Wavell compiled an anthology of poetry to which
he gave the title *Other Men's Flowers*. No other anthology
compiled since the war has been as popular and it was reprinted
many times. It is a very good book and I have learnt a lot from it.
Wavell's criterion for publication was that the poem should be
capable of being read aloud.

ROBERT SOUTHEY (1774–1843)

The Old Man's Comforts and How He Gained Them

'You are old, Father William,' the young man cried;
  'The few locks which are left you are grey;
You are hale, Father William – a hearty old man:
  Now tell me the reason, I pray.'

'In the days of my youth,' Father William replied,
  'I remembered that youth would fly fast,
And abused not my health and my vigour at first,
  That I never might need them at last.'

'You are old, Father William,' the young man cried,
  'And pleasures with youth pass away;
And yet you lament not the days that are gone:
  Now tell me the reason, I pray.'

'In the days of my youth,' Father William replied,
  'I remembered that youth could not last;
I thought of the future, whatever I did,
  That I never might grieve for the past.'

'You are old, Father William,' the young man cried,
  'And life must be hastening away;
You are cheerful and love to converse upon death:
  Now tell me the reason, I pray.'

'I am cheerful, young man,' Father William replied;
  'Let the cause thy attention engage;
In the days of my youth, I remembered my God,
  And He hath not forgotten my age.'

'You are old, Father William'

'You are old, Father William,' the young man said,
   'And your hair has become very white;
And yet you incessantly stand on your head –
   Do you think, at your age, it is right?'

'In my youth,' Father William replied to his son,
   'I feared it might injure the brain;
But now that I'm perfectly sure I have none,
   Why, I do it again and again.'

'You are old,' said the youth, 'as I mentioned before,
   And have grown most uncommonly fat;
Yet you turned a back-somersault in at the door –
   Pray, what is the reason of that?'

'In my youth,' said the sage, as he shook his grey locks,
   'I kept all my limbs very supple
By the use of this ointment – one shilling the box –
   Allow me to sell you a couple.'

'You are old,' said the youth, 'and your jaws are too weak
   For anything tougher than suet;
Yet you finished the goose, with the bones and the beak –
   Pray how did you manage to do it?'

'In my youth,' said his father, 'I took to the law,
   And argued each case with my wife;
And the muscular strength, which it gave to my jaw,
   Has lasted the rest of my life.'

from After Blenheim

'Twas a summer evening,
  Old Kaspar's work was done,
And he before his cottage door
  Was sitting in the sun,
And by him sported on the green
His little grandchild, Wilhelmine.

She saw her brother Peterkin
  Roll something large and round,
Which he beside the rivulet
  In playing there had found;
He came to ask what he had found
That was so large, and smooth, and round.

Old Kaspar took it from the boy
  Who stood expectant by;
And then the old man shook his head.
  And with a natural sigh –
''Tis some poor fellow's skull,' said he,
'Who fell in that great victory.'

*

'You are old,' said the youth, 'one would hardly suppose
   That your eye was as steady as ever;
Yet you balanced an eel on the end of your nose –
   What made you so awfully clever?'

'I have answered three questions, and that is enough,'
   Said his father; 'don't give yourself airs!
Do you think I can listen all day to such stuff?
   Be off, or I'll kick you downstairs!'

LEWIS CARROLL

The Battue of Berlin

It was a winter's morning,
   The Kaiser's sport was done;
From far and near the driven deer
   Had faced the Royal 'gun',
And all around, in grim array,
Five hundred rotting corpses lay.

From near and far, to King and Tsar
   The startled herds had fled;
And many a stag had swelled the bag,
   And many a hind lay dead.
Such things must be and will in short,
After a famous hour of sport!

It was the German Emperor
   Who slew five hundred deer;
But what he killed so many for
   Is not completely clear.
But all the journalists report
That 'twas a famous morning's sport.

'It was the English,' Kaspar cried,
   'Who put the French to rout;
But what they fought each other for
   I could not well make out;
But everybody said,' quoth he,
'That 'twas a famous victory.

*

'And everybody praised the Duke
   Who this great fight did win.'
'But what good came of it at last?'
   Quoth little Peterkin.
'Why, that I cannot tell,' said he,
'But 'twas a famous victory.'

The Widow

Cold was the night wind, drifting fast the snow fell,
Wide were the downs and shelterless and naked,
When a poor wanderer struggled on her journey,
      Weary and way-sore.

Dreary were the downs, more dreary her reflections;
Cold was the night-wind, colder was her bosom:
She had no home, the world was all before her,
      She had no shelter.

Fast o'er the heath a chariot rattled by her,
'Pity me!' feebly cried the lonely wanderer.

From left and right, in furious flight,
    The stags to slaughter came;
Each beast, deceased, by death increased
    This holocaust of game.
And, after all (you may retort),
It was a famous morning's sport.

Let sportsmen raise their hymns of praise
    To those who made such bags,
Who in an hour evinced the pow'r
    To slay five hundred stags,
While I repeat (how dare you snort?)
That 'twas a famous morning's sport!

HARRY GRAHAM

On the Tsar's visit to Berlin, the German Emperor, Wilhelm II, was
reported to have entertained his guest's suite at a battue. 'In
favourable weather,' according to the *Daily Mail*, '492 stags were
killed during an hour's shooting.'

The Friend of Humanity and the Knife-grinder

FRIEND OF HUMANITY
'Needy knife-grinder! whither are you going?
Rough is the road, your wheel is out of order –
Bleak blows the blast; – your hat has got a hole in't,
        So have your breeches!

'Weary knife-grinder! little think the proud ones
Who in their coaches roll along the turnpike-
Road, what hard work 'tis crying all day, 'Knives and
        Scissors to grind O!'

'Tell me, knife-grinder, how came you to grind knives?
Did some rich man tyrannically use you?

'Pity me, strangers! lest with cold and hunger
    Here I should perish.

'Once I had friends, but they have all forsook me!
Once I had parents – they are now in heaven!
I had a home once – I had once a husband –
    Pity me, strangers!

'I had a home once – I had once a husband –
I am a widow poor and broken-hearted!'
Loud blew the wind, unheard was her complaining,
    On drove the chariot.

Then on the snow she laid her down to rest her;
She heard a horseman – 'Pity me!' she groaned out;
Loud was the wind, unheard was her complaining,
    On went the horseman.

Worn out with anguish, toil and cold and hunger,
Down sunk the wanderer, sleep had seized her senses,
There did the traveller find her in the morning;
    God had released her.

Southey started as a Radical, being expelled from Westminster
School for an essay against flogging. He wrote this poem in 1796,
revealing a less glorious aspect of the Napoleonic Wars. It was
parodied by George Canning and John Hookham Frere in a weekly
satirical paper, the *Anti-Jacobin*, first published in November 1797.
Canning became an MP in 1793 and a junior minister in 1796. He
put into practice his belief that the devil 'Jacobinism' should not
have all the best tunes. The *Anti-Jacobin* was edited by William
Gifford, and two future prime ministers, Liverpool and Canning,
wrote for it. The 'Knife-Grinder' parody was immensely popular
throughout the nineteenth century. Incidentally, Southey's views
also changed and by the time he was Poet Laureate he had
completely renounced his radicalism – an act for which Byron was
to castigate him with gleeful energy.

Was it the squire? or parson of the parish?
    Or the attorney?

'Was it the squire, for killing of his game? or
Covetous parson, for his tithes distraining?
Or roguish lawyer, made you lose your little
    All in a lawsuit?

'(Have you not read the Rights of Man, by Tom Paine?),
Drops of compassion tremble on my eyelids,
Ready to fall as soon as you have told your
    Pitiful story.'

KNIFE-GRINDER
'Story! God bless you! I have none to tell, sir,
Only last night a-drinking at the Chequers
This poor old hat and breeches, as you see, were
    Torn in a scuffle.

'Constables came up for to take me into
Custody; they took me before the justice;
Justice Oldmixon put me in the parish
    Stocks for a vagrant.

'I should be glad to drink your Honour's health in
A pot of beer, if you will give me sixpence;
But for my part, I never love to meddle
    With politics, sir.'

FRIEND OF HUMANITY
'I give thee sixpence! I will see thee damn'd first –
Wretch! whom no sense of wrongs can rouse to
    vengeance –
Sordid, unfeeling, reprobate, degraded,
    Spiritless outcast!'

[*Kicks the Knife-grinder, overturns his wheel, and exit in a
transport of republican enthusiasm and universal philanthropy.*]

GEORGE CANNING *and* JOHN HOOKHAM FRERE

STEPHEN SPENDER (1909–   )

Airman

He will watch the hawk with an indifferent eye
        Or pitifully;
Nor on those eagles that so feared him, now
        Will strain his brow;
Weapons men use, stone, sling and strong-thewed bow
        He will not know.

This artistocrat, superb of all instinct,
        With death close-linked
Had paced the enormous cloud, almost had won
        War on the sun;
Till now, like Icarus mid-ocean-drowned,
        Hands, wings, are found.

Parachutist

I shall never forget his blue eye,
Bright as a bird's but larger,
Imprinting on my own
Tear-wounded but merciless iris
The eternal letters
Of his blond incomprehension.

He came down lightly by the lilypool
Where a bird was washing,
But he did not frighten her:
A touselled boy from the skies
Petrol should not have signed
Shamefully to his surprised dishonour;
His uniform like an obscene shroud
Fretted his hands that should have held in peace
A girl's two kind ones in a public park,
Handled a boat or fashioned simple things,
Flutes, clogs, and little wooden bears,
Or in beer gardens by the ribboning Rhine
Mirthfully gestured under linden trees.

Now these once loving-kindly hands
Cherished, like an adder picked up on a walk,
A tommy gun, cold threat to love in steel:
Icarus he stands; his silken clouds of glory
Trailing behind him – a bird's broken wing –
Still trembling from his fallen angel's flight
Down the sky weeping death.

DYLAN THOMAS *and* JOHN DAVENPORT

From *The Death of the King's Canary.*

EDMUND SPENSER (1552–99)

from The Faerie Queene, Book VI, Canto III

He was to weet a man of full ripe years,
That in his youth had been of mickle might,
And borne great sway in arms among his peers;
But now weak age had dimm'd his candle-light:
Yet was he courteous still to every wight,
And loved all that did to arms incline;
And was the father of that wounded knight,
Whom Calidore thus carried on his chine;
And Aldus was his name; and his son's Aladine.

In an immensely long letter to George and Georgiana Keats, dated 14 February to 3 May 1819, Keats tells his brother and sister: 'Brown this morning is writing some Spenserian stanzas against Mrs, Miss Brawne and me; so I shall amuse myself with him a little: in the manner of Spenser.' And he adds: 'This character would ensure him a situation in the establishment of patient Griselda.' He begins with a formula used by Spenser for the description of new characters and carries on in a vein of loose pastiche.

Stanzas on Charles Armitage Brown

He is to weet a melancholy carle:
Thin in the waist, with bushy head of hair,
As hath the seeded thistle when in parle
It holds the Zephyr, ere it sendeth fair
Its light balloons into the summer air;
Therto his beard had not begun to bloom,
No brush had touch'd his chin, or razor sheer;
No care had touch'd his cheek with mortal doom,
But new he was and bright as scarf from Persian loom.

Ne cared he for wine, or half and half,
Ne cared he for fish or flesh or fowl,
And sauces held he worthless as the chaff;
He 'sdeigned the swine-head at the wassail-bowl;
Ne with lewd ribbalds sat he cheek by jowl;
Ne with sly Lemans in the scorner's chair;
But after water-brooks this Pilgrim's soul
Panted, and all his food was woodland air
Though he would oft-times feast on gilliflowers rare.

The slang of cities in no wise he knew,
Tipping the wink to him was heathen Greek;
He sipp'd no olden Tom or ruin blue,
Or nantz or cherry-brandy drank full meek
By many a damsel hoarse and rouge of cheek;
Nor did he know each aged watchman's beat,
Nor in obscured purlieus would he seek
For curlèd Jewesses, with ankles neat,
Who as they walk abroad make tinkling with their feet.

JOHN KEATS

CAT STEVENS (1948–   )

Wild World

You know I've seen a lot of what the world can do,
  And it's breaking my heart in two.
'Cause I never want to see you sad, girl, don't be a bad
    girl,
  But if you want to leave, take good care.
Hope you make a lot of nice friends out there,
  But just remember there's a lot of bad – and beware,
    beware . . .

Oh baby, baby, it's a wild world,
  It's hard to get by just upon a smile.
Oh baby, baby, it's a wild world,
  And I'll always remember you like a child, girl.

Vile World

You know I've seen a lot of what the world can do
  And this is far worse than a bad review.
I never want to see you read, man; you'll be a dead man
  But if you want to run, take good care,
I hope you have a lot of nice police out there.
  But just remember there's a lot of bad – and
    Beware . . .

O Rushdie, Rushdie, it's a vile world,
  It's hard to get off without a trial, man.
O Rushdie, Rushdie, it's a vile world,
  You're being hounded for more than just your style,
    man.

SIMON RAE

No book, just by its publication, has caused such an international
storm as did Salman Rushdie's *The Satanic Verses*. In 1988 it
almost won the Booker Prize, and it did win the Whitbread Prize
for the best novel of the year. But it deeply offended Moslems with
its disrespectful and satirical attacks on the prophet Mohammed.
They held that it was blasphemous, and early in 1989 a copy was
publicly burnt in Bradford. In February of that year the Ayatollah
Khomeini cursed its author, who had offended even more deeply
by being an apostate, and called for his death, promising that
Rushdie's murderer would go to heaven. This appalling act was
condemned by every country in the West and diplomatic relations
between Britain and Iran were severed. Cat Stevens, the popular
singer, had become a convert to Islam and was reported in the
newspapers as supporting the Ayatollah.

ROBERT LOUIS STEVENSON (1850–94)

My Shadow

I have a little shadow that goes in and out with me,
And what can be the use of him is more than I can see.
He is very, very like me from the heels up to the head;
And I see him jump before me, when I jump into my bed.

The funniest thing about him is the way he likes to
    grow –
Not at all like proper children, which is always very
    slow;
For he sometimes shoots up taller, like an india-rubber
    ball,
And he sometimes gets so little that there's none of him
    at all.

He hasn't got a notion of how children ought to play,
And can only make a fool of me in every sort of way.
He stays so close beside me, he's a coward you can see;
I'd think shame to stick to nursie as that shadow sticks to
    me!

One morning, very early, before the sun was up,
I rose and found the shining dew on every buttercup;
But my lazy little shadow, like an arrant sleepy-head,
Had stayed at home behind me and was fast asleep in
    bed.

My Shadow

I have a sort of shadow that goes out sometimes with me,
And what can be the use of him you presently will see;
He's not the least bit like me, and in fact I'm bound to say
That whichever way *he* votes, I have to vote the other way.

The strangest thing about him is he seldom is the same,
And I never know for certain what is going to be his
    name;
Sometimes he is a Liberal who wants an evening off,
Or he may be Independent and desire a game of golf.

His one desire (and mine) is just to spend a happy day,
And this arrangement has been found the most convenient
    way;
We still receive our money, and are both as free as air,
For my shadow and myself are what is called a happy 'Pair'.

One morning I must tell you when I thought that I had
    'paired',
I stayed beneath the bedclothes till the day was nicely
    aired,
But my absent-minded shadow who I thought was safe in
    bed
Had forgotten all about me and had gone to vote instead!

W. HODGSON BURNETT

From *The MP's Garden of Verses*, published in 1920. Each poem
in it is a parody of one from Stevenson's *Child's Garden*, given a
Westminster setting, and most are eulogies of Lloyd George. This
one describes the pairing system which survives to this day and
which is very necessary for the harmonious dispatch of
parliamentary business.

S. J. STONE (1839–1901)

'The Church's one foundation'

The Church's one foundation
    Is Jesus Christ, her Lord;
She is his new creation
    By water and the Word:
From heaven he came and sought her
    To be his holy Bride,
With his own Blood he bought her,
    And for her life he died.

Though with a scornful wonder
    Men see her sore opprest,
By schisms rent asunder,
    By heresies distrest,
Yet Saints their watch are keeping,
    Their cry goes up, 'How long?'
And soon the night of weeping
    Shall be the morn of song.

'Mid toil, and tribulation,
    And tumult of her war,
She waits the consummation
    Of peace for evermore;
Till with the vision glorious
    Her longing eyes are blest,
And the great Church victorious
    Shall be the Church at rest.

The Good Church Guide gave potential worshippers advice on the
distinctive features of 2,000 different churches in this country.
There are many varied strands within the Church of England –
something for everyone!

Believers' Best Buy

The Church's publication
Is there to be explored
By those who seek salvation,
And pray they'll not be bored.
The good could do no better
Than read *The Good Church Guide*:
'The parson wears a sweater,
The verger's hair is dyed.'

Your choice may be a sermon,
A sweet and holy song,
Or something from the German
That lasts a shade too long.
To speak in tongues unites you
With Him who understands,
Or what perhaps excites you
Is laying on of hands.

If kneeling to your Maker
Is not your given role,
The Church of Kenneth Baker
Should satisfy your soul.
It may be medieval
To bow before the rich,
But if you're into evil,
Consult the April *Witch*.

ROGER WODDIS

When I was asked by the Archbishop of Canterbury to address
the General Synod on 1 February 1989, I urged the Church in its
comments on Government policies to remember that, alongside the
Catholic tradition, which emphasized a collectivist approach, there
was also a Protestant tradition, which should emphasize the
contribution that individuals can make.

JOHN SUCKLING (1609–42)

Ode to a Lover

Honest lover whosoever,
If in all thy love was ever
One wav'ring thought; if e'er thy flame
Were not still even, still the same, –
　　　Know this,
　　　Thou lov'st amiss;
　　　And to love true,
Thou must begin again, and love anew.

If, when she appears i' th' room,
Thou dost not quake, and art struck dumb;
And, in striving this to cover,
Dost not speak thy words twice over, –
　　　Know this,
　　　Thou lov'st amiss;
　　　And to love true,
Thou must begin again, and love anew.

If, fondly, thou dost not mistake,
And all defects for graces take,
Persuad'st thyself that jests are broken,
When she has little or nothing spoken, –
　　　Know this,
　　　Thou lov'st amiss;
　　　And to love true,
Thou must begin again, and love anew.

If, when thou appear'st to be within,
Thou let'st not men ask and ask again;
And when thou answer'st, if it be
To what was ask'd thee, properly, –
　　　Know this,

Ode to a Jacobin

Unchristian Jacobin whoever,
If of thy God thou cherish ever
One wavering thought; if e'er His Word
Has from one crime thy soul deterred:
    Know this,
      Thou think'st amiss;
      And to think true,
Thou must renounce Him all, and think anew.

If startled at the guillotine
Trembling thou touch the dread machine;
If, leading sainted Louis to it,
Thy steps drew back, thy heart did rue it:
    Know this,
      Thou think'st amiss;
      And to think true,
Must rise 'bove weak remorse, and think anew.

If, callous, thou dost not mistake,
And murder for mild mercy's sake;
And think thou followest pity's call
When slaughtered thousands round thee fall:
    Know this,
      Thou think'st amiss;
      And to think true,
Must conquer prejudice, and think anew.

If when good men are to be slain,
Thou hear'st them plead, nor plead in vain,
Or, when thou answerest, if it be
With one jot of humanity:
    Know this,

Thou lov'st amiss;
And to love true,
Thou must begin again, and love anew.

If, when thy stomach calls to eat,
Thou cut'st not fingers 'stead of meat;
And with much gazing on her face,
Dost not rise hungry from the place, —
Know this,
Thou lov'st amiss;
And to love true,
Thou must begin again, and love anew.

If, by this thou dost discover
That thou art no perfect lover;
And desiring to love true,
Thou dost begin to love anew, —
Know this,
Thou lov'st amiss;
And to love true,
Thou must begin again, and love anew.

Thou think'st amiss;
And to think true,
Must pardon leave to fools, and think anew.

If when all kings, priests, nobles hated,
Lie headless, thy revenge is sated,
Nor thirsts to load the reeking block
With heads from thine own murderous flock
Know this,
Thou think'st amiss;
And to think true,
Thou must go on in blood, and think anew.

If, thus, by love of executions,
Thou prov'st thee fit for revolutions;
Yet one achieved, to that art true,
Nor would'st begin to change anew:
Know this,
Thou think'st amiss;
Deem, to think true,
All constitutions bad but those bran new.

ANONYMOUS

It has not been possible to identify the author of this parody,
published in the *Anti-Jacobin* in July 1798.

JONATHAN SWIFT (1667–1745)

from The Parson's Case

Thy curate's place, thy fruitful wife,
Thy busy, drudging scene of life,
Thy insolent illit'rate vicar,
Thy want of all-consoling liquor,
Thy thread-bare gown, thy cassock rent,
Thy credit sunk, thy money spent,
Thy week made up of fasting days,
Thy grate unconscious of a blaze,
And, to compleat thy other curses,
The quarterly demands of nurses,
Are ills you wisely wish to leave,
And fly for refuge to the grave:
And, O what virtue you express
In wishing such afflictions less!
But, now shou'd fortune shift the scene,
And make thy curate-ship a dean;
Or some rich benefice provide,
To pamper luxury and pride;
With labour small, and income great;
With chariot less for use than state;
With swelling scarf, and glossy gown,
And license to reside in town;
To shine, where all the gay resort,
At consort, coffeehouse, or court;
And weekly persecute his grace
With visits, or to beg a place;
With underlings thy flock to teach,
With no desire to pray or preach;
With haughty spouse in vesture fine,
With plenteous meals, and gen'rous wine;
Wou'dst thou not wish, in so much ease,
Thy years as num'rous as thy days?

The Happy Life of a Country Parson

Parson, these things in thy possessing
Are better than the bishop's blessing:
A wife that makes conserves; a steed
That carries double when there's need;
October store, and best Virginia,
Tithe-pig, and mortuary guinea;
Gazettes sent gratis down, and frank'd;
For which thy patron's meekly thank'd;
A large Concordance, bound long since;
Sermons to Charles the First, when Prince;
A chronicle of ancient standing;
A Chrysostom to smooth thy band in;
The Polyglott – three parts – my text:
Howbeit, – likewise – now to my next:
Lo here the Septuagint, – and Paul,
To sum the whole, – and close of all.
He that has these, may pass his life,
Drink with the Squire, and kiss his wife;
On Sundays preach, and eat his fill;
And fast on Fridays – if he will;
Toast Church and Queen, explain the news,
Talk with churchwardens about pews,
Pray heartily for some new gift,
And shake his head at Doctor Swift.

ALEXANDER POPE

ALGERNON CHARLES SWINBURNE (1837–1909)

from Dolores

O lips full of lust and of laughter,
  Curled snakes that are fed from my breast,
Bite hard, lest remembrance come after
  And press with new lips where you pressed.
For my heart too springs up at the pressure,
  Mine eyelids too moisten and burn;
Ah, feed me and fill me with pleasure,
  Ere pain come in turn.

*

Cold eyelids that hide like a jewel
  Hard eyes that grow soft for an hour;
The heavy white limbs, and the cruel
  Red mouth like a venomous flower;
When these are gone by with their glories,
  What shall rest of thee then, what remain,
O mystic and sombre Dolores,
  Our Lady of Pain?

*

Fruits fail and love dies and time ranges;
  Thou art fed with perpetual breath,
And alive after infinite changes,
  And fresh from the kisses of death;
Of languors rekindled and rallied,
  Of barren delights and unclean,
Things monstrous and fruitless, a pallid
  And poisonous queen.

*

Octopus

(Written at the Crystal Palace Aquarium)

Strange beauty, eight-limbed and eight-handed,
    Whence camest to dazzle our eyes?
With thy bosom bespangled and banded
    With the hues of the seas and the skies;
Is thy home European or Asian,
    O mystical monster marine?
Part molluscous and partly crustacean,
    Betwixt and between.

Wast thou born to the sound of sea-trumpets?
    Hast thou eaten and drunk to excess
Of the sponges – thy muffins and crumpets,
    Of the seaweed – thy mustard and cress?
Wast thou nurtured in caverns of coral,
    Remote from reproof or restraint?
Art thou innocent, art thou immoral,
    Sinburnian or Saint?

Lithe limbs, curling free, as a creeper
    That creeps in a desolate place,
To enrol and envelop the sleeper
    In a silent and stealthy embrace,
Cruel beak craning forward to bite us,
    Our juices to drain and to drink,
Or to whelm us in waves of Cocytus,
    Indelible ink!

A breast, that 'twere rapture to writhe on!
    O arms 'twere delicious to feel

By the ravenous teeth that have smitten
   Through the kisses that blossom and bud,
By the lips intertwisted and bitten
   Till the foam has a savour of blood,
By the pulse as it rises and falters,
   By the hands as they slacken and strain,
I adjure thee, respond from thine altars,
   Our Lady of Pain.

    *

Dost thou dream of what was and no more is,
   The old kingdoms of earth and the kings?
Dost thou hunger for these things, Dolores,
   For these, in a world of new things?
But thy bosom no fasts could emaciate,
   No hunger compel to complain
Those lips that no bloodshed could satiate,
   Our Lady of Pain.

I have selected just five stanzas from one of Swinburne's most
notorious poems, a long-drawn-out exercise in masochistic
delirium. It goes on for pages, demonstrating Swinburne's endless
and absurd erotic fluency.

Clinging close with the crush of the Python,
    When she maketh her murderous meal!
In thy eight-fold embraces enfolden,
    Let our empty existence escape;
Give us death that is glorious and golden,
    Crushed all out of shape!

Ah! thy red lips, lascivious and luscious,
    With death in their amorous kiss!
Cling round us, and clasp us, and crush us,
    With bitings of agonized bliss;
We are sick with the poison of pleasure,
    Dispense us the potion of pain;
Ope thy mouth to its uttermost measure
    And bite us again!

A. C. HILTON

Arthur Clement Hilton (1851–77) was a don at Cambridge, where
he published a magazine called the *Light Green* as a counterblast
to the more solemn one from Oxford, the *Dark Blue*. He was
ordained in 1874, but died just over two years later, leaving behind
him some of the finest parodies of the nineteenth century.

from Itylus

Swallow, my sister, O sister swallow,
　How can thine heart be full of the spring?
　　A thousand summers are over and dead.
What hast thou found in the spring to follow?
　What hast thou found in thine heart to sing?
　　What wilt thou do when the summer is shed?

O swallow, sister, O fair swift swallow,
　Why wilt thou fly after spring to the south,
　　The soft south whither thine heart is set?
Shall not the grief of the old time follow?
　Shall not the song thereof cleave to thy mouth?
　　Hast thou forgotten ere I forget?

Sister Swallow to Swinburne

Swinburne, old Swinburne, silly old Swinburne,
    Sing me no more of that sisterly stuff!
Slink off to the city where women in sin burn,
    Swallows have swallowed enough.
And as for that songbird which 'Itys' repeats,
It is tired of providing poetical treats,
It is miffed about Milton and curt about Keats,
    And feels it is time to be tough.

For I'll tell you, poor poets, we're all simply sick of
    This maudlin approach to our practical schemes;
You clutch at a straw to make cultural brick of
    And build a pagoda of dreams,
While all that inspires our spectacular flights
Or the music that moves you on midsummer nights
Is our lust to maintain territorial rights
    With a barrage of bellicose screams.

MARY HOLTBY

NAHUM TATE (1652–1715) and
NICHOLAS BRADY (1659–1726)

from 'While shepherds watch'd their flocks by night'

While shepherds watch'd their flocks by night,
All seated on the ground,
The Angel of the Lord came down,
And glory shone around.

'Fear not,' said he, for mighty dread
Had seized their troubled mind;
'Glad tidings of great joy I bring
To you and all mankind.'

'While shepherds watched their flocks by night'

While shepherds watched their flocks by night,
All seated on the ground,
A high-explosive shell came down,
And mutton rained around.

H. H. MUNRO

Hector Hugh Munro (1870–1916) was better known as 'Saki'. In 1914 he enlisted as a private soldier in the Royal Fusiliers and kept his spirits up by writing amusing sketches for the *Westminster Gazette* and bogus letters, purporting to be from his 'Aunt Agatha', to a puzzled fellow soldier. He sent this revised Christmas greeting to his sister Ethel. Shortly afterwards, during a night march on Beaumont-Hamel, Lance-Sergeant Munro shouted to one of his men, 'Put that bloody cigarette out!' They were his last words, for a German sniper got him.

JANE TAYLOR (1783–1824)

from The Star

Twinkle, twinkle, little star,
How I wonder what you are!
Up above the world so high,
Like a diamond in the sky.

Jane Taylor and her sister Ann were the authors of *Original Poems for Infant Minds*, which appeared in 1804. In its direct appeal to juvenile sensibilities, the book was something of a revolution in children's literature and, with its successors, proved immensely popular. Although the tone of the Taylors' poems, with their pious sentiments and 'awful warnings', lent them to ridicule, 'The Star' is a relatively inoffensive item to have incurred Lewis Carroll's mockery.

'Twinkle, twinkle, little bat!'

Twinkle, twinkle, little bat!
How I wonder what you're at!
Up above the world you fly,
Like a teatray in the sky.

LEWIS CARROLL

ALFRED, LORD TENNYSON (1809–92)

The Charge of the Light Brigade

Half a league, half a league,
  Half a league onward,
All in the valley of Death
  Rode the six hundred.
'Forward, the Light Brigade!
Charge for the guns!' he said:
Into the valley of Death
  Rode the six hundred.

'Forward, the Light Brigade!'
Was there a man dismayed?
Not though the soldier knew
  Someone had blundered:
Their's not to make reply,
Their's not to reason why,
Their's but to do and die:
Into the valley of Death
  Rode the six hundred.

Cannon to right of them,
Cannon to left of them,
Cannon in front of them
  Volleyed and thundered;
Stormed at with shot and shell,
Boldly they rode and well,
Into the jaws of Death,
Into the mouth of Hell
  Rode the six hundred.

Flashed all their sabres bare,
Flashed as they turned in air
Sabring the gunners there,

The Charge of the Bread Brigade

From *The poems of Alfred Venison, the Poet of Titchfield Street*

Half a loaf, half a loaf,
Half a loaf? Um-hum?
Down through the vale of gloom
Slouched the ten million,
    Onward th' 'ungry blokes,
    Crackin' their smutty jokes!
We'll send 'em mouchin' 'ome,
Damn the ten million!

There goes the night brigade,
They got no steady trade,
Several old so'jers know
    Monty has blunder'd.
Theirs not to reason why,
Theirs but to buy the pie,
Slouching and mouching,
    Lousy ten million!

Plenty to right of 'em,
Plenty to left of 'em,
    Yes, wot is left of 'em,
Damn the ten million.
Stormed at by press and all,
How shall we dress 'em all?
    Glooming and mouching!

See 'em go slouching there,
With cowed and crouching air
    Dundering dullards!

Charging an army, while
   All the world wondered:
Plunged in the battery-smoke
Right through the line they broke;
Cossack and Russian
Reeled from the sabre-stroke
   Shattered and sundered.
Then they rode back, but not
   Not the six hundred.

Cannon to right of them,
Cannon to left of them,
Cannon behind them
   Volleyed and thundered;
Stormed at with shot and shell,
While horse and hero fell,
They that had fought so well
Came through the jaws of Death,
Back from the mouth of Hell,
All that was left of them,
   Left of six hundred.

When can their glory fade?
O the wild charge they made!
   All the world wondered.
Honour the charge they made!
Honour the Light Brigade,
   Noble six hundred!

How the whole nation shook
While Milord Beaverbrook
  Fed 'em with hogwash!

EZRA POUND

The Village Choir

Half a bar, half a bar,
Half a bar onward!
Into an awful ditch
Choir and precentor hitch,
Into a mess of pitch,
  They led the Old Hundred.
Trebles to right of them,
Tenors to left of them,
Basses in front of them,
  Bellowed and thundered.
Oh, that precentor's look,
When the sopranos took
Their own time and hook
  From the Old Hundred!

Screeched all the trebles here,
Boggled the tenors there,
Raising the parson's hair,
  While his mind wandered;
Theirs not to reason why
This psalm was pitched too high:
Theirs but to gasp and cry
  Out the Old Hundred.
Trebles to right of them,
Tenors to left of them,
Basses in front of them,
  Bellowed and thundered.

from In Memoriam

I hold it true, whate'er befall;
    I feel it, when I sorrow most;
    'Tis better to have loved and lost
Than never to have loved at all.

Stormed they with shout and yell,
Not wise they sang nor well,
Drowning the sexton's bell,
   While all the Church wondered.

Dire the precentor's glare,
Flashed his pitchfork in air
Sounding fresh keys to bear
   Out the Old Hundred.
Swiftly he turned his back,
Reached he his hat from rack,
Then from the screaming pack,
   Himself he sundered.
Tenors to right of him,
Tenors to left of him,
Discords behind him,
   Bellowed and thundered.
Oh, the wild howls they wrought:
Right to the end they fought!
Some tune they sang, but not,
   Not the Old Hundred.

                    ANONYMOUS

Footnote to Tennyson

I feel it when the game is done,
I feel it when I suffer most.
'Tis better to have loved and lost
Than ever to have loved and won.

                 GERALD BULLETT

from Maud; A Monodrama

Come into the garden, Maud,
  For the black bat, night, has flown,
Come into the garden, Maud,
  I am here at the gate alone;
And the woodbine spices are wafted abroad,
  And the musk of the rose is blown.

For a breeze of morning moves,
  And the planet of Love is on high,
Beginning to faint in the light that she loves
  On a bed of daffodil sky,
To faint in the light of the sun she loves,
  To faint in his light, and to die.

All night have the roses heard
  The flute, violin, bassoon;
All night has the casement jessamine stirred
  To the dancers dancing in tune;
Till a silence fell with the waking bird,
  And a hush with the setting moon.

I said to the lily, 'There is but one
  With whom she has heart to be gay.
When will the dancers leave her alone?
  She is weary of dance and play.'
Now half to the setting moon are gone,
  And half to the rising day;
Low on the sand and loud on the stone
  The last wheel echoes away.

                *

Queen rose of the rosebud garden of girls,
  Come hither, the dances are done,
In gloss of satin and glimmer of pearls,

Come into the Army, Maud

A.T.S. Adventure Through Service – *Daily advertisement.*

Come into the Army, Maud,
Your hours of ease are flown,
Get into the Army, Maud,
They are waiting for you alone,
And the word of command has been wafted abroad
And the fall-in finally blown.

You were blind to the ads. in the daily Press,
So they got you, sweet, on the run;
You would not pop into your battle-dress,
Though the War Office said it was fun;
You would not become an adventuress
In the ranks of adventurous A.T.S.,
Where brave girls cook for the Sergeants' Mess
And the batwoman busily bats.

You have failed to volunteer
So at last you have met your fate;
There has risen a splendid cheer
From the Commons holding debate.
The Air Force cried, 'She is near, she is near!'
But the War Office muttered, 'We wait!'
The Navy trolled, 'She is here, she is here!'
But the Army barked, 'She is late!'

Queen weed in the garden of Service girls,
You may sigh the whole war through
For gloss of ermine and glamour of pearls,
Or even a uniform blue.
De-rouge the nails, bind up the curls,
And into the A.T.S. with you!

SAGITTARIUS, December 1941

Queen lily and rose in one;
Shine out, little head, sunning over with curls,
   To the flowers, and be their sun.

There has fallen a splendid tear
   From the passion-flower at the gate.
She is coming, my dove, my dear;
   She is coming, my life, my fate;
The red rose cries, 'She is near, she is near;'
   And the white rose weeps, 'She is late;'
The larkspur listens, 'I hear, I hear;'
   And the lily whispers, 'I wait.'

She is coming, my own, my sweet,
   Were it ever so airy a tread,
My heart would hear her and beat,
   Were it earth in an earthy bed;
My dust would hear her and beat,
   Had I lain for a century dead;
Would start and tremble under her feet,
   And blossom in purple and red.

Whenceness of the Which

Come into the Whenceness Which,
  For the fierce Because has flown:
Come into the Whenceness Which,
  I am here by the Where alone;
And the Whereas odours are wafted abroad
  Till I hold my nose and groan.

Queen Which of the Whichbud garden of What's
  Come hither the jig is done.
In gloss of Isness and shimmer of Was,
  Queen Thisness and Which is one;
Shine out, little Which, sunning over the bangs,
  To the Nowness, and be its sun.

There has fallen a splendid tear
  From the Is flower at the fence;
She is coming, my Which, my dear,
  And as she Whistles a song of the Whence,
The Nowness cries, 'She is near, she is near.'
  And the Thingness howls, 'Alas!'
The Whoness murmurs, 'Well, I should smile,'
  And the Whatlet sobs, 'I pass.'

ANONYMOUS

'Come into the orchard, Anne'

Come into the orchard, Anne,
  For the dark owl, Night, has fled,
And Phosphor slumbers, as well as he can
  With a daffodil sky for a bed:
And the musk of the roses perplexes a man,
  And the pimpernel muddles his head.

ALGERNON CHARLES SWINBURNE

from Ode on the Death of the Duke of Wellington

I

Bury the Great Duke
    With an empire's lamentation,
Let us bury the Great Duke
    To the noise of the mourning of a mighty nation,
Mourning when their leaders fall,
Warriors carry the warrior's pall,
And sorrow darkens hamlet and hall.

2

Where shall we lay the man whom we deplore?
Here, in streaming London's central roar.
Let the sound of those he wrought for,
And the feet of those he fought for,
Echo round his bones for evermore.

3

Lead out the pageant: sad and slow,
As fits an universal woe,
Let the long long procession go,
And let the sorrowing crowd about it grow,
And let the mournful martial music blow;
The last great Englishman is low.

4

Mourn, for to us he seems the last,
Remembering all his greatness in the Past.
No more in soldier fashion will he greet
With lifted hand the gazer in the street.
O friends, our chief state-oracle is mute:
Mourn for the man of long-enduring blood,
The statesman-warrior, moderate, resolute,
Whole in himself, a common good.

*

from *Ode on the Death of Haig's Horse*

'The late Earl Haig's charger is dead. This famous old horse, on
which the field-marshal rode in France during the war, and which
walked in his funeral procession, has been shot at the royal stables,
where it was housed. It was suffering from pneumonia.

'Lady Haig told a *Daily Mail* reporter last night that a model of
the charger was made before its death.' — (*The Daily Mail*,
December 1929.)

I

Bury the Great Horse
With all clubdom's lamentation,
Let us bury the Great Horse
To the noise of the mourning of a horsy nation:
Mourning when their darlings fall,
Colonels carry the charger's pall,
And critics gather in smoke-room and stall.

II

Where shall we raise the statue they demand?
One in every home throughout the land.
Only thus shall all who saw him,
All who wrote long letters for him,
Recognise the work their fancy planned.

III

Set up the statue: dull and staid,
As fits an all too common jade,
Lo! our slow, slow decision's made,
And now the carping critics are dismayed
And now the public's piddling taste's displayed;
Another civic statue's made.

5

All is over and done:
Render thanks to the Giver,
England, for thy son.
Let the bell be toll'd.
Render thanks to the Giver,
And render him to the mould.
Under the cross of gold
That shines over city and river,
There he shall rest for ever
Among the wise and the bold.
Let the bell be toll'd:
And a reverent people behold
The towering car, the sable steeds:
Bright let it be with his blazon'd deeds,
Dark in its funeral fold.
Let the bell be toll'd:

*

7

A people's voice! we are a people yet.
Tho' all men else their nobler dreams forget
Confused by brainless mobs and lawless Powers;
Thank Him who isled us here, and roughly set
His Saxon in blown seas and storming showers,
We have a voice, with which to pay the debt
Of boundless love and reverence and regret
To those great men who fought, and kept it ours.
And keep it ours, O God, from brute control;
O Statesmen, guard us, guard the eye, the soul
Of Europe, keep our noble England whole,
And save the one true seed of freedom sown
Betwixt a people and their ancient throne,
That sober freedom out of which there springs
Our loyal passion for our temperate kings . . .

IV

Mourn, for with him we lose our last
Chance to redeem the errors of the past.
No more with dull assurance can we meet,
Pointing to him, our critics-in-the-street.
O friends, our chief art-oracle is mute:
Mourn for the horse of living flesh and blood,
The prototype by which we could refute
All criticism while he stood.

V

Now all's over, of course,
And small thanks to the sculptor,
England, for thy horse.
Let the bronze be cast,
And small thanks to the sculptor:
He's slighted the public taste.
Now that our judgment's passed
They're sure to curse us for ever:
Colonels, to prove themselves clever,
Will damn us, and generals blast.
Let the bronze be cast:
While an angry people, aghast,
Condemn in vain our fatal choice
Strong in the sense of a common voice,
Null, but assured, in taste.
Let the bronze be cast,

*

VII

An army's voice! We have an army yet,
Tho' all men else their warlike dreams forget,
Confused by arty snobs and high-brow Powers;
Thank Him who isled us here, and roughly set
His Briton in blown froth and storming showers.
They've got a voice, with which to pay the debt

The Merman

I

Who would be
A merman bold,
Sitting alone,
Singing alone
Under the sea,
With a crown of gold,
On a throne?

II

I would be a merman bold,
I would sit and sing the whole of the day;
I would fill the sea-halls with a voice of power;
But at night I would roam abroad and play
With the mermaids in and out of the rocks,
Dressing their hair with the white sea-flower;
And holding them back by their flowing locks
I would kiss them often under the sea,
And kiss them again till they kiss'd me
       Laughingly, laughingly;
And then we would wander away, away

Of boundless hate and ignorance and regret
To those great nags they have preferred to ours —
Preferred to ours, O God, by brute control!
O soldiers, guard us, guard the pride, the soul
Of England, keep our equine honour whole
By saving one true steed of freedom, known
To cheer the people and our aged throne —
This gallant horseflesh out of which there springs
Our loyal passion for our tasteless kings.

DOUGLAS GARMAN

from *The Laureate*

Who would not be
The Laureate bold,
With his butt of sherry
To keep him merry,
And nothing to do but to pocket his gold?

'Tis I would be the Laureate bold!
When the days are hot, and the sun is strong,
I'd lounge in the gateway all the day long
With her Majesty's footmen in crimson and gold.
I'd care not a pin for the waiting-lord,
But I'd lie on my back on the smooth greensward
With a straw in my mouth, and an open vest,
And the cool wind blowing upon my breast,
And I'd vacantly stare at the clear blue sky,
And watch the clouds that are listless as I,
        Lazily, lazily!

Then the chambermaids, that clean the rooms,
Would come to the windows and rest on their brooms,
With their saucy caps and their crispèd hair,
And they'd toss their heads in the fragrant air,

To the pale-green sea-groves straight and high,
　　Chasing each other merrily.

III
There would be neither moon nor star;
But the wave would make music above us afar –
Low thunder and light in the magic night –
　　Neither moon nor star.
We would call aloud in the dreamy dells,
Call to each other and whoop and cry
　　All night, merrily, merrily;
They would pelt me with starry spangles and shells,
Laughing and clapping their hands between,
　　All night, merrily, merrily:
But I would throw to them back in mine
Turkis and agate and almondine:
Then leaping out upon them unseen
I would kiss them often under the sea,
And kiss them again till they kiss'd me
　　Laughingly, laughingly.
Oh! what a happy life were mine
Under the hollow-hung ocean green!
Soft are the moss-beds under the sea;
We would live merrily, merrily.

William Aytoun (1813–65) was a Scottish lawyer and literary
dilettante. He collaborated with the Reverend Theodore Martin to
produce, under the joint pseudonym of 'Bon Gaultier', A Book of
Ballads in which many of their most eminent contemporaries were
accurately parodied. Here Aytoun turns one of Tennyson's juvenile
effusions against the Establishment figure the latter had become in
middle age.

And say to each other – 'Just look down there,
At the nice young man, so tidy and small,
Who is paid for writing on nothing at all,
　　　Handsomely, handsomely!'

They would pelt me with matches and sweet pastilles,
And crumpled-up balls of the royal bills,
Giggling and laughing, and screaming with fun,
As they'd see me start, with a leap and a run,
From the broad of my back to the points of my toes,
When a pellet of paper hit my nose,
　　　Teasingly, sneezingly!

Then I'd fling them bunches of garden flowers,
And hyacinths plucked from the Castle bowers;
And I'd challenge them all to come down to me,
And I'd kiss them all till they kissed me,
　　　Laughingly, laughingly.

Oh, would not that be a merry life,
Apart from care and apart from strife,
With the Laureate's wine, and the Laureate's pay,
And no deductions at quarter-day?
Oh, that would be the post for me!
With plenty to get and nothing to do,
But to deck a pet poodle with ribbons of blue,
And whistle a tune to the Queen's cockatoo,
And scribble of verses remarkably few,
And empty at evening a bottle or two,
　　　Quaffingly, quaffingly!

　　　　　'Tis I would be
　　　　　The Laureate bold,
　　　　　With my butt of sherry
　　　　　To keep me merry,
　　　And nothing to do but to pocket my gold!

　　　　　　　WILLIAM AYTOUN

DYLAN THOMAS (1914–53)

'Do not go gentle into that good night'

Do not go gentle into that good night,
Old age should burn and rave at close of day;
Rage, rage against the dying of the light.

Though wise men at their end know dark is right,
Because their words had forked no lightning they
Do not go gentle into that good night.

Good men, the last wave by, crying how bright
Their frail deeds might have danced in a green bay,
Rage, rage against the dying of the light.

Wild men who caught and sang the sun in flight,
And learn, too late, they grieved it on its way,
Do not go gentle into that good night.

Grave men, near death, who see with blinding sight
Blind eyes could blaze like meteors and be gay,
Rage, rage against the dying of the light.

And you, my father, there on the sad height,
Curse, bless, me now with your fierce tears, I pray.
Do not go gentle into that good night.
Rage, rage against the dying of the light.

Do Not Go Sober

Do not go sober into that dim light.
Young bards should burp and belch at end of day;
Rage, rage against that crabby, Abbey site.

Though poets at their end know wrong is right
Because their words have left them legless they
Do not go sober into that dim light.

Good men, who know what sweat it is to write,
And cheat and sponge and get their end away
Rage, rage against that crabby, Abbey site.

Wild men who did their best when they were tight
And languished when they kept the booze at bay
Do not go sober into that dim light.

Grave men, now dead, who know, as well they might,
Memorial plaques diminish human clay,
Rage, rage against that crabby, Abbey site.

And you, Lord Byron, lying on my right,
Proving that dissolution rules OK,
Do not go sober into that dim light.
Rage, rage against that crabby, Abbey site.

                              ROGER WODDIS

Written on the occasion of Dylan Thomas's being granted a
memorial in Westminster Abbey.

from Poem in October

It was my thirtieth year to heaven
Woke to my hearing from harbour and neighbour wood
    And the mussel pooled and the heron
        Priested shore
      The morning beckon

With water praying and call of seagull and rook
And the knock of sailing boats on the net webbed wall
    Myself to set foot
      That second
    In the still sleeping town and set forth.

Christopher Robin Changes Guard
with Dylan Thomas

It was my fifth year to heaven
Palm of my charmed hand in the nook of nurse's fingers
    And the palace palings by busby head in
        Pointed shelter
    The guard hardened fast though still lingers
The lips of nurse on his pursed face as long legs drill
To march at charge of sock-sergeant's changing call
        While helter-skelter
Scribbles the busy king in depth of the palace's sea
    With a wrong face to falter
On the salt lip of a distant window sill
Until Time grips my wrist to wheel us back to a bleating
    tea.

                                        BILL GREENWELL

EDWARD THOMAS (1878–1917)

Adlestrop

Yes. I remember Adlestrop –
The name, because one afternoon
Of heat the express-train drew up there
Unwontedly. It was late June.

The steam hissed. Someone cleared his throat.
No one left and no one came
On the bare platform. What I saw
Was Adlestrop – only the name

And willows, willow-herb, and grass,
And meadowsweet, and haycocks dry,
No whit less still and lonely fair
Than the high cloudlets in the sky.

And for that minute a blackbird sang
Close by, and round him, mistier,
Farther and farther, all the birds
Of Oxfordshire and Gloucestershire.

Willesden Gree

Yes, I remember WILLESDEN GREE.
(That's what it said, the night the train,
Somewhere along the Jubilee,
Pulled up, and failed to start again.)

We sat in silence, face to face
(For that is what the British do),
While over all the air, apace,
Stole twilight scents of North-West Two.

But as I looked, I grew aware
Not everything outside was dark;
In each back room, a livid square –
The telly-screens of Brondesbury Park!

And lo! at that I seemed to sense
An age-old stirring in my side –
The nation's heart, benign, immense,
At one, in thrall to *Nationwide*.

JIMMIE PEARSE

JAMES THOMSON (1700–1748)

from On Beauty

This happy place with all delights abounds,
And plenty broods upon the fertile grounds . . .
The nibbling flock stray o'er the rising hills,
And all around with bleating music fills;
High on their fronts tall blooming forests nod,
Of sylvan deities the blest abode;
The feathered minstrels hop from spray to spray,
And chant their gladsome carols all the day,
Till dusky night, advancing in her car,
Makes with declining light successful war.

from Of a Country Life

How sweet and innocent are country sports,
And, as men's tempers, various are their sorts.
    You, on the banks of soft meandering Tweed,
May in your toils ensnare the watery breed,
And nicely lead the artificial flee,
Which, when the nimble, watchful trout does see,
He at the bearded hook will briskly spring;
Then in that instant twitch your hairy string,
And, when he's hooked, you, with a constant hand,
May draw him struggling to the fatal land.
    Then at fit seasons you may clothe your hook
With a sweet bait, dressed by a faithless cook.
The greedy pike darts to't with eager haste,
And, being struck, in vain he flies at last;
He rages, storms, and flounces through the stream,
But all, alas! his life can not redeem.

Jack and Jill

So, up the steep side of the rugged hill,
Companions in adventure, Jack and Jill
With footing nice and anxious effort hale
To the moist pump the necessary pail.
The industrious pair their watery task divide,
And woo the bashful Naiad side by side.
The sturdier swain, for arduous labour planned,
The handle guiding in his practised hand,
With art hydraulic and propulsion stout
Evokes the crystal treasure from the spout,
The maid attentive to the useful flow,
Adjusts the apt receptacle below;
The gelid waves with bright reflections burn,
And mirrored beauty blushes in the urn.
Now down the slope, their task accomplished, they
The liquid plunder of the pump convey,
And seek the level sward; incautious pair!
Too soon, alas, too soon shall ye be there.
The hero first the strong compulsion feels,
And finds his head supplanted by his heels;
In circles whirled he thunders to the plain,
Vain all his efforts, all his language vain,
Vain his laced boots and vain his eyebrow dark,
And vain, ah! vain, his vaccination mark.
The inverted pail his flying form pursues,
With humid tribute and sequacious dews:
(So, through affrighted skies, o'er nations pale,
Behind the comet streams the comet's tail).
The prudent fair, of equilibrium vain,
Views, as he falls, the rotatory swain.
Exhilaration heaves her bosom young,

At other times you may pursue the chase,
And hunt the nimble hare from place to place.
See, when the dog is just upon the grip,
Out at a side she'll make a handsome skip,
And ere he can divert his furious course,
She, far before him, scours with all her force:
She'll shift, and many times run the same ground;
At last, outwearied by the stronger hound,
She falls a sacrifice unto his hate,
And with sad piteous screams laments her fate.
See how the hawk doth take his towering flight,
And in his course outflies our very sight,
Beats down the fluttering fowl with all his might.
See how the wary gunner casts about,
Watching the fittest posture when to shoot:
Quick as the fatal lightning blasts the oak,
He gives the springing fowl a sudden stroke;
He pours upon't a shower of mortal lead,
And ere the noise is heard the fowl is dead.

Tilts the fine nose, protrudes the vermeil tongue,
Bids from her throat the silvery laughters roll
And cachinnations strike the starry pole.
Gnomes! her light foot your envious fingers trip,
And freeze the titter on the ruby lip;
The massy earth with strong attraction draws,
And Venus yields to gravitation's laws;
From rock to rock the charms of Beauty bump,
And shrieks of anguish chill the conscious pump.

A. E. HOUSMAN

Housman's satire is aimed not so much at any single poet as at the
Augustan style in general, with its tendency to long-windedness
and complacency. But Thomson in his juvenilia exhibits its
characteristics as clearly as anyone.

ISAAC WATTS (1674–1748)

from The Sluggard

'Tis the voice of the sluggard, I heard him complain
'You have waked me too soon, I must slumber again.'
As the door on its hinges, so he on his bed,
Turns his sides and his shoulders, and his heavy head.

*

I passed by his garden and saw the wild brier,
The thorn and the thistle, grow broader and higher;
The clothes that hang on him are turning to rags;
And his money still wastes till he starves or he begs.

I made him a visit, still hoping to find
That he took better care for improving his mind.
He told me his dreams, talked of eating and drinking;
But he scarce reads his Bible, and never loves thinking.

Dr Isaac Watts, a dissenting clergyman, published his *Divine Songs Attempted in Easy Language for the Use of Children* in 1715. His *Moral Songs* were added later, and together they became required nursery and schoolroom reading for the best part of a century. Although he was held in the highest esteem in his own day, earned a monument in Westminster Abbey and wrote a number of hymns which are still sung, his fall from eminence in the sphere of children's literature was abrupt and apparently final. He is now probably best known for having given Lewis Carroll the opportunity to parody him.

''Tis the voice of the Lobster'

'Tis the voice of the Lobster; I heard him declare,
'You have baked me too brown, I must sugar my hair.'
As a duck with its eyelids, so he with his nose
Trims his belt and his buttons, and turns out his toes.
When the sands are all dry, he is gay as a lark,
And will talk in contemptuous tones of the Shark:
But, when the tide rises and sharks are around,
His voice has a timid and tremulous sound.

I passed by his garden, and marked, with one eye,
How the Owl and the Panther were sharing a pie:
The Panther took pie-crust, and gravy, and meat,
While the Owl had the dish as its share of the treat.
When the pie was all finished, the Owl, as a boon,
Was kindly permitted to pocket the spoon:
While the Panther received knife and fork with a growl,
And concluded the banquet by —

LEWIS CARROLL

from Against Idleness and Mischief

How doth the little busy bee
  Improve each shining hour,
And gather honey all the day
  From every opening flower!

How skilfully she builds her cell!
  How neat she spreads the wax!
And labours hard to store it well
  With the sweet food she makes.

'How doth the little crocodile'

How doth the little crocodile
   Improve his shining tail,
And pour the waters of the Nile
   On every golden scale!

How cheerfully he seems to grin,
   How neatly spreads his claws,
And welcomes little fishes in
   With gently smiling jaws!

LEWIS CARROLL

WALT WHITMAN (1819–92)

For You O Democracy

Come, I will make the continent indissoluble,
I will make the most splendid race the sun ever shone
   upon,
I will make divine magnetic lands,
        With the love of comrades,
            With the life-long love of comrades.

I will plant companionship thick as trees along all the
   rivers of America, and along the shores of the great
   lakes, and all over the prairies,
I will make inseparable cities with their arms about each
   other's necks,
        By the love of comrades,
            By the manly love of comrades.

For you these from me, O Democracy, to serve you ma
   femme!
For you, for you I am trilling these songs.

from *Variations on an Air*

Me clairvoyant,
Me conscious of you, old camarado,
Needing no telescope, lorgnette, field-glass, opera-glass,
    myopic pince-nez,
Me piercing two thousand years with eye naked and not
    ashamed;
The crown cannot hide you from me;
Musty old feudal-heraldic trappings cannot hide you from
    me,
I perceive that you drink.
(I am drinking with you. I am as drunk as you are.)
I see you are inhaling tobacco, puffing, smoking, spitting
(I do not object to your spitting);
You prophetic of American largeness,
You anticipating the broad masculine manners of these
    States;
I see in you also there are movements, tremors, tears,
    desire for the melodious,
I salute your three violinists, endlessly making vibrations,
Rigid, relentless, capable of going on for ever;
They play my accompaniment; but I shall take no notice
    of any accompaniment;
I myself am a complete orchestra.
So long.

G. K. CHESTERTON

From a set of parodies of a number of poets in which Chesterton
used the nursery rhyme 'Old King Cole' as the theme for his
stylistic variations.

OSCAR WILDE (1854–1900)

from The Ballad of Reading Gaol

I

He did not wear his scarlet coat,
　For blood and wine are red,
And blood and wine were on his hands
　When they found him with the dead,
The poor dead woman whom he loved,
　And murdered in her bed.

*

I never saw a man who looked
　With such a wistful eye
Upon that little tent of blue
　Which prisoners call the sky,
And at every drifting cloud that went
　With sails of silver by.

I walked with other souls in pain,
　Within another ring,
And was wondering if the man had done
　A great or little thing,
When a voice behind me whispered low,
　'That fellow's got to swing.'

Dear Christ! the very prison walls
　Suddenly seemed to reel,
And the sky above my head became
　Like a casque of scorching steel;
And, though I was a soul in pain,
　My pain I could not feel.

*

from *The Gourmand*

He did not wear his swallow tail,
  But a simple dinner coat;
For once his spirits seemed to fail,
  And his fund of anecdote.
His brow was drawn and damp and pale,
  And a lump stood in his throat.

I never saw a person stare,
  With looks so dour and blue,
Upon the square of bill of fare
  We waiters call the 'M'noo',
And at every dainty mentioned there,
  From *entrée* to *ragout*.

With head bent low and cheeks aglow,
  He viewed the groaning board,
For he wondered if the chef would show
  The treasures of his hoard,
When a voice behind him whispered low,
  'Sherry or 'ock, m'lord?'

Gods! What a tumult rent the air,
  As with a frightful oath,
He seized the waiter by the hair,
  And cursed him for his sloth;
Then, grumbling like some stricken bear
  Angrily answered, 'Both!'

For each man drinks the thing he loves,
  As tonic, dram, or drug;
Some do it standing, in their gloves,
  Some seated, from a jug;

Yet each man kills the thing he loves,
   By each let this be heard,
Some do it with a bitter look,
   Some with a flattering word,
The coward does it with a kiss,
   The brave man with a sword!

Some kill their love when they are young,
   And some when they are old;
Some strangle with the hands of Lust,
   Some with the hands of Gold:
The kindest use a knife, because
   The dead so soon grow cold.

Some love too little, some too long,
   Some sell, and others buy;
Some do the deed with many tears,
   And some without a sigh:
For each man kills the thing he loves,
   Yet each man does not die.

He does not die a death of shame
   On a day of dark disgrace,
Nor have a noose about his neck,
   Nor a cloth upon his face,
Nor drop feet foremost through the floor
   Into an empty space.

    *

I I
Six weeks our guardsman walked the yard,
   In the suit of shabby grey:
His cricket cap was on his head,
   And his step seemed light and gay,
But I never saw a man who looked
   So wistfully at the day.

    *

The upper class from thin-stemmed glass,
  The masses from a mug.

    *

Some gorge forsooth in early youth,
  Some wait till they are old;
Some take their fare off earthenware,
  And some from polished gold.
The gourmand gnaws in haste because
  The plates so soon grow cold.

Some eat too swiftly, some too long,
  In restaurant or grill;
Some, when their weak insides go wrong,
  Try a post-prandial pill,
For each man eats his fav'rite meats,
  Yet each man is not ill.

He does not sicken in his bed,
  Through a night of wild unrest,
With a snow-white bandage round his head,
  And a poultice on his breast,
'Neath the nightmare weight of the things he ate
  And omitted to digest.

I know not whether meals be short
  Or whether meals be long;
All that I know of this resort,
  Proves that there's something wrong,
And the soup is weak and tastes of port,
  And the fish is far too strong.

The bread they bake is quite opaque,
  The butter full of hair;
Defunct sardines and flaccid 'greens'
  Are all they give us there.
Such cooking has been known to make
  A common person swear.

    *

He did not wring his hands nor weep,
  Nor did he peek or pine,
But he drank the air as though it held
  Some healthful anodyne;
With open mouth he drank the sun
  As though it had been wine!

    *

V

I know not whether Laws be right,
  Or whether Laws be wrong;
All that we know who lie in gaol
  Is that the wall is strong;
And that each day is like a year,
  A year whose days are long.

    *

The vilest deeds like poison weeds,
  Bloom well in prison-air;
It is only what is good in Man
  That wastes and withers there:
Pale Anguish keeps the heavy gate,
  And the Warder is Despair.

    *

VI

And all men kill the thing they love,
  By all let this be heard,
Some do it with a bitter look,
  Some with a flattering word,
The coward does it with a kiss,
  The brave man with a sword!

To dance to flutes, to dance to lutes,
    Is a pastime rare and grand;
But to eat of fish, or fowl, or fruits
    To a Blue Hungarian Band
Is a thing that suits nor men nor brutes,
    As the world should understand.

*

Six times a table here he booked,
    Six times he sat and scanned
The list of dishes badly cooked
    By the chef's unskilful hand;
And I never saw a man who looked
    So wistfully at the band.

He did not swear or tear his hair,
    But drank up wine galore,
As though it were some vintage rare
    From an old Falernian store;
With open mouth he slaked his drouth,
    And loudly called for more.

He was the type that waiters know,
    Who simply lives to feed,
Who little cares what food we show
    If it be food indeed,
And, when his appetite is low,
    Falls back upon his greed.

For each man eats his fav'rite meats,
    (Provided by his wife);
Or cheese or chalk, or peas or pork,
    (For such, alas! is life!).
The rich man eats them with a fork,
    The poor man with a knife.

HARRY GRAHAM

CHARLES WOLFE (1791–1823)

The Burial of Sir John Moore after Corunna

Not a drum was heard, not a funeral note,
   As his corpse to the rampart we hurried;
Not a soldier discharged his farewell shot
   O'er the grave where our hero we buried.

We buried him darkly at dead of night,
   The sods with our bayonets turning,
By the struggling moonbeam's misty light
   And the lanthorn dimly burning.

No useless coffin enclosed his breast,
   Not in sheet or in shroud we wound him;
But he lay like a warrior taking his rest
   With his martial cloak around him.

Few and short were the prayers we said,
   And we spoke not a word of sorrow;
But we steadfastly gazed on the face that was dead,
   And we bitterly thought of the morrow.

We thought, as we hollowed his narrow bed
   And smoothed down his lonely pillow,
That the foe and the stranger would tread o'er his head,
   And we far away on the billow!

Lightly they'll talk of the spirit that's gone,
   And o'er his cold ashes upbraid him –
But little he'll reck, if they let him sleep on
   In the grave where a Briton has laid him.

But half of our heavy task was done
   When the clock struck the hour for retiring;
And we heard the distant and random gun
   That the foe was sullenly firing.

Not a Sous Had He Got

Not a *sous* had he got, – not a guinea or note,
    And he look'd confoundedly flurried,
As he bolted away without paying his shot,
    And the Landlady after him hurried.

We saw him again at dead of night,
    When home from the Club returning;
We twigg'd the Doctor beneath the light
    Of the gas-lamp brilliantly burning.

All bare, and exposed to the midnight dews,
    Reclined in the gutter we found him;
And he look'd like a gentleman taking a snooze,
    With his *Marshall* cloak around him.

'The Doctor's as drunk as the d—,' we said,
    And we managed a shutter to borrow;
We raised him, and sigh'd at the thought that his head
    Would 'consumedly ache' on the morrow.

We bore him home, and we put him to bed,
    And we told his wife and his daughter
To give him, next morning, a couple of red
    Herrings, with soda-water.

Loudly they talk'd of his money that's gone,
    And his Lady began to upbraid him;
But little he reck'd, so they let him snore on
    'Neath the counterpane just as we laid him.

We tuck'd him in, and had hardly done
    When, beneath the window calling,
We heard the rough voice of a son of a gun
    Of a watchman 'One o'clock!' bawling.

Slowly and sadly we laid him down,
    From the field of his fame fresh and gory;
We carved not a line, and we raised not a stone,
    But we left him alone with his glory.

After an incident in Spain which might be described as the Dunkirk
of the Peninsular War. Sir John Moore commanded an
outnumbered British army, forced to retreat by the unexpected
arrival on the scene of Napoleon and a force of 200,000 French
veterans.

Slowly and sadly we all walk'd down
   From his room in the uppermost story;
A rushlight we placed on the cold hearth-stone,
   And we left him alone in his glory.

R. H. BARHAM

R. H. Barham (1788–1845), a churchman, was also the author of
the enormously popular volume, *The Ingoldsby Legends*.

WILLIAM WORDSWORTH (1770–1850)

'She dwelt among the untrodden ways'

She dwelt among the untrodden ways
     Beside the springs of Dove,
A maid whom there were none to praise
     And very few to love:

A violet by a mossy stone
     Half hidden from the eye!
Fair as a star, when only one
     Is shining in the sky.

She lived unknown, and few could know
     When Lucy ceased to be;
But she is in her grave, and, oh,
     The difference to me!

London, 1802

Milton! thou shouldst be living at this hour:
England hath need of thee: she is a fen
Of stagnant waters: altar, sword, and pen,
Fireside, the heroic wealth of hall and bower,

He Lived amidst th' Untrodden Ways

He lived amidst th' untrodden ways
  To Rydal Lake that lead;
A bard whom there were none to praise,
  And very few to read.

Behind a cloud his mystic sense,
  Deep hidden, who can spy?
Bright as the night when not a star
  Is shining in the sky.

Unread his works – his 'Milk White Doe'
  With dust is dark and dim;
It's still in Longman's shop, and oh!
  The difference to him!

HARTLEY COLERIDGE

Hartley Coleridge (1796–1849) was the eldest son of Samuel
Taylor Coleridge. He was unsuccessful as a schoolmaster and went
to live in the Lake District, where he wrote minor poetry. In this
sharp piece, he turns on his father's old friend and co-author of
Lyrical Ballads, the revolutionary collection of poems which in
1798 signalled the birth of the Romantic movement in literature.

Sonnet to the 'Most Distinguished Chancellor' that Oxford Has Had

Curzon! thou shouldst be living at this hour;
Harold hath need of thee; the Viscount Cave,
Plodding through parchments down into the grave,
Takes not his fancy, and he sees thee tower

Have forfeited their ancient English dower
Of inward happiness. We are selfish men;
Oh! raise us up, return to us again;
And give us manners, virtue, freedom, power.
Thy soul was like a Star, and dwelt apart;
Thou hadst a voice whose sound was like the sea:
Pure as the naked heavens, majestic, free,
So didst thou travel on life's common way,
In cheerful godliness; and yet thy heart
The lowliest duties on herself did lay.

from Resolution and Independence

Now, whether it were by peculiar grace,
A leading from above, a something given,
Yet it befell, that, in this lonely place,
When I with these untoward thoughts had striven,
Beside a pool bare to the eye of heaven
I saw a man before me unawares:
The oldest man he seemed that ever wore grey hairs.

*

High o'er that dallier in Amanda's bower,
The so-called Iron Duke; we hear him rave
Against the folly that to Oxford gave
A sad old Cecil's presence for her dower.
Thy soul was like a Star, and like a Garter;
Thy brow was as a great calm Eagle's egg,
And, like Sir Willoughby, thou hadst a leg;
So didst thou awe earth, sky, clouds, azure main;
And Harold would incontinently barter
His pure young soul to see thee rise again.

MAX BEERBOHM

Beerbohm wrote this shortly after Lord Cave had defeated Asquith
in the election to the Chancellorship of Oxford University in 1925.
He sent it to Harold Nicolson, who was to write a study of
Curzon, Chancellor from 1907 to 1925. He refers to two former
prime ministers who had also held that post, the Duke of
Wellington (1834–52) and Robert Cecil, Marquis of Salisbury
(1869–1903). Sir Willoughby was a character in Meredith's *The
Egoist*. Asquith is not the only Prime Minister to have been
defeated for the Chancellorship: Edward Heath lost to Roy Jenkins
in 1986. Curzon was much caricatured by Beerbohm, for he had
great style and presence, but he never became Prime Minister,
losing to Stanley Baldwin.

'I'll tell thee everything I can'

I'll tell thee everything I can:
    There's little to relate.
I saw an aged aged man,
    A-sitting on a gate.
'Who are you, aged man?' I said.
    'And how is it you live?'
And his answer trickled through my head,
    Like water through a sieve.

Such seemed this Man, not all alive not dead,
Nor all asleep – in his extreme old age:
His body was bent double, feet and head
Coming together in life's pilgrimage;
As if some dire constraint of pain, or rage
Of sickness felt by him in times long past,
A more than human weight upon his frame had cast.

A gentle answer did the old Man make,
In courteous speech which forth he slowly drew;
And him with further words I thus bespake,
'What occupation do you there pursue?
This is a lonesome place for one like you.'
Ere he replied, a flash of mild surprise
Broke from the sable orbs of his yet vivid eyes.

    *

His words came feebly, from a feeble chest,
But each in solemn order followed each,
With something of a lofty utterance drest –
Choice word and measured phrase, above the reach
Of ordinary men; a stately speech;
Such as grave Livers do in Scotland use,
Religious men, who give to God and man their dues.

He told, that to these waters he had come,
To gather leeches, being old and poor:
Employment hazardous and wearisome!
And he had many hardships to endure:
From pond to pond he roamed, from moor to moor;
Housing, with God's good help, by choice or chance,
And in this way he gained an honest maintenance.

He said 'I look for butterflies
   That sleep among the wheat:
I make them into mutton-pies,
   And sell them in the street.
I sell them unto men,' he said,
   'Who sail on stormy seas;
And that's the way I get my bread —
   A trifle, if you please.'

But I was thinking of a plan
   To dye one's whiskers green,
And always use so large a fan
   That they could not be seen.
So, having no reply to give
   To what the old man said,
I cried 'Come, tell me how you live!'
   And thumped him on the head.

His accents mild took up the tale:
   He said 'I go my ways,
And when I find a mountain-rill,
   I set it in a blaze;
And thence they make a stuff they call
   Rowland's Macassar-Oil —
Yet twopence-halfpenny is all
   They give me for my toil.'

But I was thinking of a way
   To feed oneself on batter,
And so go on from day to day
   Getting a little fatter.
I shook him well from side to side,
   Until his face was blue:
'Come, tell me how you live,' I cried,
   'And what it is you do!'

The old Man still stood talking by my side;
But now his voice to me was like a stream
Scarce heard; nor word from word could I divide;
And the whole body of the Man did seem
Like one whom I had met with in a dream;
Or like a man from some far region sent,

My former thoughts returned: the fear that kills;
And hope that is unwilling to be fed;
Cold, pain, and labour, and all fleshly ills;
And nightly poets in their misery dead.
Perplexed, and longing to be comforted,
My question eagerly did I renew,
'How is it that you live, and what is it you do?'

He with a smile did then his words repeat;
And said, that, gathering leeches, far and wide
He travelled; stirring thus about his feet
The waters of the pools where they abide.
'Once I could meet with them on every side;
But they have dwindled long by slow decay;
Yet still I persevere, and find them where I may.'

While he was talking thus, the lonely place,
The old Man's shape, and speech – all troubled me:
In my mind's eye I seemed to see him pace
About the heavy moors continually,
Wandering about alone and silently.
While I these thoughts within myself pursued,
He having made a pause, the same discourse renewed.

And soon with this he other matter blended,
Cheerfully uttered, with demeanour kind,
But stately in the main; and when he ended,
I could have laughed myself to scorn to find
In that decrepit Man so firm a mind.
'God,' said I, 'be my help and stay secure;
I'll think of the Leech-gatherer on the lonely moor!'

He said 'I hunt for haddocks' eyes
   Among the heather bright,
And work them into waistcoat-buttons
   In the silent night.
And these I do not sell for gold
   Or coin of silvery shine,
But for a copper halfpenny,
   And that will purchase nine.

'I sometimes dig for buttered rolls,
   Or set limed twigs for crabs:
I sometimes search the grassy knolls
   For wheels of Hansom-cabs.
And that's the way' (he gave a wink)
   'By which I get my wealth –
And very gladly will I drink
   Your Honour's noble health.'

I heard him then, for I had just
   Completed my design
To keep the Menai bridge from rust
   By boiling it in wine.
I thanked him much for telling me
   The way he got his wealth,
But chiefly for his wish that he
   Might drink my noble health.

And now, if e'er by chance I put
   My fingers into glue,
Or madly squeeze a right-hand foot
   Into a left-hand shoe,
Or if I drop upon my toe
   A very heavy weight,
I weep for it reminds me so
Of that old man I used to know –
Whose look was mild, whose speech was slow,
Whose hair was whiter than the snow,

from To the Cuckoo

O blithe New-comer! I have heard,
I hear thee and rejoice.
O Cuckoo! shall I call thee Bird,
Or but a wandering Voice?

Thoughts of a Briton on
the Subjugation of Switzerland

Two Voices are there; one is of the sea,
One of the mountains; each a mighty Voice:
In both from age to age thou didst rejoice,
They were thy chosen music, Liberty!
There came a Tyrant, and with holy glee
Thou fought'st against him; but hast vainly striven:
Thou from thy Alpine holds at length art driven,
Where not a torrent murmurs heard by thee.
Of one deep bliss thine ear hath been bereft:
Then cleave, O cleave to that which still is left;
For, high-souled Maid, what sorrow would it be

Whose face was very like a crow,
With eyes, like cinders, all aglow,
Who seemed distracted with his woe,
Who rocked his body to and fro.

And muttered mumblingly and low,
As if his mouth were full of dough,
Who snorted like a buffalo —
That summer evening long ago,
   A-sitting on a gate.

LEWIS CARROLL

'O Cuckoo, shall I call thee Bird'

O Cuckoo, shall I call thee Bird,
Or but a wandering Voice?
State the alternative preferred,
With reasons for your choice.

attributed to A. E. HOUSMAN

A Sonnet

Two voices are there: one is of the deep;
It learns the storm-cloud's thunderous melody,
Now roars, now murmurs with the changing sea,
Now bird-like pipes, now closes soft in sleep:
And one is of an old half-witted sheep
Which bleats articulate monotony,
And indicates that two and one are three,
That grass is green, lakes damp, and mountains steep:
And, Wordsworth, both are thine: at certain times
Forth from the heart of thy melodious rhymes,
The form and pressure of high thoughts will burst:

That Mountain floods should thunder as before,
And Ocean bellow from his rocky shore,
And neither awful Voice be heard by thee!

from We Are Seven

I met a little cottage Girl:
She was eight years old, she said;
Her hair was thick with many a curl
That clustered round her head.

She had a rustic, woodland air,
And she was wildly clad:
Her eyes were fair, and very fair;
– Her beauty made me glad.

'Sisters and brothers, little Maid,
How many may you be?'
'How many? Seven in all,' she said
And wondering looked at me.

'And where are they? I pray you tell.'
She answered, 'Seven are we;
And two of us at Conway dwell,
And two are gone to sea.

'Two of us in the church-yard lie,
My sister and my brother;
And, in the church-yard cottage, I
Dwell near them with my mother.'

At other times – good Lord! I'd rather be
Quite unacquainted with the A. B. C.
Than write such hopeless rubbish as thy worst.

J. K. STEPHEN

Wordsworth on Lloyd George

I met a little cottage-girl;
She strutted by my side.
'Now tell me, little maid,' asked I,
'Whence comes such sinful pride?'
'Why, Lloyd George knew my father, sir,'
This innocent child replied.
'And father knew Lloyd George,' said she,
'And mother did as well.'
Her childish laughter in my ears
Rang like a silver bell.
He whom a wise child honours thus
Must sure in heaven dwell.

MARY VISICK

W. B. YEATS (1865–1939)

The Lake Isle of Innisfree

I will arise and go now, and go to Innisfree,
And a small cabin build there, of clay and wattles made:
Nine bean-rows will I have there, a hive for the honey-
    bee,
And live alone in the bee-loud glade.

And I shall have some peace there, for peace comes
    dropping slow,
Dropping from the veils of the morning to where the
    cricket sings;
There midnight's all a glimmer, and noon a purple glow,
And evening full of the linnet's wings.

I will arise and go now, for always night and day
I hear lake water lapping with low sounds by the shore;
While I stand on the roadway, or on the pavements grey,
I hear it in the deep heart's core.

The Cockney of the North

I will arise and go now, and go to Inverness,
  And a small villa rent there, of lath and plaster built;
Nine bedrooms will I have there, and I'll don my native
    dress,
  And walk about in a d— loud kilt.

And I will have some sport there, when grouse come
    driven slow,
  Driven from purple hilltops to where the loaders quail;
While midges bite their ankles, and shots are flying low,
  And the air is full of the grey-hen's tail.

I will arise and go now, for ever, day and night,
  I hear the taxis bleating and the motor-'buses roar,
And over tarred macadam and pavements parched and
    white
  I've walked till my feet are sore!

For it's oh, to be in Scotland! now that August's nearly
    there,
  Where the capercailzie warble on the mountain's
    rugged brow;
There's pleasure and contentment, there's sport and
    bracing air,
  In Scotland – now!

                                        HARRY GRAHAM

EPILOGUE

from The Tempest

Our revels now are ended. These our actors,
As I foretold you, were all spirits and
Are melted into air, into thin air:
And, like the baseless fabric of this vision,
The cloud-capp'd towers, the gorgeous palaces,
The solemn temples, the great globe itself,
Yea, all which it inherit, shall dissolve
And, like this insubstantial pageant faded,
Leave not a rack behind.

                    WILLIAM SHAKESPEARE

Our Parodies Are Ended

Our parodies are ended. These our authors,
As we foretold you, were all Spirits, and
Are melted into air, into thin air.
And, like the baseless fabric of these verses,
The Critic's puff, the Trade's advertisement,
The Patron's promise, and the World's applause, –
Yea, all the hopes of poets, – shall dissolve,
And, like this unsubstantial fable fated,
Leave not a groat behind!

HORACE TWISS

ACKNOWLEDGEMENTS

For permission to reprint copyright material the publishers gratefully acknowledge the following:

Anne Anderton for 'Marking of Folders'; Faber and Faber Limited and Random House, Inc. for ' "O where are you going?" said reader to rider' and lines from 'Miss Gee' from *W. H. Auden: Collected Poems* edited by Edward Mendelson (Faber, 1976)/(Random House, 1976) copyright © 1976 by Edward Mendelson, William Meredith and Monroe K. Spiers, Executors of the Estate of W. H. Auden; Faber and Faber Limited and Random House, Inc. for lines from *The Dog Beneath the Skin* by W. H. Auden and Christopher Isherwood (Faber, 1989) Copyright 1935 and renewed 1963 by W. H. Auden and Christopher Isherwood; Mrs Eva Reichmann for 'After Hilaire Belloc', 'Chorus of a Song that Might Have Been Written by Albert Chevalier', 'Same Cottage – but Another Song, of Another Season', 'A Prayer', 'A Luncheon (Thomas Hardy Entertains the Prince of Wales)', 'Time, you thief, who love to get', 'P.C., X, 36', 'Sonnet to the "Most Distinguished Chancellor" that Oxford Has Had' and lines from ' "Savonarola" Brown' by Max Beerbohm; The Peters, Fraser & Dunlop Group Ltd. for 'Noël', 'Tarantella', 'Fatigue' and 'But how much more unfortunate are those' from *Complete Verse* by Hilaire Belloc (Duckworth, 1970); The Peters, Fraser & Dunlop Group Ltd. for 'Place Names of China' by Alan Bennett; Gerard Benson for 'Ben Barley'; John Murray (Publishers) Ltd. for 'How to Get On in Society', 'On Seeing an Old Poet in the Café Royal' and 'Business Girls' from *Collected Poems* by John Betjeman (John Murray, 1970), and 'The Ballad of George R. Sims' from *Uncollected Poems* by John Betjeman (John Murray, 1982); G. P. Putnam's Sons for 'Ozymandias Revisited' from *Spilt Milk* by Morris Bishop (Putnam, 1942); Mrs Rosemary Seymour for 'Footnote to Tennyson' from *Collected Poems* by Gerald Bullett (Dent, 1959); David Higham Associates Limited for 'Betjeman 1984' from *Collected Poems* by Charles Causley (Macmillan, 1975); Allen & Unwin Australia Pty.

Ltd. for 'The Accounting Cat', 'Jenny Hit Me', 'There was an old man with a beard' and 'The Story So Far' from *The Complete Book of Australian Verse* by John Clarke (Allen & Unwin Australia, 1986); Wendy Cope for 'Variation on Belloc's Fatigue' and 'Strugnell's Bargain', and Faber and Faber Limited for lines from 'Strugnell's Rubáiyát', 'Usquebaugh', 'Budgie Finds His Voice', 'Mr Strugnell' and 'The Lavatory Attendant' from *Making Cocoa for Kingsley Amis* by Wendy Cope (Faber, 1986); Random Century Group Ltd. for 'To a Fat Lady Seen from a Train' from *Collected Poems* by Frances Cornford (Cresset Press, 1954); Methuen, London, for lines from 'Mrs. Worthington', lines from 'The Stately Homes of England', lines from 'Let's Do It' and 'Contours' by Noël Coward from *The Lyrics of Noël Coward* (Methuen, 1983); Roger Crawford for lines from 'The Love Song of Tommo Frogley'; Grafton Books, a division of The Collins Publishing Group and Liveright Publishing Corporation for 'o pr' from *Complete Poems* by e. e. cummings Vol. I (MacGibbon & Kee, 1968)/*No Thanks* by e. e. cummings, edited by George James Firmage (Liveright, 1978); Copyright 1935 by e. e. cummings. Copyright © 1968 by Marion Morehouse Cummings. Copyright © 1973, 1978 by the Trustees for the E. E. Cummings Trust. Copyright © 1973, 1978 by George James Firmage. John Desmond for 'When We Two Parted'; Watkins/Loomis Agency, Inc. for 'Poets have their ear to the ground' from *The Tents of Wickedness* by Peter de Vries (Gollancz, 1959) © 1959, Peter de Vries; Tom Disch for 'Poems' from *Burn This* by Tom Disch (Century Hutchinson, 1982); Faber and Faber Limited and Harcourt Brace Jovanovich, Inc. for lines from 'Little Gidding' in *Four Quartets*, lines from 'Gerontion', lines from 'Ash Wednesday', lines from 'Choruses from "The Rock"', lines from 'The Love Song of J. Alfred Prufrock', lines from 'The Waste Land' and lines from 'Lines for Cuscuscaraway and Mirza Murad Ali Beg' from *Collected Poems 1909–1962* by T. S. Eliot (Faber, 1963)/ (Harcourt Brace, 1963) copyright 1936 by Harcourt Brace Jovanovich, Inc., copyright © 1964, 1963 by T. S. Eliot, and lines from 'Macavity: The Mystery Cat' from *Old Possum's Book of Practical Cats* by T. S. Eliot (Faber, 1939)/(Harcourt Brace, 1939) copyright 1939 by T. S. Eliot and renewed 1967 by Esme Valerie Eliot; Lady

Empson and Harcourt Brace Jovanovich, Inc. for 'Just a Smack at
Auden' and 'Villanelle' from *Collected Poems* by William Empson
(The Hogarth Press, 1955)/(Harcourt Brace, 1949) copyright 1949
and renewed 1977 by William Empson; Random Century Group Ltd
for 'Invasion' and 'Not Wavell but Browning' from *The Complete
Little Ones* by Gavin Ewart (Hutchinson, 1968), and 'Nursery
Rhyme', and 'Jubilate Matteo' from *The New Ewart: Poems 1980–
1982* by Gavin Ewart (Hutchinson, 1982); Martin Fagg for lines
from 'Mrs Nightingale', 'The Golden Road to Barcelona: 1992' and
'Elegy on Thomas Hood'; The Estate of Robert Frost and Henry Holt
& Co. Ltd. for lines from 'New Hampshire' by Robert Frost from *The
Poetry of Robert Frost* edited by Edward Connery Lathem (Cape,
1971)/(Holt, Rinehart & Winston, 1969); Oliver D. Gogarty for 'On
First Looking into Krafft-Ebing's *Psychopathia Sexualis*' by Oliver St
John Gogarty; Bill Greenwell for 'Christopher Robin Changes Guard
with Dylan Thomas'; Paul Griffin for 'New Tarantella' and 'To His
Importunate Mistress'; Louise H. Sclove for 'Sea-Chill' from *Gaily
the Troubadour* by Arthur Guiterman (E. P. Dutton, 1936); The
Peters, Fraser & Dunlop Group Ltd. for 'Breaking the Chain' from
Selected Poems by Tony Harrison (Penguin International Poets
Series, 1989); Faber and Faber Limited and Farrar, Straus & Giroux
Inc. for 'Oysters' from *Field Work* by Seamus Heaney (Faber, 1979)/
(Farrar, Straus & Giroux, 1979) Copyright© 1976, 1979 by Seamus
Heaney; Mary Holtby for 'Answer to a Kind Enquiry', 'Dawn
Chorus' and 'Sister Swallow to Swinburne'; Faber and Faber Limited
and Harper & Row, Publishers, Inc. for 'That Moment' from *Crow*
by Ted Hughes (Faber, 1970)/(Harper & Row, 1971) Copyright©
1971 by Ted Hughes; Joyce Johnson for 'The bat that blocks at close
of play'; Curtis Brown Ltd., London, for 'Summer Time on Bredon'
and 'What, still alive at twenty-two' by Hugh Kingsmill from *The
Best of Hugh Kingsmill* edited by M. Holroyd (Gollancz, 1970)
Copyright Dorothy Hopkinson, 1970; *Punch* for 'Upon Julia's
Clothes' by E. V. Knox; Unwin Hyman Ltd. for 'The New Jerusalem'
and 'This Railway Station' from *Bank Holiday in Parnassus* by Allan
M. Laing (Allen & Unwin, 1941); Faber and Faber Limited for 'Mr.
Bleaney' from *The Whitsun Weddings* by Philip Larkin (Faber,

1964); Tom Lehrer for 'The Elements'; Christopher Logue for 'I Shall Vote Labour' from *Ode to the Dodo* (Cape, 1981); Faber and Faber Limited for lines from 'Bagpipe Music' by Louis MacNeice from *The Collected Poems of Louis MacNeice*, edited by E. R. Dodds (Faber, 1966); The Society of Authors as the literary representative of the Estate of John Masefield for 'Sea-Fever' and extract from 'No Man Takes the Farm' from *Collected Poems* by John Masefield (Heinemann, 1923); Methuen, London, for lines from 'The King's Breakfast', lines from 'Vespers' and lines from 'Disobedience' from *When We Were Very Young* by A. A. Milne (Methuen, 1924); *The Daily Express* for 'Someone Asked the Publisher', 'Hush, hush', 'John Percy' and 'Another Canto' by J. B. Morton ('Beachcomber'); The Estate of Eugene O'Neill and Houghton Mifflin Co. Inc. for 'To a Bull Moose' and 'Lament of a Subwayite' from *Poems 1912–44* by Eugene O'Neill (Cape, 1980)/(Ticknor & Fields, 1980); Gerald Duckworth & Co. Ltd. and Viking Penguin Inc. for 'Resumé' by Dorothy Parker from *Collected Dorothy Parker* (Duckworth, 1973)/ *The Portable Dorothy Parker* (Viking Press, 1973); Eric O. Parrott for 'More Bagpipe Music'; *The New Statesman* for 'Willesden Gree' by Jimmie Pearse; Campbell Thomson & McLaughlin Limited for 'It was in the Spring of 1825', 'There's a breathless hush on the Centre Court' and 'The Great Poll-Tax Victory of '88' by Noël Petty; *The New Statesman* for 'God made the sex-shop keeper' by Fiona Pitt-Kethley; The Estate of William Plomer for lines from 'The Playboy of the Demi-World' from *Collected Poems* by William Plomer (Cape, 1960); Warner Chappell Music Ltd for lines from 'Let's Do It' by Cole Porter from *Music and Lyrics by Cole Porter*; Faber and Faber Limited and New Directions Publishing Corporation for 'Ancient Music', lines from 'Moeurs Contemporaines' and 'The Charge of the Bread Brigade' from *Collected Shorter Poems* by Ezra Pound (Faber, 1952)/*Personae* (New Directions, 1956) Copyright 1926 by Ezra Pound; Kay Gee Bee Ltd. for 'All Things Dull and Ugly' by Monty Python; Simon Rae for 'Pulling the Chain' (first published in *Poetry Review*) and 'Vile World' (first published in *Weekend Guardian*); Oxford University Press for 'The Garden' from *The Onion, Memory* by Craig Raine (OUP, 1978) © Craig Raine 1978; John Tydeman,

Executor of Henry Reed Estate, for 'Chard Whitlow' and 'Naming of Parts' from *A Map of Verona* by Henry Reed (Cape, 1946); *The New Statesman* for 'Into concrete mixer throw' by Barbara Roe; Jonathan Miller for 'Servant of the House', 'Freedom is in Peril', 'Croaked the Eagle: "Nevermore"' and 'Come into the Army, Maud' by Sagittarius (Olga Katzin Miller); Methuen, London, for 'How I Brought the Good News from Aix to Ghent, or Vice Versa' from *Horse Nonsense* by Walter Carruthers Sellar and Robert Julian Yeatman (Methuen, 1933); Feinman & Krasilovsky for the Estate of Robert Service for lines from 'The Shooting of Dan McGrew' by Robert Service from *Collected Verse of Robert Service* (Benn, 1930); Stanley J. Sharpless for 'Sonnet', 'Chaucer: The Wogan's Tale', 'Pied Beauty' and 'There's a breathless hush on the Centre Court'; The Gallery Press for 'Cavalier Lyric' from *Poems 1956–1986* by James Simmons (Gallery, 1986) © James Simmons 1986, poems; David Higham Associates Limited for 'Said King Pompey' from *Collected Poems* by Edith Sitwell (Macmillan, 1957); James MacGibbon, Executor, and New Directions Publishing Corporation for 'Not Waving but Drowning' by Stevie Smith from *The Collected Poems of Stevie Smith* (Penguin Modern Classics, 1983) Copyright © 1972 by Stevie Smith; Faber and Faber Limited and Random House, Inc. for 'Airman' from *Collected Poems 1928–1985* by Stephen Spender (Faber, 1985) Copyright © 1986 by Stephen Spender; Cat Stevens for 'Wild World'; David Higham Associates Limited and New Directions Publishing Corporation for lines from 'Poem in October' and 'Do not go gentle into that good night' from *The Poems of Dylan Thomas* (Dent, 1971)/(New Directions, 1971) Copyright 1945 by the Trustees for the Copyrights of Dylan Thomas, 1952 by Dylan Thomas; The Trustees for the Copyrights of Dylan Thomas and the Executors of John Davenport for 'Request to Leda' and 'Parachutist' from *The Death of The King's Canary* by Dylan Thomas and John Davenport (Hutchinson, 1976); André Deutsch Ltd. and Alfred A. Knopf, Inc. for 'Dea ex Machina' from *Facing Nature* by John Updike (Deutsch, 1986); N. J. Warburton for 'The Snake on D. H. Lawrence'; Roger Woddis for 'A Moral Tale', 'The Doctor', 'The Rolling Chinese Wall', 'Final Curtain', 'Rewards and Fairies', 'Eat Your Heart Out, Edward

Lear!', 'I Shall Vote Centre', 'Believers' Best Buy' and 'Do Not Go
Sober'; Random Century Group Ltd and A. P. Watt Ltd on behalf of
the Trustees of the Wodehouse Estate for 'The Outcast' from *The
Parrot and Other Poems* by P. G. Wodehouse (Hutchinson, 1988).

Faber and Faber Limited apologize for any errors or omissions in the
above list and would be grateful to be notified of any corrections that
should be incorporated in the next edition or reprint of this volume.

INDEX OF POETS

INDEX OF PARODISTS